SOUL OF A KNIGHT

The Knight's Birth

By: M.J. Felder

Soul Of A Knight: The Knights Birth
©2020 M.J.Felder

Published by: **M.J. Felder** in association with Tanisha Mackin Publishing, LLC.

I Praise GOD, for all that HE has given me; gifts far too numerous to number, but the gift of writing is both my passion, and responsibility.

I DEDICATE this book, to the two SoulKnights that are my everything: **BRENDAN & JAXON**. You two are my daily inspiration.

Thanks to My parents, Valorie DuBois Gardner and Willie Felder Jr. as well as the memory of my late grandfather Pastor Glenn H. DuBois

Lastly, I am forever grateful for my plethora of family and friends, many of you will see your names in my book(s).

Without further ado,

WELCOME to the Epic that is

SOUL OF A KNIGHT

Prologue:

Watching Over London

Slowly exhaling smoke from his nose; James needed this. He closes his eyes and lifts his head trying to relax. He had just spent two and a half hours watching what he considered to be a spectacle. One big show, that's what he often said. Loud, colorful, funny, serious, stand, sit, babies crying, music, and dancing! James wasn't raised in church. As a kid, he and his family would only visit seasonally; that meant Easter, Mother's Day, and Watch night service. But even then, he would either fall asleep or play with the toys he'd snuck in his pockets. He and his siblings hated being made to go. It didn't matter that it was only three times a year.

James felt that Tammy, his wife, was the one trying to make him go now. She'd hit him with guilt trips and lecture to him. He couldn't understand why she wanted him to go so badly. It's not as if he was an atheist. He just felt he was a good enough person. He was a good father, a good husband, and thus an all-around good man. What else was there?

James was standing on the side of the house where he couldn't be seen. Tammy would have a fit if she knew he had lit one up. As far as she knew, he'd quit the habit cold eight months ago. For the most part she'd be correct. He only gives in when he's really stressing. This is one of those times. James takes a long drag on his cigarette, holds it, and then exhales. He felt that if church is so important to her then she should be satisfied going without him. After all, she wouldn't be alone. She can always take London. *I'm not going to keep doing this*, he thinks to himself. He takes a few more puffs and drops what's left on the ground. He stomps it out and looks at his watch.

"I'm missing the game!"

Tammy opens the door to London's playroom, puts him in his playpen, and then walks to her bedroom. She takes her earrings, necklace, and other jewelry off, then walks to the closet. She begins taking her dress off. She is visibly irritated. Tammy wanted to be a good wife to her husband: submit, follow his lead, and even though many women considered it out of date, obey. But how can she continue doing these things for a husband that refuses to keep his promise? It's been three years now! He keeps saying he'll try to embrace his spirituality, but there are very few if any signs of such. James is a good man, and a lot of women would be more than happy, but Tammy needed more. How can they raise their eight-month old son when the two don't agree on what's most important? Tammy grabs something out of the closet then walks to the bathroom and locks the door. A few minutes pass and she hears James coming in *from the corner store*. She turns on the shower.

James quickly climbs the stairs and heads for the bedroom. He looks around before realizing Tammy must be in the master bathroom, plus he could hear the water running. He walks to the door and twists the doorknob. It's locked. He knocks.

"Tammy, James knocks, Tammy…"

"I'm in the shower."

"I'm just letting you know I'm back. I'll be downstairs watching the game."

"Check on the baby before you go down."

"Alright."

Once Tammy hears James leave the room, she walks to the sink and picks up a small device. She holds it up to the light, and then slowly closes her eyes. She takes a deep breath, and then boxes the device back up. She takes off the remainder of her clothes and gets in the shower. Every thought she'd been having, every feeling, every frustration, was now enhanced by a small plus sign.

Now all the time that James and Tammy were stressing about their circumstances, little London was carefree. He sat in his playpen having a ball with all his favorite toys. There were things he liked to put in his mouth, stuffed animals, and cartoon characters. But his most favorite was his plastic basketball. He would roll it around the playpen. Sometimes he'd even throw it over the side. When this would happen, he'd cry until his mother or father would come and either put it back or take him out and let him play with the ball on the floor. This must've been what baby London was now thinking. It seemed he'd gotten tired of rolling the ball around in the small area he was given. He picked the ball

up and tossed it over the side. He watched as the ball bounced then

rolled out of the room. This was the first time this had happened.

Any other time the ball would hit a wall or bounce low and roll

short. He couldn't even see the ball! He immediately cried. His

parents needed to come to the rescue right now! He cried and

cried. No one came. Eventually London cries himself out. Where

are his parents, how is he going to get his ball? Baby London

grabs the sides in the corner of his playpen and pulls himself into a

standing position. Fresh off of crying, he's pouting and breathing

fast. He stares toward the doorway that has taken his basketball.

He reaches with both arms, but the playpen is holding him back.

London begins to whine and kick at the sides. He reaches harder

with his arms over the top. This turns into a bit of a tantrum and

London starts hopping up and down with his top half leaning

forward. All of a sudden, the room flips, and little London's back

is hurting. He screams out! Luckily the room has thick carpeting,

so he isn't badly hurt. More than anything he is scared. He lays

there for a minute and calms from a screaming sob to a whine. He

rolls over and sees the doorway. He's on the floor! London stops

whining and crawls as fast as he can to the doorway. He is now in the middle of the upstairs hallway. He has never crawled this far. Little London is just about to cry again, then he sees his ball. He races toward it. It's resting against the railing where the hall turns into a balcony overlooking the downstairs. London makes it to the ball and sits up. He was set to roll it down the hall, until he looks through the railing and sees an open and endless canyon. He can't resist. Little London crawls closer and easily pokes his head through the railing. He pushes and gets his left shoulder through. He pushes again to look lower and pops his right shoulder through. Once again, the room flips. But instead of being followed by back pain, it just keeps flipping! Air rushes at him from every angle, and with each second he speeds faster toward a hardwood floor. One flip from tragedy, one flip from certain death, one flip from destiny destroyed. One flip remained. Then, just before his next flip would be his last, he begins to move in slow motion. His momentum stops, and he is now sitting right side up. London starts to laugh. He of course has no idea how close he had come to the end of all laughter. And he of course has no idea of *what* kept him from that end. He'd fallen from upstairs but didn't exactly make it to the lower level. He was sitting in midair. Then, as London continues to laugh, he slowly begins to rise. On an invisible elevator he ascends the way he came down. Instead of going through the railing, this time he rises over it. London is now back in the upstairs hall, but still sitting in midair. And there sitting where it was when London fell through the railing, was the little plastic basketball that started all of this. Suddenly, it rolls in the direction of London's playroom. London is lowered to the floor. He chases after the ball. It comes to a stop right in front of his playroom. Now close enough to grab the ball, he reaches for it. But before he can touch it, it rolls into the room. London follows it. The door closes behind him.

Several minutes later, James comes back upstairs during a commercial break and approaches the baby's playroom to check on him. He's surprised to see the door is closed. He opens the door and gets an even bigger surprise.

"Tammy!"

Tammy was allowing the hot shower water to dance on her face hoping to affect some mental escape. James calls her name. She ignores him.

"Tammy!"

Tammy sighs. She steps out of the shower and leaves the water running. She puts on her robe, opens the door and walks toward her husband's voice. Hair dripping and tying her robe she asks...

"What's the matter James?!"

He motions toward London's playroom. She walks up to look into the room.

"What?"

"*I* didn't put the baby on the floor."

"Is he alright?"

Tammy immediately picks London up and checks him out.

"He's fine, but that's not the point."

"What do you mean?"

"Why was the door closed?"

"Closed, I know for a fact I left the door open. I always do."

"Well how do you explain it?"

"I don't know James, maybe London… "

"Tammy, you know how thick the carpet is. There's no way London could push it closed."

"I said I left the door *open* James. What do you want me to say?"

Walking toward the stairs, "I don't want you to *say* anything. I want you to watch my son."

Tammy puts London and the ball back inside of the playpen. She walks after James and cuts him off before he can go downstairs.

"Okay James, I'll tell you what, since… she sniffs. *You've been smoking*!"

"Your fellow church members catching the Holy Ghost and what not, drove me to it!"

"Whatever James, but since I obviously don't do a good job watching *your* son, then you can do it for the rest of the night."

She then walks past James and heads back for the bedroom.

"I'm going to my sister's house."

"Baby hold on!"

James chases after Tammy.

Neither parent notices London once again throwing the ball over the side of his playpen. Nor do they notice the ball being tossed back into the playpen.

"I'm sorry baby, I shouldn't have …"

"No, you were right James. So, I want you to give London the kind of supervision he needs tonight. And maybe in nine months, I'll be as good as you with *your* next child."

Tammy closes and locks the door.

"Nine months, baby what are you talking about?"

He knocks on the door. No answer.

Tammy gets back in the shower and once again tries to affect some mental escape. At least until she physically escapes to her sister's house.

Chapter One:

Eyes are the Soul (Part A.)

"Would you like a beverage ma'am?"

"Yes, what kind of juice do you have?"

"Excuse me, can I get by please? I need to get to the rest room."

A few feet in front of the woman, a young man grabs a pillow from an overhead compartment. He sits down and reclines his seat. He's glad he isn't as tall as some of his teammates. They struggle to get comfortable on planes. He rests his head on the wall, and chin in his hand as he stares out of the window. His dark brown eyes reflect. They perfectly match his skin. As he relaxes, the noise on the capacity filled plane starts to fade. His mind wanders. His imagination begins to mold sculptures with the clouds: exotic animals, expensive cars and trucks, and even the shape of the continent of Africa. The next object he imagines makes him reminisce. He is now focused on a cloud that resembles a bike. Not just any bike, but a 1984 BMX dirt bike. The same

kind he'd gotten seven years ago on his eighth birthday. This was

back when his family was complete and perfect. Or at least he'd

thought so. He was still reminiscing 20 minutes later when the

flight attendant asked if he had any garbage.

Ironically, London is on his way to California to spend the

next several weeks with his father. This was the summer routine

for London and his brother. Donald was already with their father.

London had to come later due to basketball camp. After almost

four hours, the plane began its descent. The sight of the cloud bike

was bitter-sweet. It seemed London could still feel the tension that

was evident between his mother and father on that day. He didn't

remember much, but he did remember that it was the beginning of

the end. He always avoided what little memory he did have of this

time when it began to creep into his mind. The thought of it all

made him uneasy. Even though he'd become comfortable with the

way things developed, it was still painful. London sighs, and then

decides to allow himself a taste of the past. He can see the bike

clearly as his hands rip the wrapping off. It crunches loudly. He

throws it to the ground. Both parents are there. The images are very sporadic. Next, he sees himself bike riding along with his friends. Suddenly he's alone and out of breath. He seems panicked; riding hard and reckless. An unimaginable sound, almost like a roar explodes in the air and seems to actually touch London! A line of trees topples over with a continuous crashing sound. A large and very fast-moving animal flashes into view. It appears to be a shade of blue. London falls from his bike and hits the ground hard. He can feel the creature quickly closing in! Then all at once a piercing headache forces London to treat the memory with the same cold shoulder he'd been giving it for the last seven years. What was all of that? This was the longest he'd allowed himself to linger in quite some time. But he had never before had this experience.

The plane reaches its' gate at LAX

London unbuckles his seat belt and gathers his carry-on items. Just as he enters the airport, he hears his name called. Expecting to see his father, London turns and sees a middle-aged guy wearing a business suit exiting from the same plane he was just on.

"London Bishop, I thought that was you. You play the point for Bennett High School, right?"

Shaking the man's hand, "Yes. I do."

"You're a great talent kid. I watched you play back in February. I think it was against McKinley."

"Yeah, we lost that game."

"But you had forty-seven! That's a freshman record."

The man notices another guy standing in the background, obviously awaiting London.

"Well, I'm glad to have met you. I'll sure keep an eye on your career son."

"Thank you, sir."

Walking over to London, "A fan huh? Did he want an autograph?"

"Funny Dad." James' bald head was covered with a black leather baseball cap. He wore a dark grey zipped sweat suit. His goatee was perfectly shaped from the mustache down the sides of his lips and on his chin.

"What's up Donald" the brothers embrace.

"Hey London." Donald was ready to swim. He was wearing trunks and a T shirt.

The three make their way to the parking lot. James presses a couple buttons on his car remote. The trunk on his new Jaguar opens. London throws his bags in. Father and sons jump in the car and drive off. James' house is thirty minutes from the airport. After filling his father in about school, basketball, and girls, London calls his mother.

"Hey Ma, it's me London. I made it in safely. I'm with Dad and Donald now. Okay I will, here Donald", he hands the phone to his younger brother."

"Hey Ma, I'm good. Yes, yes, I miss you too. Hold on I'll ask him. Dad, Mommy said how's the business?"

James is now the senior vice president of one the most successful architectural firms on the west coast.

"She knows as well as I do. James laughs. Tell her I have a few new projects on the horizon, and to say a prayer for my negotiations."

"She said she will, but to tell you that you need to say your own prayer too."

Donald continued talking with his mother. He'd been with his father for weeks now and he wanted to do some catching up of his own. What James had meant when he said Tammy knew as well as he did about how his business was doing, was concerning her monthly check. James and Tammy had uncharacteristically negotiated the terms of alimony and child support. They did so without the assistance of representation. Tammy wasn't motivated by greed, and James wasn't interested in getting off cheap. They remained friendly.

James and his sons finally make it to the house. James and Donald help London with his bags. As London follows, he abruptly stops. A disturbing feeling comes over him. He slowly turns and looks around. He first looks to the street. It's empty and quiet. London then looks at the neighboring houses. A woman is watering her front lawn with her back turned to London.

Everything in him tells him that he's being watched. He drops his bag on the ground and walks down the driveway carefully surveying as he goes. When he reaches the street he looks right, nothing to see. He turns and looks left, nothing to see. But as he turns to go back, the feeling intensifies and draws his attention back left. He zeros in on a street pole fifteen feet away, and freezes. Several large snakes are wrapped around it. Each one has glowing red eyes and are locked in on London. Fear and adrenaline rush through London's veins. He carefully backs away keeping his eyes on the pole. Just as he begins his turn to run up the driveway, he hears a low growl from his right. He looks but sees nothing.

"London! What are you doing?"

The voice startles him. He looks up the driveway and see his brother, then back in the direction of the growl, still nothing. London looks back at the phone pole and even the snakes are gone. He swallows hard and then jets back to his bag. He quickly grabs it and joins Donald.

"Dude, what's wrong?"

"Yo!! There were like ten huge snakes wrapped around that phone pole just now! "

"What? Donald laughs. I know they have snakes here and there but the ones I've seen aren't big enough to wrap around a pole London."

"These were huge! And their eyes were red!"

Donald laughs and walks down the driveway to look.

"Dude there's nothing here."

"I know, they were gone when I, I heard..."

"You heard what? Did they start talking?" Laughing harder.

"No of course not. Let's just put these bags in the house."

"But seriously London, hold on. I have seen a few snakes since I've been here. If any tells you to eat any fruit, just say no!"

They both crack up laughing and London playfully shoves Donald. High at the top of the phone pole several large snakes watch the brothers enter the house. They then turn their red eyes down in the direction of the growl and nod their heads in unison. A growl sounds in response from an invisible presence; followed by the sound of something heavy fleeing the area.

The house is immense. There are five bedrooms, three full bathrooms, a game room, a balcony, a heated pool & Jacuzzi, basketball court, and a three-car garage. Every summer the boys felt like celebrities.

The next day London and Donald swam for over two hours. When they were finished, they changed their clothes and headed for the kitchen.

"Hey dad, What's for lunch? London and I are..."

They boys stopped at the large breakfast nook and smiled. There sitting in the center were several assorted bowls filled with various vegetables, cheese, chicken, and ground beef. There were also two plates, one presented soft shell taco shells for London's chicken tacos, and the other soft taco shells for Donald's beef tacos.

"THANKS DAD!" The boys shout in unison.

James walks in. "Your welcome boys, I didn't think you guys would ever get out of that pool. Save me a couple I have to make an important call. Drinks are in the 'fridge"

"No problem Dad."

London fixed a plate for his father and put the rest of the food away. When he was done, he looked around for Donald and found him playing video games in the finished basement.

"Start it over and let me get in."

"Your game is hoops this is football, a real man's game. You're not ready for this bro."

"Oh really, I'll let you pick whatever team you want, and I'll still spank you!"

Donald tosses London the other joystick.

"Then come get some! I'll show you what it's going to be like when you go back home. I can't wait to cash in from our bet."

"The only thing you'll be doing with that bet is paying up; and you better not cry to Ma when I come to collect."

Saturday night James and the boys were out at a fancy restaurant. James had to help the boys order. They all laughed as Donald tried to pronounce some of the dishes on the menu.

"Before the food gets here, I have a surprise for you guys."

"Alright Dad! You finally decided to give me the keys to the Jag."

"Uhh… funny."

"You got us Ravens season tickets!"

"What? No boy. Something is wrong with ya'll! No, I have someone that I want you guys to meet. "

London saw the look on his father's face. His father had been waiting for this moment. His hands are folded and he's smiling… hard. It required real effort to keep from showing teeth. James always hated smiling with teeth showing. He thought it made smiles look forced. London knew this.

"Who are you talking about Dad?"

James stood up and tuned to his left. An attractive woman stood up from the bar and walked toward him. James takes her by the hand. "London, Donald, this is Evelyn."

London went numb. He was speechless.

"Do you guys mind if she eats with us?"

"We don't mind. "

London looks Donald square in the face.

"It's a good thing there are four chairs here. Is she your girlfriend Dad?"

James and Evelyn laughed. London clenches his teeth and stares to make sure Donald saw him this time. Donald frowns.

"Well, Evelyn is a really good person and a very close friend of mine. We've known each other for some time now and we're getting closer. I thought it was time for you and London to meet her.

"Your father's told me so much about the two of you. You guys are really handsome."

"I like her Dad. I'm Donald."

Again, James and Evelyn laughed.

She spoke with Donald for a few minutes. She then turns to London.

"So, I guess that means you're London. Your father tells me that you're a star basketball player at your school."

London forces a smile. Nearly all his teeth are showing. It doesn't go unnoticed.

"I'm alright."

When their meals arrived, everyone dug in, everyone except London. He just picked over his food. It was clear that London was uncomfortable. He continued to force the occasional smile, and even some phony laughter. James and Donald tried several times to include him in the conversations and re-energize him but were forced to concede to London's withdrawal. When dinner was over Evelyn said her goodbyes and James walked her to the door.

"So, you don't like her huh?"

London looks in the direction that his father and his new friend had just gone in. Suddenly he is overcome with the same feeling of being watched. The last time it was snakes. His heart races, he looks left and right but there are only tables of other families eating and conversing. He pulls the tablecloth up and frantically searches under the table.

"London? Dude what's really going on with you? What are you looking for?"

He then looks overhead. All is normal, no snakes and no growling. But his feelings are not betraying him. Two sets of eyes are carefully watching his every move. One set is keeping watch from a far table inside the restaurant, and the second set is watching from outside of a window. London looks towards the window and sees nothing. But for some reason he keeps staring. He's feels drawn.

"Umm... Brother London, is there something you want to tell me? Do you see dead people or...?"

And then just before he turns away, something outside the window beats him to it. A huge translucent figure quickly moves laterally to the right, until it was out of sight of the windows. London stands in awe.

Now the one staring is Donald; at his suddenly insane older brother.

"Sir, is everything okay? May I help you?" Asks the server.

"God I sure hope so." Donald replies.

"What was... umm, no nothing. I just... thought I saw someone I knew. What did you ask me a minute ago?"

"I think this west coast heat is getting to be too much for you London. You're scaring me man, for real! But anyway, I was asking you about Dad's friend Evelyn."

"Oh yeah... her," he says as he takes his seat. London forgets what he'd just seen and remembers his father's smile when he introduced her. "I can't say I don't like her. We don't even know her. But I can say that I'm not ready for her."

In the far corner of the room a second set of eyes are fixed on London. This set of eyes is also the only other set in the restaurant that had seen what London had. The body that housed these eyes stood from the table and walked out of the restaurant to rendezvous with the translucent figure.

"It is him. He is the touched."

The next morning James drove the knife in the rest of the way and twisted it. He walked into the boys' room and woke them up earlier than he ever had on a Sunday.

London yarns, "What's up Dad is everything alright?"

"Everything is fine. I just thought it would be nice if we could all go to Church together."

"Church? Are you serious Dad?"

"Yes, I'm serious; is it too late for a man to get close to the Lord?"

London and Donald looked at each other in wonder. London stood up and began stretching. He was shaking his head in amusement until…

"You guys are going to love Evelyn's Church. The Pastor is something special, and the choir is out of this world. I'm telling you... "

London's chest tightens. His breathing begins to race, and his mouth dries up. Being introduced to his father's new girlfriend was nearly unbearable. But witnessing his father do for another woman what he refused to do for his mother was unforgivable. For the remaining two weeks London hides behind a constant show of teeth. He can't wait to leave.

By the fourth week of July, James and Donald are once again helping London with his bags. He's headed back home. Football try outs are being held at high school back home and London was planning to try his hand. Even though basketball was always his passion, he was always a fan of football. London had never played, other than in the neighborhood. He wasn't sure if he had what it took to make the team, but he wanted to give it a shot, and he wanted to shut Donald up. James and Donald walked London to the security line.

"Alright bro, have a safe flight." They slapped each other five and hugged. I'll see you in a couple weeks."

"Thanks man see you soon."

"Dude, you don't really have to go through with that bet," Donald whispers.

London smiles, "You're not getting out of it that easy."

"Oh, okay well have my money when I get home."

James walks up. He hands London an envelope, as he always does when their summers together were over.

"I enjoyed you son. I wish we didn't have to cut it short this year."

"I enjoyed you too Dad. I just want to see if I can make the team."

"No, I get it, it's cool. I hope you make it. Actually, I know you'll make it."

"Thanks Dad."

"Hey, I know meeting Evelyn was a little awkward. I should have warned you guys. I apologize for that."

"You don't need to apologize for that Dad."

London stuck his hand out to shake his father's hand. James looked at his son's outstretched hand. He took a second before eventually shaking it. He then pulled London close and hugged him.

"I love you son."

"Love you too Dad."

James let go of his first-born child and for the first time looked into the eyes of a young man.

"Be good son."

"I will."

London walks away thinking, but you should've apologized for Sunday. Not that it would've mattered.

London's flight has a layover in Chicago. O'Hare is crowded as usual. The layover is expected to last about an hour, so London sits and waits. He thinks about his father. They have a great relationship. He's always been able to talk to him about anything. His father is the one who had gotten him interested in basketball. James coached his son and spent a lot of time teaching him life lessons at an early age. Even now he flies back to Maryland at least twice a year to watch London play. But what now, London is furious with his father. He rests his head in his hands.

London is totally zoned out when he overhears a couple talking.

"... I can't believe this. Every time I've flown this year it's been delayed!"

London looks at his watch to discover that he'd been waiting for forty minutes already. He decides to walk to the ticket counter to ask if there are any updates on the arrival of his flight. The lady at the counter says it would unfortunately be another two hours; maybe longer. She said the plane had run into some pretty bad weather and was forced to turn around. London sighs and heads back to his seat. He takes his phone out and calls his parents to inform them of the news. After hanging up, he decides to eat something. There are several fast food spots, but given the time he has to waste, London figures he might as well go to a more upscale place. A couple gates down he finds the perfect place. There's a *Please wait to be seated* sign. After a couple of minutes, he's taken to his seat. He places his bag in between his feet, like his father always showed him, and then opens his menu. Good thing his father had given him some money when he dropped him off. London orders a grilled chicken sandwich and a Pepsi. He opens his bag looking for a book when he hears…

"*London Bishop.*"

He looks up to see a familiar face smiling at him. He can't quite remember where he knows the man from.

"Remember me? We met a few weeks ago at LAX."

"Oh yeah, I remember."

"The name's Pat. Are you eating alone?"

"Yeah, actually I am. My flight was delayed so I'm really just wasting time."

"Tell me about it. My flight was delayed and delayed until it was finally cancelled. You mind if I sit?"

"No, feel free."

When the server returned with London's drink, Pat orders his meal without looking at the menu.

"I guess you've been here before?"

"Yeah, I do a lot of traveling. I'm a college recruiter. That's why I know so much about you. I know talent when I see it kid, and you've got it."

"Thanks. I really appreciate it."

This really piques London's interest. One of his biggest goals is to play college ball.

"Who do you recruit for?"

"I started at Georgetown, but now I'm like a free Agent. Schools get in touch with me when they need reinforcements.

When school starts back, you'll be entering your second year right?"

"That's right."

"How are your grades?"

"I mostly get A's."

"Good. Keep it up and you can play for whatever school you want."

They go on talking basketball while they eat for almost an hour. When they finish eating, London realizes that he still has at least an hour of time to waste.

"Well it's about time I try to find a hotel room. Like I said before, I'll be watching your career. Good luck with that flight."

Just before walking out of the restaurant, Pat turns as if he's forgotten something.

"London, if you're interested, there's a sport's memorabilia shop that I like to visit whenever I'm in Chicago. It's around gate 18."

London thanks Pat and is relieved that he'll be able to occupy the rest of his time by doing something he is genuinely interested in. Walking toward gate 18, he passes by a man carrying two bags over his shoulder; he's thankful that his has wheels. He arrives at the gate then turns and sees the shop. Several people are inside either making purchases or browsing around. London walks in. He is immediately attracted to a trophy case displaying autographed jerseys. He stares inside. They have a number of the legends like Charles Barkley, Moses Malone, and Larry Bird. London grins as he looks them over. He looks for the price tag knowing it would be unreasonable. Suddenly, there's a loud noise that draws his attention away from the case… the loud sound of silence. No commotion, an eerie stillness. London looks around. He is surprised to see that the several customers that were all but surrounding him just seconds ago are now out of sight. And so are all of the others. But he is not alone.

"May I help you son," Asks a man whose back is facing him from behind the counter.

"Umm, did I miss something? When did everyone run out of the door?"

"What door?"

London looks in the direction from which he'd entered the shop. There is no door. He looks over the entire store and sees no exit whatsoever. He can hear his heartbeat. He fearfully looks back at the clerk.

"What's going on?"

"What do you mean London?"

Upon hearing the clerk call his name, London freezes. The clerk turns around. London knows him. It's Pat. London's heart skips a beat.

"Hey, Mr. Pat. What's the joke? Where is everybody? And how did you beat me here?"

"Joke? Where there's no laughter, there's no joke."

London swallows hard and once again looks for a way out. Once again, he does not find one.

"There's no way-out kid."

"What do you want man, money? *Here*, he fishes $170 out of his pocket, it was the rest of the money his father had given him, it's all I have, it's yours!"

"Foolish mortal, I'm not here for your money."

As Pat speaks these words, his face begins to change. His eyes grow larger and darker until the white parts disappear and leave two completely black reflecting orbs. His hair also thins. His teeth grow longer and sharper. Pat's fingernails turn to claws, and he grows to slightly over seven feet. London is terrified.

"Help, somebody help!" London yells.

The creature laughs.

"Who… what are you, what do you want from me?"

"What I want, I will take!"

Pat jumps on top of the counter smashing the glass. It's so sudden that London falls over trying to escape. Again, Pat laughs.

"What do you want?!"

"Silence! Speak no more coward!"

London rolls to his left and kicks in a glass display housing an autographed Wayne Gretzky hockey stick. He pulls it out and stands up holding it in a defensive stance.

"So, you're not a coward. No matter, your bravery is no savior."

Savior... The word is an epiphany to London. But before he can focus on it, Pat leaps from the countertop and lands in front of him. He back hands London sending him flying across the shop. London crashes into a wall with shelves holding baseballs. He cries out and grimaces in pain. It feels like something is broken. The thing that was Pat casually walks toward London. All is lost. It is then that London acts on his epiphany. He closes his eyes and whispers...

"Savior... deliver me"

Just then, a color distortion in the midst of nothing, drips downward painting the figure of a man on a canvas of air. This man stands behind London's attacker whole. Shock now takes the place of London's fear. He can't believe what he is seeing; and *somehow, it's not the first time.* This can't be happening, can't be real!

The thing that was Pat, notices that London's attention is now directed behind him. He looks at a display case a few feet from London and sees the reflection of a man standing behind him. Pat spins around with incredible speed striking the mystery man on the right side of his face. The man stumbles into a nearby wall, cracking it. However, the man looks unaffected. He simply straightens up. Pat is now facing the man. He speaks to him in a foreign tongue. London sees an opportunity. He pulls himself along the floor away from the action, protecting his hurt arm. The mystery man doesn't speak to Pat, but he does respond. He performs his own spin, ducking low with an outstretched leg sweeping Pat's feet from under him. He then looks directly at London who is attempting to escape. Although London felt he'd somehow seen this mystery man before, he felt no sense of déjà vu as the two make eye contact. Where the thing that was Pat has solid black eyes that reflect perfectly; this guy who was obviously no mere guy, has eyes that glow! Neither of them had pupils, but the mystery man's eyes are the color of the sky on a cloudless day.

And they have life. Pat's eyes are dead. The mystery man's eyes moved like water, never still. They waved and shimmered. The man points in the direction of where London entered the shop. The last time London had looked, a wall was standing there. But now he looks and sees that the wall is blinking in and out of sight. Pat climbs to his feet.

"Don't move boy!"

He then turns to the mystery man.

"Care to try that maneuver again?"

He lunges at the man knocking him to the floor. The two wrestle around smashing glass, and sending balls flying. London wastes no time. He crawls to the blinking wall as fast as he can. He reaches out and his arm passes through the wall. It's an illusion! London crawls out of the shop. He looks up and sees gate 18. He turns around to see if the wall is still blinking. Not only is it not blinking, it is no longer a wall. It's an open threshold. And that's not all; the shop is still under construction.

London is still on the floor.

"Are you okay son? Who's with the special needs child?"

"I think he's having a seizure; quick somebody get a doctor before he swallows his tongue!"

London barely hears them. He rises to his feet and begins to run in hopes of putting distance between himself and the two… whatever they are with the eyes! Even though one of them had saved his life, he still wanted nothing to do with him. He couldn't explain it, but as he ran, the pain in his arm melted away. A voice sounds on the loudspeaker.

"Code red, code red, security report between gates 20 and 30, Code red."

London looks up and sees that he is approaching gate 24. He realizes that he no longer has his bags; no bags and he's running. It was apparent, *he's* the code red. He slows down and passes several people pulling their wheeled luggage. London looks left and sees the restrooms. He dips into the women's restroom hoping no one is in there.

"Hello, is anyone in here. I need to clean up in here."

He is alone. He jumps in the stall, aware that if they happen to search the lady's restroom, this is undoubtedly the first place that they will look. He needs to collect his thoughts; he has to figure something. What's really going on?

Out of breath, "I'm losing my mind. There's no other explanation. I'm losing my young mind!"

The sight of the mystery man's eyes is burned into London's head. Panting uncontrollably, London slowly begins to focus on what he had seen before making eye contact with the mystery man. It was like a waterfall; A series of colors dripping down some kind of disturbance. It was familiar. London's mind begins to dig deep within itself. Until it found what it was looking for. London was only a child, and a party was going on...

AWAKENED

MEMORIES

Memory 1:

A bike and a bracelet

"Surprise happy birthday," yells a crowd of adults and children.

Its London's birthday and he had been led to believe that he was going to be taken to his favorite restaurant. However, his parents, his mother anyway, had been planning this surprise for weeks now. His friends from school, his closest cousins, his two aunts, an uncle, and his six-year-old baby brother Donald were all there. London couldn't stop smiling.

"How old are you, how old are you, how old are you …"

"I'm eight years old; I'm eight years old …"

"Blow out the candles London. And don't forget to make a wish."

Under his breath, "If London can't make one, I can pinch hit."

"Chill out James, she's going to hear you."

"She never hears me, that's the problem. She doesn't listen!"

"Not so loud, let's go in the kitchen."

James' friend ushers him out of the room.

"What's going on James? Why are you talking about Tammy like that?"

"Things just aren't the same man. All she does is complain. That and spend my money!"

"I hear you Bro. I told you, I'll never get married, too much of a hassle. What you need is a little something on the side."

"Oh, believe me, I've been considering it, he sighs. But I couldn't do that."

"So, what's she complaining about?"

"What isn't she complaining about? I work too much, I need to stop smoking… and it never stops with the Church! Now she knew when we were dating that I loved football. But for the last couple years she's been acting brand new. I'm not missing the game just so you can jump around and wear your hats!"

The two friends laugh hard.

Tammy walks into the kitchen. "James what are you doing, London is about to open his presents?"

"We're coming."

"Open this one. It's from your Aunt Reba."

London rips the wrapping off.

"Ooh London, That's a nice outfit. You can wear it to church tomorrow. Tell your Auntie thank you."

"Thank you, Aunt Reba."

London opens presents from his other Aunt, friends, and cousins. He received books, cards, money, toys and, more clothes.

"Open mine next little man." His Uncle Terrance hands him a square box.

London rips the wrapping off.

All the kids react, "Ooooh!"

"Stephen Curry, and LeBron James jerseys! Thanks Uncle T!"

"You're welcome L.B."

James walks to the next room. He makes the sound of a drum roll with his mouth. He then comes out walking a big red and white plastic bag.

"What's that Dad? What's in the bag?!"

Tammy storms into the kitchen, "No he didn't. No, he didn't."

Tammy's two sisters follow her into the kitchen.

"What's wrong?"

"I can't believe him!"

"What girl, what?"

"He's out there acting like that present was all his idea!"

"I'm missing something?"

"James and I were supposed to give London his gift together. We were going to stand on each side and lift him. But no, he's out there doing his own thing. He always has to do his own thing. He's so damn selfish!"

London runs over to his father and tears the bag off his present. He can't believe what he sees. He was sure they knew he wanted a bike, but he didn't know they knew the exact kind!

"Dad, how did you know?"

"I don't know; I guess I was lucky."

Back in the kitchen "… and he's dumber than I thought if he thinks I didn't hear him talking to Terrance earlier."

"What did he say?"

"While we were singing, he was making smart comments about his wishes for me."

"But Tammy, I thought you two were… well, relatively happy."

"We were, but to tell you the truth, ever since Donald was born, we've been growing further apart. And on top of that he's still smoking! He lied. He told me ... "

Kitchen door swings open. "Mommy look what Daddy got me!"

"Oh, *Daddy* got you that?"

James walks in. "Actually London, your mother helped me pick it out."

"Oh, I helped you huh?"

"Alright Tammy, you picked it out, you bought it, and it was your idea."

"That's right. It was my idea. If it weren't for me, you wouldn't have known which bike to get!"

Terrance turns to the children. "Hey kids, why don't we let London change into one of his new jerseys and we'll all go out back and shoot some hoops."

This excites the kids and they all eagerly run to the back with London's uncle.

Meanwhile, James and Tammy argue for another twenty minutes while Tammy's sisters clean up, all the while eavesdropping.

This is Terrance's first time seeing his nephew play ball. He is in awe. London isn't good for his age; he's *too* good for his age! He played with a physical ability that shouldn't have been possible until he was a teen. He was seven just yesterday! After watching the kids for forty-five minutes, Terrance takes the kids back inside. He convinces himself that London appearing to be so talented is due to the amount of beer that he and James had been drinking. Terrance, Tammy's sisters, and everyone else exchange pleasantries and make their way home.

An hour later, James and Tammy are finally calm, but obviously ignoring one another. London and Donald pretty much stay in their room and play with London's new toys. When 8:30pm rolls around, James and Tammy come in separately to see the kids to bed. Each parent apologizes for what happened earlier.

Tammy reads the boys a bedtime story before leaving their room. Donald immediately falls asleep. London can't get comfortable. His pillow feels like it has a hard lump in it. After tossing and turning for what seems like forever, he finally lifts his pillow and looks underneath. There, on his bed lies a small wooden box. He picks it up and stares at it. It doesn't look like any gift box he's ever seen. It looks *old and rugged.* He looks for the separation in the box and opens it.

Meanwhile, James and Tammy lay in the bed, backs facing each other. James looks over his shoulder to see if his wife is asleep; she is. He slowly rolls out of bed and heads downstairs. It occurred to him, that in all of the drama from earlier, he didn't get any cake. He goes to the kitchen opens the refrigerator and grabs a plate. As he begins cutting a slice, he shakes his head. He can't help but think of the problems he and Tammy have been having. He sighs.

"I don't know how much more of this I can take."

James eats a couple slices and drinks a soda. He makes sure to clean up before heading back upstairs. As he reaches the top of the stairs, he notices light coming from under the boy's bedroom door.

"London turn the light out and go to sleep."

The light immediately goes out. James slowly crept back into bed; convinced he didn't wake his wife. On the other side of the bed, Tammy rolls her eyes.

As soon as London opened the box, he was blinded by a strange light. All of a sudden, he hears his father's voice. He immediately closes the box. The light goes out. London waits patiently to hear his father's bedroom door close. Once he hears the sound, he pulls the covers over his head. When he is sure he's hidden, he re-opens the box. Once again, blinding light emerges, but it diminishes after a few seconds. London slowly takes the covers off. He looks in the box. Lying there inside, is a simple bracelet. It isn't even jewelry; how did it light up? It's a braided piece of cloth, dark in color. It looks cool. He puts the bracelet on his left wrist and places the box under his bed. London figures any one of three people had hidden the present: his mother, father, or his Uncle T. He smiles and goes to sleep.

Memory 2:

Blue Nightmare

London sat next to his mother and Donald. His Aunts sit behind them. He wore one of his new outfits. London always liked church. He liked to sing from the pews with the choir. He and Donald would stand and clap. But what they loved more than anything else was pretending to catch the *Holy Ghost!* London wished his father would come. It had been a long time since the whole family went together. He felt his father didn't know what he was missing. Whether it was Sunday school, or morning worship, London paid attention and even understood. More importantly, he believed.

For the next few weeks London spends all of his free time riding his bike. As long as his homework was finished, and he was in before the streetlights came on, his parents were okay with it. He mostly rides with his best friend John. They ride around in the neighborhood park a couple blocks down. Two kids they know from school sometimes come to the park and the four of them race.

One day after school, London finished his homework and chores then rode his bike to John's house. They ride to meet their friends at the park. They were expecting two but are greeted by three. Warren went to the same school as the rest of the boys, but he was a little older than they were. London and John learn that Warren didn't live far from the park. They are also told of Warren's big idea. The older kids in school often talked about a certain bike trail. A trail that is said to be a dirt biker's fantasy. They keep the location secret. They don't want just anyone riding there. Warren was one of the Keepers of that secret. Turns out, three of the regulars that ride there, two brothers and another, all re-located within the last several months. Warren was recruiting! He invited the four boys to come with him and experience the height of dirt biking! The boys are all excited and ready to go. London had a question.

"Where is the trail?"

"I can't just come out and tell you. You just have to follow me."

"Well how far away is it? How long will it take?"

"What difference does it make? Do you want to go or not?"

"Yeah, I do, but I can't stay out too late."

"It's not that far if we ride fast. Whoever's coming let's go!"

Warren turned around and peddled off. The other two boys fell in line behind him.

"London what are you going to do?"

"I want to go, but my father …"

"You heard what Warren said. If we ride fast …"

"What if we don't ride fast enough?"

John contemplates then suddenly says, "I'm going!"

John turns his bike around and chases after the others. London is torn.

"John, hold on. I'm coming!"

The boys have the time of their lives. Warren was right; this was the best bike trail that any of them had ever ridden on. Warren was also right about riding fast. They made it back before curfew with time to spare. The boys kept this up for the next week. No one was the wiser.

The following week, London and company again sped their way to the secret trail. The road that led to the trail was surrounded by woodland. By now they were all familiar with the sights and sounds on the route. But today was different. Today they were being watched. Especially London, his every move was under a microscope. When they arrived, the other *members of the secret trail* were waiting for them. They had even more fun than they normally did. In fact, they rode around so long, that when London finally took a break, he realized they'd been riding for much longer than they normally would.

"Hey, Warren, what time is it?"

Warren looks at his watch.

"I don't think you really want to know."

"We've got to get out of here!"

"London hold on, think about it, we're already late; we might as well ride some more if we're going to get in trouble anyway."

The other boys overheard London and Warren.

"We can make it if we leave now." John says.

"I don't think so John."

"I agree with Warren and Ronnie."

"The rest of ya'll can stay, come on John."

The sun was going down. London and John sped off. John rode as hard as he could. London was capable of riding much faster but was forced to hold back so as not to leave John. London knew that if he were riding alone, he really had a chance of making it back in time. He couldn't explain it, but he had the ability to do many things better than his friends, a lot better. But something told him to keep it to himself.

"London. London, I need to stop! I need to rest."

They pull their bikes to the side of the road to rest. John is so tired he drops his bike and sits on the road. He breathes heavily. London could use a rest, so he didn't protest, although he was indeed capable of continuing on. As they rested, London hears a tree branch snap. After hearing a second one, he's suspicious.

"John, did you hear that?"

John, who's relieved to be resting, reluctantly lifts his head. "Hear what?"

Just then, several branches snap in succession.

"That! Come on, something isn't right."

"Alright, but let's go slow. I'm still tired."

As they ride, more branches brake. It's apparent that someone is following them. London and John speed up. The snapping of trees speeds up in response. The boys are scared. They ride harder. A couple minutes pass. The tree snapping seemed to stop.

"I don't hear it anymore."

"I think we're faster than whoever it was."

Then suddenly, as if cued, they hear a crash behind them. They look back. What they see pumps cold fear through their veins. They both scream! The thing pursuing them roars! This thing was no animal; it was enormous and dark blue! It was a nightmare. The creature was about half a mile back, but it closed the distance between them as if they weren't moving. The boys are terrified! The creature's mouth is wide open, revealing teeth that looked like hunting knives. It was the size of a minivan. A minivan with huge black eyes. Its' roar was painful! However, the most out of the ordinary feature, of the many, was its' six legs!

London was now well ahead of John, his fear made him ride as fast as he could. John calls out to him. He doesn't know what to do. Then, London's loyalty to his friend kicks in and he kicks up dust bringing his bike to a complete stop. John catches up, but unfortunately this also brought the creature within fifty yards. London sat on his bike staring in the direction of the creature. He couldn't break his stare.

"London let's go! London come on! London!"

John rides past London. He was too scared to stop. He can't believe London is trying to be a hero! However, John never turned to see exactly what it was that held London's attention. Though it made since for John to conclude that his friend was looking at the beast, there was much more that met London's eye. There was something, *happening*. Something was between London and the beast, a kind of disturbance. There was an area in midair, though transparent, that was sort of blocking his view of the creature. Then, before London's eyes, a series of colors dripped down this disturbance like a waterfall. When this it ended, it had painted the appearance of a man. London sat perched on his bike in a state of shock. The creature saw the same disturbance and stopped in its' tracks. It roars its' painful roar! The beast paces back and forth just several feet from the figure in midair. The man, or whatever it is, is motionless. The creature is visibly agitated. But then, it seemed to be contemplating … figuring. Then without warning, it ends its' pacing by leaping directly over the motionless being. London falls off his bike! It heads straight for him. His entire body throbs with anticipation of a horrible death. The beast lets off its' most painful roar yet, as its jaws swing open. London closes his eyes. He hears a thump… but doesn't feel anything. He slowly opens his eyes. The beast is struggling and tumbling around on the ground with the man like being that was, until seconds ago, motionless. The creature eventually frees itself. Then, it does something that defies logic, as if everything else happening isn't doing that already. It speaks. It isn't English, but it's definitely speech. The tongue it speaks in is understood by the mystery figure. He responds in the same tongue. The two obviously weren't seeing eye to eye, because they were hollering. The blue nightmare of a creature charges the mystery being. The being dodges the creature at the last possible moment. The beast's momentum propels it into the woods. The mystery man runs over to London and places one hand on his shoulder, and the other on his bike. The man, London, and his bike all disappear. When the creature thrust its' way back into the open, it is furious to find London and his attacker are gone. It throws its' head back and once again lets out a powerfully painful roar. In the distance, John is still riding when he hears this last roar. He peddles faster. All he can think is, "how and why would London try to fight"?! He feels guilty for leaving his best friend behind, but what could he have done?

Meanwhile, a block away from London's home, something was happening; a disturbance that dripped living color like a rainbow waterfall. Only this time, when it finished its' downpour, it revealed a man, a boy, and a bike. The man never looks directly at London; never in the eye. He simply stands and picks London and his bike up off the ground. He then turns and walks off. As he walks, he fades out of existence as if he were never there. He never spoke a word. Well, not to London that is. London looks around. What had just happened? He realizes he is back in his own neighborhood. But that's impossible, he was at least fifteen minutes away from home even if he rode with all his true might! He nervously walks his bike home. He'd had enough of riding today. His mind is full of the impossible events he'd witnessed; too many to number! London opens his front door pulls his bike into the front hall and locks up. The streetlights pop on. He'd beaten curfew.

"London is that you?"

"Yes Dad, it's me."

"Boy where have you been?"

"The streetlights just came on Dad."

"I didn't ask you about any streetlight! I asked you where you were!"

London didn't know how, but his father knew he wasn't where he was supposed to be. He was already in trouble. He didn't want to make it worse by lying, plus he didn't know just how much his father knew. Tammy hears the commotion and comes to the front.

"James is that London you're talking to?"

She rounds the staircase and sees her first-born standing in front of her husband.

"London?!"

She grabs him and hugs him tightly.

"Are you alright? We were worried sick, where were you?"

"Answer your mother boy!"

"I-I, my friends and I went to the secret bike trail," he stutters.

"What? What secret bike trail?"

"You follow the road through the woods."

"Oh really! I'll tell you what, you want to go further than the park huh, let's see how far you get without this!"

James grabs London's bike and walks out of the back door with it. He takes it to the garage.

"London, go to your room while your father and I talk about this."

When he got to his room, Donald was playing with *his* toys, on *his* bed. Ordinarily, London would be all over his brother for this, but after the day he'd had, all he could say was…

"Off my bed."

London jumps in the bed and stares at the ceiling.

"How did they know I wasn't at the park?"

"Dad got off early and stopped by there to surprise you."

London just shakes his head.

Tammy is on her way to join her husband in the kitchen, when there is a knock on the door. She looks out. It's John. He is frantic and out of breath. She opens the door.

"*Mrs. Bishop, Mrs. Bishop…*"

"What is it John? Is everything okay?"

"It's London Mrs. Bishop."

She crosses her arms anticipating a lie.

"What about London?"

"We got chased by a giant blue monster with six legs and big teeth! I got away, but I think it got London! He tried to fight!"

"Umm hmm, he tried to fight huh? Look John, I'm glad my son has a friend he can count on but lying doesn't help him. He's upstairs right now. I guess he got back from *the secret bike trail* before you huh? You should probably head home. Your parents were looking for you too."

John is speechless. He turns and heads home. He is more confused than ever.

Hours later, London is awakened by his mother. She tells him of the punishment she and his father agreed on. Two weeks grounded, three without his bike. She explains why it is so harsh. She tells him of how scared they were when they couldn't find him, and how dangerous his trek was. She also reminds him that he knew where he was supposed to be. He wasn't happy, but he understood and apologized. Tammy kisses him on the cheek and tucks him in. She leaves the room. Five minutes later, James enters the room.

"London, you sleep?"

"No."

"Did your mother tell you what we decided?"

"Yes."

"Listen son, sorry I yelled at you. But this situation could've been really serious. We love you London. I don't want to see anything happen to you or Donald."

Once again London apologizes. James hugs him and then turns to Donald giving him a high five before leaving their room. London rolls over and closes his eyes. Ten minutes later he hears voices outside of his window. He gets up and peeks out of his curtain. Warren, Ronnie, and Michael are laughing and riding down London's street. They were just now returning from the trail.

Memory 3:

A Deeper Disturbance

Two weeks later, London was finally allowed to go outside and play. However, he still had another week until he could ride his bike again. He walks to John's house. For the past two weeks, London could do little more than think about that day, the day his nightmares became reality. He always believed monsters had to exist, no matter what his parents said. The one thing he couldn't account for was the man; the man who came from out of nowhere and saved his life. Why did he save his life? Was he an Angel, a ghost, or maybe some new super high-tech cop? Yeah, that's it, like Men in Black or something. He was there to get that alien thing!

He didn't speak or even look at me though, London thinks to himself. He must be like a ninja too. He would've had to kill me if I saw his face.

Two blocks from home, London trots up John's front stairs and rings the bell. John's mother answers the door.

"Hello Mrs. Reilly. Can John come out?"

She gives him a long hard look, and then tells him to hold on.

John comes to the door and like his mother, gives London a long hard look.

"Can you come out?"

John doesn't reply.

"What's the matter, are you still on punishment? John remains silent. Are you going to say anything?"

"How did you get away?"

"I'll tell you if you come out."

"Mom, I'm going out with London."

"Bring your ball!"

They head toward the park.

"First of all, before I tell you anything, you have to promise not to tell anyone!"

"Okay, I promise."

"What did you tell your mother?"

I told her we got chased by something. I told her it was a monster. I told her everything."

"What did she say?"

"She didn't believe me. She said the only large animals around here are deer. But she did say that my grandfather always said, wherever there's a deer, there's a bear."

"A bear, have you ever seen a blue bear? What kind of bear has six legs?"

"Yeah I know. She didn't believe me anyway. That's why I still got in trouble. Your mother didn't believe me either."

"My mother, when did you talk to my mother?"

"I went straight to your house that day. Your mother said you were already home. Now how is that? How did you get away?"

"It was crazy. I couldn't move. That thing was just about to eat me! Then, there was this man. He just appeared out of nowhere. I opened my eyes and he was fighting the blue thing."

"I thought that's what *you* were doing!"

"I'm not stupid! Anyway, the man faked the creature out. Then, he grabbed me and did something to make us disappear."

"Disappear? What are you talking about?"

"Just listen. After he let me go, we were down the street from my house. Then *he* disappeared."

London and John enter the park.

"I think I know what happened."

"What?"

"He was like, a Men in Black Ninja or something. You know, if you find out who they really are they'll have to kill you."

"I knew that movie was real!"

"We're the only ones who really know about this John. We have to keep it secret. I've seen what they can do. We have to be smart. I don't think we should talk about this again. They may be able to hear us. What do you think?"

John swallows hard and looks around nervously.

"I think you're right."

London and John head to the courts. They play games of around the world, 50, and then one on one. They'd been at the park for a little over an hour, when they heard a car horn blow. It came from a burgundy SUV. London knew who it was when he heard the rhythm of the horn. It was his father. The boys run over to the car.

"How's it going guys, who's winning?"

"Hey Mr. Bishop, I'm up," he says laughing.

"Yeah you wish. Hey Dad, what are you doing here?"

"I got off early and came home. Your mother told me you were here. I'm on my way to the mall, actually, Donald and I, he says while pointing to the back seat, are on our way to the mall."

"Donald's back there? What's up Donald?"

"What's up John, hey London."

"I wanted to see if you guys wanted to tag along. We're going to get pizza and ice cream."

"Yeah we want to go!"

"John, I talked to your mother. She said you can come if you like."

"Thanks Mr. Bishop."

"You boys jump in and buckle up."

When they arrived at the mall, James took the boys to the arcade. They played for forty-five minutes. From there he took them to the mall's toy store. He bought a couple of toys for Donald, a video game for London, and even bought a joystick for John. Their last stop was the food court. Just as James had promised, it was pizza and ice cream to go around. They had medium sodas to wash it all down. London didn't know why their father was being so nice, but he sure wasn't going to ask. He was having too much fun! That night when London said his prayers, he thanked God for giving him the best father in the world.

The very next day after lunch, again James was home early. London wondered how his father was able to keep getting off early from work. He asked him.

"I needed a break, so I took some time off. But if you want, I can make a couple calls and go in."

"No, no, no I'm glad you took off."

"Are you sure?"

"Yes, I'm sure, I was just wondering."

"Okay, well in that case, I think you may like my next idea."

"What's your next idea Dad," Donald asks with a full smile.

"The sooner you guys get your chores done the sooner you'll see."

The boys finished their chores faster than ever before. James was amused. The three of them get into the SUV and headed out. When the vehicle stopped, they were in the parking lot of the area's most popular water park. London and John bounced and cheered when they saw the signs. They spent hours there. It was some of the most fun they'd ever had.

"What do you guys want to do tomorrow?"

"Let's go to the movies."

"Yeah, that sounds good, I'm with Donald!"

Back at home, just before falling asleep, London figured what it was that had his father acting like father of the year, summer vacation was almost over. The next day after returning from the movies, James calls his sons into the living room. When they come down the stairs their parents are sitting on one of the couches.

"You fellas come and have a seat. Your mother and I need to talk to you."

James is uneasy. He tries to hide it as his children sit.

"Guess what."

Fully anticipating another day of fun, the boys perk up, "What Dad?"

"I've got a new job."

"You do?   Asks London. Congratulations Dad."

"Yeah, congratulations Dad."

"Thank you, guys. They gave me what you call a promotion. That means the people I work for like the way I work so much, that they gave me a better job."

"Did you get a new job too Mommy," Donald asks.

"No baby," Tammy says to her son as she smiles at his innocence.

"This new job is in California."

"*California*… isn't that a long way away?"

"Yes, it is London."

"Does that mean we're moving?" London asks.

Donald is excited "We're moving?"

"Well, listen boys, it's kind of tricky. I'm going to be moving by myself for right now. My new bosses have an apartment waiting for me. There's only room enough for one person. But once I get there, I can start looking for a big house. Then you boys can come whenever you want! We can have the same kind of fun we've been having these last few days, just the fellas."

London knew what fellas meant. However, he didn't know why his father had just called his mother a *fella.*

"Dad, you just called mommy a fella. I thought a fella was a boy or a man."

"You're a very smart boy London. You always have been. (James took a deep breath) Your mother's going to stay here and take care of this house."

"But who's going to take care of this house when we all go to the new house in California?"

"London, Donald… Mommy and Daddy aren't going to be living in the same house anymore. Tammy says. We still love you both, and we do still love each other. But the best thing for Mommy and Daddy is to ..."

Donald didn't totally understand what this all meant, London did. His heart instantly breaks. That night when London prayed, he prayed hard. He asked God to keep his parents together. He repeated this prayer every day until his father moved out. Then London prayed no more. He couldn't think of a single reason why his prayer wouldn't have been granted. He was betrayed. There was only God to blame.

Eyes are the Soul

(Part B.)

London wipes tears from his eyes. How had he forgotten so much? Then he remembers something he once read about trauma. Trauma has the potential to cause one to repress certain memories, especially emotional traumas. He immediately realized the separation and subsequent divorce of his parents was his trauma. He accepted that. That was real. But how is everything else real? London takes a deep breath and tries to relax.

Boom! The bathroom door is forced open. London freezes.

"We have you surrounded. Come out with your hands up! We know you're in one of these stalls. Unless you want us to figure which one, a series of clicks and other sounds that are obviously guns sound off. I suggest you put your feet down and slowly come with us."

London slowly puts his feet down.

London thinks to himself; *they're going to put me in the Looney bin when I tell them my story. Bad thing is I may belong there.*

"Good, now do exactly what I tell you. First slowly unlock the stall door."

London did as he was told. He waits for his next instruction. A full minute passes and London still hasn't received his next instruction.

"Should I come out now?"

No reply.

"I'm coming out with my hands up. I do not have a weapon; *I repeat*; I do not have a weapon."

He opens the door slowly as he possibly can. It opens slightly. He pushes a little harder. An airport officer is standing there pointing a gun directly at him! London closes his eyes. Nothing happens. He opens his left eye keeping the right one tightly shut. There are other cops pointing guns in his direction. They're all silent. London steps out. He stands next to the stall he was just in. But the cops are still pointing their guns at the stall;

completely motionless. London approaches the lead officer's face.

He reaches out to touch him, then …

"London, son of James…"

The voice startles London. He falls into the cop knocking

them both to the floor. When the cop hit the floor, he remained in

the very same position that he was in while standing frozen-like.

The voice had come from above the stalls. London looked up.

There in midair, over the stall's wall dividers was the mysterious

man with the water-like eyes.

"Greetings London son of James, fear not, for my purpose

is peace."

London didn't speak. What could he say? The man

descended to ground level. He reaches down to help London up.

All London can do is stare at his disturbing yet mesmerizing eyes.

"Others will soon come."

The man retracts his hand when it becomes apparent that

London has no intention of taking it.

"Come with me or by them be taken."

Just then, voices from outside, "They went into the Ladies room after the guy who was running!"

London jumps up.

"Okay, I'll go with you."

The man touches his shoulder and the two of them fade out of sight.

Simultaneously, reinforcements kick the door in half a second later. The first cops on the scene regain motion and consciousness. They are in no way wise to their recent condition.

"Sam are you hit?!"

"What, no, no I don't think so."

"Why are you on the floor?"

The first cops were still waiting for the suspect to follow the lead officer's instructions.

Sam stands up. "Slowly open the door and come out with your hands up!"

When there is no response, "You have until the count of three! One, two, three…"

The lead officer kicks the stall door in revealing an empty toilet.

"What the… we just saw his legs; where could he have gone?!"

London is all of a sudden standing in the middle of a large unfurnished studio apartment; He and the man with the eyes. The only things in the room with them are a fold up chair and an echo. The man walks over to one of the windows and peers out.

"Ask what you will. I will answer what I can."

"Where am I?"

"Safe."

"Can I leave?"

"Soon."

"Why not now?"

"You were brought here for a reason, for answers. Ask what you will."

London thinks a minute. "What are you?"

"I am the Fourth Corner."

"What? What is that supposed to mean?"

"I am guardian of the Fourth Corner of the Earth."

"O-okay, umm, well who or what was that thing that just tried to kill me?"

"He is a demon disciple. The other is his enforcer."

"The other? What other?"

"Dozorn, he is the six legged one."

London didn't respond. He didn't want to accept the fact that this has been going on since he was ten years old! And he still can't believe he'd forgotten it all!

"You fall silent."

"Six legs, I don't know what you're talking about."

"I am not deserving of your lies."

London felt guilty. Who was he kidding; it was time to 'fess up.

"Sorry. But, why are they after *me*?"

"You have been chosen. The attempts on your life have not and will not end."

"I've been chosen to be killed?!"

"No. You've been chosen for a purpose."

"What purpose?"

"The Knight's Birth."

"The Knight's what?"

"You shall become a warrior against the principalities of this world, a device of the Most-High: The *SoulKnight*. You will seek out, confront and destroy the evil."

"*Excuse me*? You sound like a movie trailer. Speaking of movies, am I on some kind of reality show or something? Where are the cameras, am I getting paid for this?"

London realizes that the 4th Corner isn't finding his sarcasm amusing in any way.

"Back in the shop, I know for sure I injured and maybe even broke my arm. But now it feels as if nothing's happened, good as new."

"Thank the gift giver for the gift that was given."

"What gift and what gift giver?"

"Seven years you've worn the gift. And there is but one gift giver."

"Seven years? What, the bracelet?" He lifts his sleeve; "My uncle gave me this."

"So, you thought. Sit. The bracelet is one of several gifts. It will heal your body of whatever ails you, broken bones, lacerations, bruises, and more."

London can't remember the last time he was sick.

"You said several gifts. What are the others?"

"You have physical abilities beyond normal man. Your strength, foot speed, and endurance are all touched."

"Strength, speed, and endurance; those are what I use to play ball."

London admits to himself the fact that he's always had a feeling of a deeper ability but was fearful of tapping into it. He could never explain the feeling.

"You've done well."

"Wait a minute, I work hard! Are you saying that my success is due to these so-called gifts?"

"As I have said, you have done well to suppress your true abilities. I will say, the majority of your athletic accomplishments are not related to your gifts."

London sat and wrestled with his thoughts. The 4th Corner went back to staring out of the window. What was going on? This made no sense! A few minutes pass, and London thinks of another question.

"As much power as you have, why would you need me? You're a much more powerful man than I'll ever be!"

"I am a guardian, not a Knight. And I am not a man."

"Just what are you? And who chose me. Who is this mighty gift giver?"

"What you have been told thus far, is sufficient; for now. Much you must learn on your own. Arise. He points, "That door is your exit. We will meet again."

The 4th Corner faded out of existence right before London's eyes. London is confused. He didn't know what to believe. He apprehensively walks to the door and opens it. Miraculously he finds himself inside of a small restroom, and the door in which he'd entered is nowhere to be seen. London opens the new door and steps out. He takes a few steps and realizes he's between two columns of seated people. He's on a plane.

"Sir you need to be seated; we're descending!"

How did he end up on an airplane?

"Where is this plane headed?!"

"Are you suffering from motion sickness? We're going to Maryland. Now please sit down!"

Breathing heavily, London sits down and tries to calm himself. Had he fallen asleep? He didn't believe that was likely. He tried to dispel everything that had just happened. None of this made any sense! Unless… could he have been drugged? He looks around. There are only six people within ten feet of him, and they're all seniors. He had never suffered from motion sickness before, but is that what's going on? The only other explanation was too hard to accept. London gazed out of the window. He was just too young to be losing his mind!

Chapter Two:

Sight is Belief

The plane touched down at BWI airport. London was still trying to rationalize the days' events when the other passengers started unloading their overhead compartments.

Whispering, "I must be going Schizoid!"

The same flight attendant walks up ten minutes later.

"Sir, are you okay?"

He sighs. "I don't know anymore."

He notices he's the only passenger still on the plane.

"Are you feeling sick?"

"Yeah, in the head."

London gathered his things and exited the plane.

Two days later, London had concluded that the combination of a lack of sleep, no breakfast, and a sudden attack of motion sickness were to blame for his episode on the plane. And by now, all confusion had given way to excitement. The day for football try-outs had arrived. London, John, and the whole crew rode with Warren to school.

"Listen up London, you may be the man in basketball but now you're entering into my domain," Warren boasts.

Warren was already a defensive starter. He was one of the team's best players. He was anxious to finally be able to outshine London.

"I don't want any hard feelings after practice fellas. When I do what I do, it's just business, never personal."

When the boys arrived, they followed Warren to the field. Twenty minutes later the Head coach explained to everyone what the day would consist of. He also told them of his expectations After the speech, Warren walked up to the coach and the two joked. It was obvious that Warren was one of his favorites.

After the stretches and warm-ups, the first test (so to speak), was the forty-yard dash. Everyone gives their all. They run with every fiber of their being. The third group lines up. London is included. Just before the assistant yells go, the Head coach stops him. Warren wants in. He lines up right next to London. London was not naïve. He knew what Warren was trying to do. He was able to quickly re-focus. Although he was convinced that he'd imagined the whole 4th Corner thing, he had decided that he would act on the feeling that he could do more. He was not going to suppress his abilities on this day. The assistant yells go. Warren takes off! His muscles flex and his lungs burn. He swung his arms like a technician. He remembered every tip he'd ever been told about speed; *long strides, lean forward, head down.* He flew down field, focused on the task at hand. In fact, he's so focused, that when he finally lifts his head, he sees one of the assistants at the finish line. He paid Warren no attention; and for that matter he pays the other runners no attention either. He was in conversation. When Warren crossed the finish line, he saw who the assistant was talking to. Warren's momentum carries him past London and the assistant coach. He bends over and tries to catch his breath. After his lungs get relief, he walks toward the two. It started to occur to him, in order for the assistant to be speaking to London while he himself was still running, would mean that London won the race. And not only won it, but he would have had to have smashed the race! Warren's personal best was 4.6 seconds. He was sure that he'd run even faster today. What did London run? Warren walked up and stood next to London. The Head coach and other players crowded around all wanting to know the time on the stopwatch. There was a lot of commotion. It was hard to hear what the coaches were saying. The only thing Warren could make out was *"That's impossible!"*

"Alright let's break it up, show's over. Everyone line up for the catching drills!"

Warren was the last one standing. He made his way to the assistant with the stopwatch.

"Coach Bobby."

"Yeah?"

"I have to know."

Sighing, "I don't know. It doesn't make sense."

"What are you talking about; come on what was his time?"

Coach Bobby handed him the stopwatch.

"That's impossible! There's no way!"

Warren threw the stopwatch in the grass. It read 2.7 seconds.

London didn't know what to say. Everyone gave him sideway looks as he joined them for the next drill. He didn't want to seem arrogant, so he hung back as the drills began. 2.7 seconds, how can that be? No one can run forty yards in 3 seconds, 3.9 would have been impossible, but 2.7, that has to be a mistake. London's name is called. He had faded so far into the background that he didn't hear it.

"Where's cheetah boy?"

London heard the commotion and jogged over.

"There he is. Where've you been? Did you take a quick trot around the globe?" everyone laughs.

"Sorry Coach, I ran for water."

"Alright son let's test those hands."

The drill went like this: one man in the middle surrounded by several, *hope to be* quarterbacks standing ten yards away in radius. The player in the middle stands ready to catch the first ball thrown. However, as soon as he catches the ball, he must immediately drop it to the ground in order to turn facing the next quarterback who will immediately throw the next ball. This goes on until the circle is completed twice.

Everyone's attention turned to watch London. What would he do this time? London felt all eyes squarely on him as he walked to the middle. After what happened earlier, he was no longer excited. He was nervous, very nervous. How would he follow that up?

"Go!"

The first ball went flying. It was a bullet, that is, to everyone except London. The second ball came, another bullet, third, fourth, all bullets! London wondered when they were going to start really whipping the balls at him. He had warmed up enough! He took a closer look. Each quarterback was visibly putting their all into their throws. But when he caught the balls, it was like they were just tossing them to him. London was catching the balls without the slightest level of difficulty. It occurred to him that if he kept this up, he'd be looked at like a freak! The last two balls thrown to him before completing the first circle, he intentionally drops. The second time around, he purposely drops every third ball. For The rest of tryouts he continues a similar pattern. Each tackle, each block, each pass, each catch, each and every drill was as simple as breathing to London. Yet, he kept his performance at an average level. The only justification he allowed himself to accept for this was to not be considered a freak. But he knew that there was something more. He couldn't explain it, but he felt … something.

London was relieved when try outs were over. It wasn't because of fatigue though; he was tired of holding back! All the players went to the locker room to shower and change. Since London was curbing his abilities, Warren was the main stand-out. He was eager to remind everyone, especially London.

"Good try out London. I talked to the coach. He said not to worry about the problems with your forty time."

"What problems with my forty time?"

"He said the stopwatch they used had been giving them problems and they'd been meaning to get a new one but just didn't get a chance. Not to worry though, I think you'll definitely make the *practice squad*."

London responds sarcastically, "Yeah I hope so."

"You won the race fair and square though, I have to give it to you. I reacted too slowly. We have to do it again sometime."

Visibly irritated, "Yeah whatever!"

London walked over to John, who also had an average performance.

"I think I'm going to take the bus home."

"The bus, why?"

"I don't want to hear any more of his mouth."

John laughs hard, "Yeah I hear you! I'll come with you."

"No, that's alright, I have some things on my mind anyway."

"You sure?"

"Yeah I'm cool."

After his shower, London got dressed and headed for the bus stop. He hadn't been there for three minutes before Warren's car pulled up.

"Hey London, just because you can't be a two-sport star is no reason to be depressed!"

"I'm not depressed. I just have some things going on right now. I need to do some thinking."

"Whatever... see you around."

Warren and the others drive off. Not long thereafter, the bus comes. London walks to the back of the bus and takes a seat. *What does this all mean?* Before he can speculate, he remembers the empty studio apartment. How can this all be? This is real life not a sci-fi movie! After the bus made a few stops, London began to look at the other side of the coin. He could've easily shown not just Warren up, he could've shown a whole NFL team up! What are the limits of his abilities? He signals to let the driver know he's getting off at the next stop. London gets off and waits until the bus is out of sight. He pulls the sleeves up on his shirt and starts the timer on his wristwatch. He knows that at his present location, he's a good twenty-minute walk from home. He takes off! First, he runs down the street. He watches as the trees and parked cars whiz by in a blur. He then jets down a residential driveway. Once he gets to the backyard he jumps vertically and lands standing straight up atop the metal fence at the rear of the yard. Without stopping his momentum, he bounces off the fence into a double front somersault landing in the next yard sprinting in full stride! He then takes two large steps up the back of the house in the yard, springing himself into a tree. Hanging from a branch, he swings himself around and around building up speed. When he is satisfied with his force, he let's go! This action sends him flying into the tree in the next yard! He catches a branch and climbs until he is standing. Next, he leaps out of the tree landing on the roof of the home on the property. Houses in the neighborhood are rather close, so he hops from rooftop to rooftop as easily as if he was a child hopping from square to square on the sidewalk. When he reaches the fifth house, he jumps to the front yard and keeps running. Seconds later he's home, he stops the timer on his watch as he stands in front of his side door. He is exhausted, but remarkably he catches his breath in half the time it should've taken. London notices that his bracelet is slightly glowing. Not as brightly as it did when he had first found it, but it is glowing. He stops the timer on his watch and sees only six minutes have passed. If this was a movie, he was definitely the star.

It is now Thursday. School resumes on Monday. Almost a week has passed since London tested the level of his abilities. This he could accept, after all, he'd always felt a deeper capability. But as for the 4th *Corner,* London refused to acknowledge any such memory; at least consciously. He was preoccupied with coming up with new extravagant shortcuts home. He was having the time of his life! Daily he challenged himself to not only up the ante, but to also remain unseen. London couldn't wait for his mother to send him to the corner store. He'd be there and back before she knew he was gone. He played ball in his backyard with a new-found vigor. He was always an elite player, but now he was unbelievable! He wanted people to see but decided against it.

Tammy and London went to the airport to pick Donald up. Although London had decided to keep his abilities secret, he felt he'd be safe sharing with Donald. As far as London was

concerned, the only decision to be made was whether to tell

Donald straight out or just show him. It would be more fun to just

show him. They parked the car in short term. They were about

forty minutes early. They sat and talked. London was close to his

mother. Part of him wanted to also share with her.

"You never told me how your football tryouts went."

London had to bite his tongue to keep from spilling his

guts.

"London, I know you hear me talking to you."

"I didn't make the team."

"Oh, I'm sorry honey. Well at least you tried your best

right?"

"Uh, where are the restrooms?"

"I'm not sure; I think I saw a sign back toward the

entrance."

"I'll be back."

London was glad he'd gotten out of answering that last question. He didn't want to lie to his mother. He walked outside to waste a little time, and hopefully make his mother forget her line of questioning. London watched as car upon car stopped and dropped people off. He looked at his watch. Donald's plane should be landing in another ten minutes or so.

"Has thou found fulfillment?"

London turns around. The 4th Corner stares back at him. He also sees that the dozens of people who are all around, now stand motionless. London swallows hard and stands still in disbelief.

"Come now London, thou were unsuccessful in fooling thyself, surely ye think not to fool me."

London takes a deep breath and rubs his eyes. He slowly walks past the 4th Corner and sits on a bench.

"What was your question?"

"Hast thou found fulfillment? You toy with your abilities and long to show them."

"I guess you, and all that you said was true."

"Indeed."

"I have more questions."

"It is known however; you must first be tested."

"Tested, what kind of test?"

"A test of trust; and whether or not you can be trusted. You must keep your abilities secret from all, even your brother."

"How'd you know I'd tell him?"

"All is known."

"What's that supposed to mean? No one knows everything."

"Your questions shall all be answered. First prove worthy. Tell no one and use extreme discretion even when thou believeth that thou art alone, eyes are ever watchful. Thy mother calleth."

London turns to look behind him. Everyone is back in motion. He turns back and the 4th Corner is gone.

"London come on. I see Donald. What have you been doing out here?"

In the car, Donald did all the talking. He told his mother and London of all the things he and his father had been doing. After fifteen minutes of non-stop talk, Donald noticed that London was quiet all the while.

"What's wrong with London?"

"He didn't make the team"

"Oh, sorry to hear that."

"I'll be alright."

"Good. Uh, so when can I get paid bro?"

Saturday rolled around. It was noon. London was still lying in his bed. He couldn't stop thinking about what the 4th Corner had told him. He wanted to know everything there was to know. He vowed to keep all that he'd been told guarded. It wouldn't be easy, but he would make it happen. The decision was made.

That night when both Tammy and Donald were asleep, London snuck out back and fulfilled his craving to indulge in backyard acrobatics. His only audience was the night stars, and the neighbor's cat. London knew he couldn't stop altogether; he'd just have to play in the dark.

Chapter Three:

Introductions Are in Order

It's the third week of school. London is a sophomore. He doesn't hate school, but he isn't its biggest fan either. His thing is the vast majority of what's being taught he'll never need in real life. Still, London is smart. He receives very good grades. His goal is to be accepted into a college with both a respectable basketball program for him, and a good academic program for his parents. In fact, if it wasn't for his parents, especially his mother, he wouldn't have had nearly the grades he had. She was adamant about him receiving good grades in order to continue playing ball.

Like most guys, the one class he did love was gym class. One day in particular, London showed out! He was always known as the school's top basketball player, but he wasn't known to do things like, dunk! At lunch he was the talk of the school. It was then that he realized he made an error in judgment. He was far from discreet on this day. The only thing he had going for him was the fact that there weren't as many students in gym class as there normally would be. This meant that he could more easily dismiss his rumored performance as exaggeration. Whenever someone

asked him about the rumors, he'd severely downplay them:

"I heard you dunked!"

"I really just got some of the rim."

"I heard you were pulling up from half court!"

"I made a prayer or two off the backboard."

"They said you made every shot!"

"I had it going, but I did miss a few."

When the bell rang at the end of the day, London couldn't

wait to get out of the building. He was the first one through the

door. It was hard work fixing what he almost sabotaged! When

John called him at home, he had to once again play the extra

humble role. It took the rest of the week and two more highly

attended gym classes to cool things down, but things finally got

back to normal.

In the next couple of years, London had gotten it down to a

science. He did just enough to remain a star player, but nothing approaching his true abilities. When the urge to indulge would arise, he would borrow the keys to the school gym from the coach (one of the perks of being the star player). He would just tell him that he had some things he wanted to work on.

London was now eighteen and beginning his freshman year of college. He earned a full athletic scholarship to play in Philadelphia. It was a school that fit the bill for himself and his parents. It wasn't considered a national powerhouse, but it was D-1. Pro scouts didn't even have it on their radar. It was perfect. It meant that as long as he didn't score 100 points, he should be able to get away with having a couple pretty big games a year.

It's been years since London's seen the 4th Corner. The only proof that they'd ever met, were the abilities that London kept hidden. He often wondered whether he'd failed the test. He figured this was most likely the reason he hadn't seen or heard anything in so long. It's been a long time since he's seen his father as well. London hadn't gone back to visit his father in California since meeting his new girlfriend. London made sure he was too busy with either basketball camp or preparing for the next semester. He'd speak to his father on occasion, but even that would only last briefly. London was fazing his father out of his life.

It is now the second semester. Things are going well. London's team had just won their third straight game. It's Friday night and the team had a small party to celebrate. London made it back to his dorm room late. He drags himself to the shower and then to bed. He's only asleep for fifteen minutes when he's awakened by his roommate. When London looks up, he sees his roommate is still lying down, so he decides to ignore him. Ten minutes later, his name is called again.

"Man, what do you want?"

No answer. Again, London dozes off. After another ten minutes London's name is called for the third time. He is irritated. He gets up, rips the covers off of his roommate, and voices his displeasure!

"Dude what is your problem?! Wake me up again and you'll be waking up in the hospital!"

"What, what's wrong? What's going on?"

London sees that his roommate's eyes are completely red. He had been sound asleep.

"My fault, bad joke, go back to … "

He was asleep before London could finish. London looks around the room. Is there an intruder? No, it had to be the 4th Corner! He whispers his name. There's no response. He gets back in bed. He wasn't going to kid himself. He knows his name was called. If it wasn't the 4th Corner, then who? He feels fear begin to creep. Just before he dozes back off, he remembers a story he'd heard in Sunday school as a kid. It was about Samuel. Then sleep overtakes him.

"LONDON."

London wakes and sit ups. This time he doesn't look to his roommate.

"Speak… Lord, for your servant heareth." (1st Samuel 3:9 King James Version Holy Bible)

The response he receives is so immediate and powerful, it shakes him.

"I AM ALPHA AND OMEGA, THE BEGINNING AND THE END, THE FIRST AND THE LAST, WHICH IS AND WHICH WAS, AND WHICH IS TO COME, THE ALMIGHTY!" Rev. 1: 8

London cannot move. It isn't only his fear (which is great), he is physically paralyzed. His heart beats faster than he thought possible. It is the only part of him that can move. All is silent. Then out of nowhere the voice repeats the same powerful statement.

"I AM ALPHA AND OMEGA, THE BEGINNING AND THE END, THE FIRST AND THE LAST, WHICH IS AND WHICH WAS, AND WHICH IS TO COME, THE ALMIGHTY!"

The voice continued.

"IT WAS I WHO CHOSE YOU. IT WAS I WHO GAVE YOU YOUR GIFTS, AND IT IS I WHO CAN TAKE THEM AWAY. YOUR CONCERNS ARE KNOWN. ALL IS AN OPEN BOOK BEFORE ME! AS A CHILD YOU DOUBTED ME NOT, BUT AT THE SEPARATION OF YOUR PARENTS YOU REJECTED ME HENCEFORTH. FROM THERE YOU HEARD

114

THE SUGGESTIONS OF THE WORLD AND GREW WITH THEIR BELIEFS.

THY EARTHLY FATHER DOES NOT SERVE ME. THOUGH THE OPPORTUNITY HAS BEEN HIS MANY TIMES, TIME AND TIME AGAIN HE HAS REFUSED ME. HOWEVER, THY MOTHER IS MY CHILD. SHE LOVED YOUR EARTHLY FATHER AND LIVED RIGHTEOUSLY BEFORE HIM. THROUGH NO FAULT OF HER OWN, SHE WAS UNSUCCESSFUL IN WINNING HIM. IN TIME, THIS DIVISION WOULD'VE HINDERED YOUR PURPOSE. THEIR SPLIT WAS NECESSARY AND PROFITABLE FOR YOU. IT WAS I WHO MADE SURE THEIR MUTUAL PRIORITY WAS THE UPBRINGING OF YOU AND YOUR BROTHER. I ALSO ALLOWED A SPIRIT OF FRIENDSHIP TO DWELL BETWEEN THEM.

I ALONE, AM GOD. VERILY I SAY UNTO YOU, WHETHER THEY BE CARVED, MOLDED, MANUFACTURED, DRY BONES IN A GRAVE, OR WALKING THE EARTH, THEY ARE IDOLS! THERE IS NONE BESIDE ME. THE SCIENCE OF MAN CANNOT

STAND UP TO ME. THEY KNOW WHAT I LET THEM KNOW, THEY LEARN WHAT I ALLOW THEM TO LEARN. "I AM THE WAY, THE TRUTH, AND THE LIFE, NO MAN COME UNTO THE FATHER, BUT BY ME!" John 14. 6

THOUGH YOU SOUGHT TO REJECT ME, YOUR HEART HAS SOMEWHAT CLINGED TO MY WORD. ALL IS AN OPEN BOOK BEFORE ME! THE FAITH YOU HAD AS A CHILD HAS NOT WHOLLY ABANDONED YOU. THE GIFTS THAT I HAVE GIVEN YOU, YOU WILL USE TO SERVE ME. THERE ARE MORE GIFTS STILL THAT ARE NOT YET GIVEN. YOU ASK, AS MANY HAVE ASKED BEFORE YOU, WHY YOU? VERILY I SAY UNTO YOU, THE GROUND DOES NOT ASK THE FOOT, WHY DID YOU CHOOSE TO WALK IN THIS DIRECTION; ALL OF THE GROUND IS THE FOOT'S TO WALK, SO TOO IS THE EARTH AND EVERYTHING IN IT, MINE TO DO WITH WHAT I WILL!

FOLLOW THOSE I SEND. UNTIL THEN, BE SPIRIT LED, AND REKINDLE YOUR FAITH. SERVE ME AND BE BLESSED. I ALONE, AM GOD."

The moment the voice stopped; London was able to move. He jumps out of bed and crashes into his dresser. He knocked everything that was on top to the ground. The noise awakes his roommate.

"London what are you doing? Were you drinking at the party or what?"

London sees his mouth moving, but he doesn't hear a word. He is too worked up. He has to get out!

"I need some air, I'll be back."

He leaves the room, jogs down the steps, and is out on the street in 5 seconds. Wearing shorts, a T-shirt, and house shoes, London shoots down the street. He's in a panic. Everything he'd experienced up until then, he'd been able to handle. He would've considered governmental experiments, or even the paranormal. He would've even considered a possibility that he was losing his mind; but God? And not just a supreme being, but the very God of the bible! In a dazed state, London speed walks with no destination. The only thing that breaks his blind quest is the horn of a car that almost hits him as he crosses an intersection without looking. He had been walking for over forty minutes. Hearing the horn snaps

London out of his daze. As the car passes by, London looks

around and sees a city park across the street. He walks up to a

water fountain and splashes his face. He sits down on a bench next

to the fountain. London hadn't been to church in years, but there

was no denying what had just happened to him. Part of him always

wanted to believe. But his common sense and knowledge of how

the world worked always dismissed the urge. He began

reminiscing about when he was a child in church, the stories, the

songs, the lessons, the sermons. The truth? He now had the

answer. The proof that all scientists demanded; an indisputable

personal encounter.

London's panic finally gave way to a measured calm. He

understood and accepted what had happened. What he didn't

know, was what he would now do. He was a ball player, not some

warrior Knight! Warriors go to war. The closest thing he'd seen to

war was a road game.

London attempts to walk back to his dorm. It occurs to

him that in his panic, he had obviously made a turn or two that he'd

never before taken. He is lost. Nothing looks familiar, not a street, a house, or a landmark. The wind starts to pick up. Or so he thought. Something is wrong, very wrong. London's clothes start to blow in the wind. Debris and streetlights began to blow around. But the problem was there was no sound. There is absolutely no noise, just movement. London picks up the pace. He's being watched. He can feel it. He has to get out of the open. London turns the corner and stands with his back against a wall. His heart is in an invisible race against his thoughts. Mugged, or murdered which one was it going to be? He just wanted to play ball how was all this happening?! London peers back the way he'd come to see if anyone was following him. He looks everywhere, under cars, behind trees, and even on top of buildings. There's no one. Afraid, and standing with his back to the wall, London is suddenly blown into the open and to the ground by a silent wind. He rolls and springs up into a double back flip landing on his feet. Terrified, London runs at top speed toward another corner. He rounds it, but his escape is defeated by a dead end. He immediately turns around and heads in the opposite direction. He doesn't get ten feet. London stops cold. There, not five feet away, stood his past. The past he'd forgotten. The impossible six-legged beast from his childhood, emerged from a sea of blackness. London's heart skipped a beat. He back peddles in disbelief.

"You should really watch your step London," says a voice from behind him.

London turns around. The thing he'd formally known as Pat stood there with a scowl on his face. Whoever came up with the saying *between a rock and a hard place*, didn't understand its' meaning as well as London now did. Pat and Dozorn slowly circled around London. How was he supposed to be a warrior against such foes? Where was the 4th Corner? Was this another test? London circled even slower trying to figure which one would attack first. Why were they waiting? He was defenseless, a sitting duck in stew! Then, as if he had read London's mind, Pat ended the mystery.

"Be grateful the Dark Author has given us instruction to leave you with your life. Otherwise we would've snatched your soul from your flesh!"

Thinking to himself, Dark who?

London swallows hard. He decides to stand strong and look brave. Especially since Pat said they aren't going to kill him.

"State your business or let me go beasts!"

Pat laughed.

"Your bluffing needs work coward, your fear is almost tangible; However, our business in an introduction."

"I don't want to know anyone that you know!"

"Silence mortal! Growls the beast. Behold, the Dark lord of the under!"

The simple fact that the blue creature called Dozorn, spoke in English this time, was terrifying enough, but the sight London sees when he turns, gives birth to new fear. London laid his eyes upon what could only be described as perfect evil. On a huge throne, made from a rotted tree, sat a monstrosity. Every inch of London's body seized up. Around the bottom of the throne were eight scale armored spider legs. They were connected to an almost human waste that wore a fiery red chain link belt. Underneath the belt on the very seat of the throne, legs folded one over the other.

Above the belt was a torso that was similar to that of a silverback gorilla. The arm rests of the throne supported two hairless human arms, the ends of which were like unto lizard claws. At the top of the torso was a cobra hood wide enough to block the shine of the moon. Folded behind the monstrosity, but still visible, were a pair of humongous eagle wings. The actual head of this monstrosity was covered by a lion's mane. The face was spotted like a leopard. There were snake pits instead of a nose, and a mouth full of fangs, no lips. Just above his huge black reflective eyes stretched two bull horns wide. It spoke without opening its' mouth.

"I am the Earth's nightmare, the Dark Author known by many names. I bring chaos to perfection, evil to righteousness, and death to life. I agreed to the terms of your God this day, in order to meet with you. As long as you are not threatened, he will not interfere. Thus, you will not be harmed on this night. But be ye sure, another day like this will not come! Decline your God's offer. You cannot prevail against me. He wishes you to be a warrior… I am war! Refuse him and spare your mortal existence. Join me, for it is I who will rule the future. Consider this wisdom, no more shall be given!"

The Dark Author turns to Pat.

"Open his eyes."

Pat looks at London and points to the dead end. London looks. The wall of the dead end disappears. He can now see his way. When he turns back, he is alone. He runs back to the dorm with every bit of speed he possesses! For the rest of the night he doesn't sleep a wink.

The next day, London's roommate, Tommy, who's also on the team, exited a bus and climbed the stairs of the dorm. It is after 4pm. He opens the door and sees the same mess that greeted him when he woke that same morning. Everything is as it was; including London who is still asleep. He's dead to the world getting the sleep he'd missed last night.

"London, London wake up... London!"

"Yeah, yeah what's up?"

"What was going on last night? First you kept waking me up, then you jumped out of bed and ran out of the room. Now I find you still in bed sleep close to 4:30pm. Man, coach is going to kill you when he finds out you're on that stuff!"

"What?! London sits up and looks at the clock. You know good and well I'm not on anything. I'll tell you what though; I had the craziest dream ever! I was lying here... "

Just then, a picture of the Dark Author popped in London's head.

"And what happened?"

"On second thought, you don't want to know."

That weekend, London takes a bus home to Maryland. He needed to see his mother. When he arrives, he's so happy to see her that he almost forgets the reason he's there. Tammy cooked London's favorite dish, steak and lobster tails. He would have been glad to be eating anything other than cafeteria food, but this was heaven! The two played catch up for about two hours, including dinner. Donald was with friends in New York. When dinner was over, London cleaned up and he and his mother went into the living room.

"So, lay it on me. I can tell it's pretty serious."

"What, how do you know I have something on my mind?"

"Well first of all, I know my son; second, you never clean up without having to be told. So, like I said, lay it on me."

London sighs.

"London, you didn't get anybody pregnant, did you?"

"No, no nothing like that."

"Whew, Okay good."

"But they are loving the boy!"

"What? Boy I know you better have your attention on those books and not those fast…"

Laughing loudly, "Ma, I'm just playing I'm focused out here. You have no reason to worry."

"Don't play with me boy."

"But seriously, I've been kind of thinking about… God lately."

Tammy's face lights up. She remembers when her son loved going to church. And she knew that the split of she and her husband had changed all that.

"Is that right? And what brought this about?"

"A bunch of different things, for one, I've been reminiscing a lot lately. I remember stories from Sunday school. I remember saying our prayers at night, learning new bible verses; I even remember parts of sermons."

"Train up a child in the way he should go, and when he is old, he will not depart from it." Prov. 22: 6. This moment is proof positive."

"But I think it's fair to say that I departed. I haven't been to church in years. And up until recently, I haven't really thought about God."

"Listen, you and I both know that what you've been doing is ignoring him. You've always known that he was there. And more importantly, you've always known *who* he is; what you did was stray. But what was dormant in you, is now awakening. You're coming back."

"I understand what you're saying, but I don't know what to think."

"Wait here."

Tammy went to the kitchen and made a phone call. The call lasted no more than two minutes. Tammy returns to the living room.

"Let's go. Don't ask any questions, just come on." She grabs her keys and heads for the door. London followed.

After a rather short drive, they pulled up to an unfamiliar brick house. London was clueless.

"Go and ring the side bell."

London glances at his mother, before following her direction. He stepped out of the car and walked up the driveway. 248, the address sounded familiar. Just as he reached to ring the bell, the door opens. London couldn't believe his eyes when he saw who stood there. It was a face he'd nearly forgotten. A face barely touched by time. It was Rev. Glenn H. DuBois, his Pastor as a child, and his mother's pastor to this day.

"Pastor DuBois?"

"Hello LB." Not many people could get away with calling London LB.

London heard the car pulling off. He turned around and saw his mother driving away.

"Don't worry son. I'll take you home. Come on in. Have a seat."

Mrs. DuBois came in the room.

"Hello London, would you like something to drink?"

London couldn't help but smile. Everyone loved Mrs. DuBois. He hadn't seen her in so long.

"Hello Mrs. DuBois, how are you? No thank you I'm fine."

"Well I guess you'd like to know why you're here. Your mother called me. She says you're confused about some things and have some questions. She thought it would be a good idea if we had a talk. Is that okay with you?"

"Yes. I'm glad she called you. I don't know where to start."

"The beginning always works for me."

London laughs. He'd forgotten how funny Pastor DuBois could be.

"Have a seat."

"How do I know if God is really talking to me?"

The Pastor folds his hands. "That's a very good question. It's also a very common one. The Lord speaks to different people in different ways. For some, he speaks with signs obvious to only that individual. To others he may speak by dreams or even visions. He speaks to all through Pastors and preachers. He also speaks through the bible, his holy Word."

"What about out loud, like you and I are talking now?"

"Too many times we make the mistake of waiting or hoping for the Lord to *speak* to us literally. I say that because most times we can get so caught up looking for that, that we ignore his many other attempts to communicate with us. However, the Lord spoke words to his servant Moses. They conversed. There are other instances; God also spoke to Adam and Eve. He spoke to Abraham. There are still others."

"Yeah, but those times were all a long time ago. What about now, does he still speak to people?"

"Jesus Christ is the same yesterday, today, and forevermore." Heb. 13: 8. He is all powerful. I have no doubt that when the Lord deems it necessary to converse with someone, or instruct them audibly, he'll do just that. It's just rare because it's usually unnecessary. The things we need to know for salvation; and life in general, are in his Word. He gives Pastors to help us understand. I will say this, whenever the Lord does decide to actually speak, it is of monumental importance."

London swallowed hard. "Monumental importance."

"No doubt."

"If you don't mind Pastor, I have another question."

"No problem. What is it?"

"What if God wants me to do something, and I refuse?"

"Well LB, God told Jonah to go to Nineveh and give them the message that God wanted them to change their wicked ways. But Jonah refused, he ran and hid in the side of a ship. His punishment was first being thrown overboard into a raging sea. Then, he was swallowed by a big fish! Jonah 1: 1-17. But to bring it closer to home, your uncle, the late Rev. Henry Ford, is an example. When the Lord first called him to preach, he refused. The Lord blinded him until he accepted the call."

"What, I was never told that!"

"The Lord's will... will be done."

London was blown away! He and Pastor DuBois talked for another forty minutes before London ran out of questions. The wise preacher man took London back to his mother's house. London thanked him for everything.

"You're very welcome London. Here, this is the number of a very good Pastor friend of mine who lives up in Philadelphia. My numbers on the back. Call anytime."

London thanked him again. He felt honored that Pastor DuBois would extend such an open door to him. London got out of the car and went in the house. Tammy was sitting in her

bathrobe waiting for London. She was half sleep. She awoke

when London closed the door.

"You're back. How did everything go?"

"It was excellent! He had the answers I needed. Thanks

for taking me."

"You're welcome. I'm glad it went well. I'm going to bed

I'll see you in the morning."

Tammy hugged her son and went to bed. She was both

happy, and proud of him. But mostly, she was thankful to God.

London went to his room and did a lot of thinking. He got

on his knees and prayed for the first time in years. He made a

decision. He would accept The Knight's Birth. Besides, he wasn't

trying to go blind, or get swallowed by any mutant fish!

Chapter Four:

Hear the desert, *Hear* the jungle

A few months later, spring break had begun; and not a
moment too soon. London needed to get away. He remained in
contact with his best friend John, who was enrolled in school back
home in Maryland. The two of them had planned a trip, along with
the rest of their old crew, to Cancun Mexico. London finished up
his last-minute packing. He grabs his plane ticket, zips and straps
his bags, and heads downstairs to load his taxi. His phone rings.
Normally he would check to see who it is. He is immediately upset
with himself for not doing so the moment he hears the voice on the
other end.

"Hello"

"Well hello there. It's been a long time since I've heard
from you son. How are things?"

He raises his head in the air in irritation. "Hey Dad, yeah
you're right it has been a while. But I'm good, how are you?"

"Things are going well but I'm sure missing my oldest son."

"I miss you too Dad. You know I've just been so busy with school, studying, practice, and the games."

"Yeah, I understand all of that, but it doesn't excuse you from making time for family. I've only seen you play once since you've been in college. You don't communicate."

A horn blows.

"Dad you're right. I promise I'll make some time, but Dad you caught me at a bad time I have a cab outside that's about to leave me. I'll call you soon."

"Okay London, I hope so."

London secures his phone and opens the door. He stares directly into perfectly blue water. At least that's what it seemed like. The weight of his luggage made London fall backward when he flinched. The waters that startled him were the eyes of the 4th Corner. It had been years.

"Greetings London, son of James."

"Well, well, long time no see. London gathered his bags and stood up. I guess we know who you are now. You're my guardian angel or something right?"

"I am not."

London stands and gathers his bags. "You're not? Well... Listen man I talked to the big guy. I think you can tell me who you really are. What is all this 4th Corner stuff?"

"I am gatekeeper to the fourth corner of the Earth."

"Okay, so you're a lot of people's guardian angel."

"Simply what has been told to you is what I am."

"Where have you been," London asks as he walks down the stairs.

"Guarding my corner."

"You're a great conversationalist. You should host a talk show. Since you're here now, who's standing your post now?"

"I am."

"What? How… Never mind, I don't even want to know. Well what message do you have for me today?"

"I'm not reading enough scriptures right, do I need to join a church, am I praying right?"

"No message. I am here to escort you."

"Escort me? That's alright I'm looking forward to relaxing on the flight. But thank you anyway."

London approaches the cab. The 4th Corner places his hand on London's shoulder. When he removes it, they are standing in an entirely different environment. London knew what had happened. This was a feat the 4th Corner had performed with him on two other occasions. He had transported them; but where? London looked around. They were in the middle of nowhere. The blazing sun in all of its' fury, was the only thing that greeted them. They stood atop endless acres of sand. They'd transported to a desert.

"What the… Where are we, where'd you bring me? The only sands I'm supposed to be standing on are on the beaches of Mexico!"

"The Knight's Birth begins."

"I still don't know exactly what that means!"

"For your beginning ... heareth."

"Heareth? I need you to heareth me. I really need this time to relax and recharge! I know you haven't been around, but I have a lot going on Mr. 4th Corner. I ..."

POW!

London hits the ground unconscious. Sometime later, he comes to. Once his eyes regained their focus, he slowly lifts his head. He's lying prone on the ground. He looks around. The light is dim. He's in an empty room in what appears to be a small cabin. The only thing around is a nearby bookshelf. What happened? The last thing he remembered was standing in some desert alongside the 4th Corner. He had been hit with something. Did the 4th Corner hit him? No. He was hit from behind. *For your beginning, heareth* that's what the 4th Corner had said. But he never told him just what to listen to. Where was he now? London was just about to get up off the ground, when he notices someone quietly sitting with their back facing him in the next room. This had to be the man who had attacked him! He was being tested to determine just how much training he really needed. He had to figure a way to disable his attacker. London looks around for a weapon. The bookshelf... London's eyes lit up when he notices two blunt and heavy bookends. He looks back in the direction of the stranger. He is none the wiser. London pushes himself up to his hands and knees. The ground is hard and rough, but it doesn't keep London from crawling toward the bookshelf. He again glances at the stranger, and then reaches for a bookend as quietly as he possibly can. He knows he can't walk up to the man and hit him over the head. The wooden floor would most certainly betray his approach. He inches up just enough then throws the bookend at the stranger's head. It flies through the air end over end. The only thing that keeps it from hitting the seated stranger is a blind dodge. The heavy bookend slams into the wall and rips out a chunk of wood. It lands on a plate of food atop a small table.

How did he do that? He couldn't have seen it. How did he dodge it?

"If you could've done what I just did, you could've walked, instead of being carried in here. Actually, if you could've done what I just did, you never would've been brought to me."

"Who are you, and why did you kick, hit, or do whatever you did to me? And, where are we?"

"Shame... you asked three questions, none of which were the questions that a wise man would've asked."

"Oh really? Well what should I have asked?"

"You should have asked how I dodged your weapon, and can I teach you."

London thought about what the stranger said. He was right. London should've been more concerned about the possibilities of possessing such a skill. His anger from missing his Spring break trip was consuming him. He wiped his hand over his face and took a deep breath. He closed his eyes before speaking. He cleared his mind and then stood up.

"How did you dodge my weapon? And please, will you teach me?"

The stranger turned around. This was London's first time seeing the man's face. He was a short elderly Native American man.

"I am known as Sun Ray. What I did to you, was throw a small weapon common to my tribe. It was to see just how deaf to sound you are. And where you are, is safe. Now to answer your questions of a wise man; I was able to dodge your weapon because I can truly *hear*. And yes, I will teach you. My question is, will you learn? Do not answer."

"Thank you. How long does it take to learn?"

"In my tribe, we learn to hear from the time we are little ones. You are deaf to sound; it will take many seasons."

"Seasons, what do you mean seasons? We don't, I know I don't have that much time!"

Sun Ray stands.

"This skill you have asked me to teach, will assuredly take many seasons to learn. It will take even more to master them. How many all depends on the sensitivity of your focus. Now, the next step of a wise man would be to eat. Each day there will be three meals prepared for you. Your clumsily thrown bookend has beaten you to your supper tonight. I hope it has saved some for you."

"Where are the menus?"

"That same wise man would then get some rest. Being unconscious does not take the place of sleep."

"Oh wow, very funny."

Sun Ray walked out of the room and returned dragging a small cot with two folded blankets and a small pillow. He drops them at London's feet.

Again, Sun Ray leaves the room. This time, he returned with a large pail of water.

"There is a well. Drink deeply, you must do this every day. You will sweat you will cry, and you will bleed. You must be hydrated."

"I will cry and bleed? I thought I was learning to heareth."

"The books on the shelf are for your reading pleasure. You will find no other comfort or recreation."

"Tomorrow you begin your first exercise in sound. Sleep well."

"Where do you sleep?"

"Elsewhere." "There is but one rule, do not open that door."

Sun Ray points to a door on the other side of the cabin.

"Oh, I take it that's where your room is huh?"

London looks back in the direction of Sun Ray, but he is gone. London walks to the front door and opens it. He is greeted by the darkest black he has ever seen. He closes the door and takes a deep breath to calm himself. London eats what his unsuccessful bookend left him and did his best to drink from the large bucket. He then followed the second step of a wise man and settled in his cot. He has no idea what is in store; neither for tomorrow, nor for the rest of his life.

The next morning, Bong, Bong, Bong! London springs from his blanket awakened from a dream, that if given a choice, he would've stayed in forever.

"What the... what was that!"

"So, you're not completely deaf" (He lowers the brass gong to the floor).

London looks up. Sun Ray drops a brass gong to the ground.

"Good to see you didn't drink all of the water. Whatever you leave is what you bathe with."

"Bathe? This isn't enough water to bathe with!"

"Next time drink less. Everything you need is there (he points to a small table and chair). Bathe, change, and eat; outside, I await you."

Sun Ray walks out the front door. London shakes his head and walks over to the table. London glances at the door on the other side of the room. Sitting on top of the chair was a crude set of shorts, and a matching T-shirt. Sitting still on top of those, was something that he guessed was soap. There was also a rag. There was a bowl of something on the table that actually smelled pretty good. London grabbed what he needed and bathed with the water that was left. He then got dressed and ate. As he pushed his chair back, he sees that there is a pair of moccasins underneath it. He puts them on. They're comfortable. As he walks toward the door, he is filled with excitement; but equally nervous.

London opens the door. He is in shock as he looks out. The empty cabin in which he had spent the night in had no windows, so he had no idea that he'd see the sight that he now sees. He thought he was in some kind of a village. He was mistaken. London gazes at the same barren desert wasteland that replaced his Mexican beach vacation. He looks past his shock and sees Sun Ray standing about a blocks' distance away. He gathers himself and makes his way to his new teacher. Sun Ray stands motionless staring at London. London turns to see that the desert is endless in all directions. And it's hot!

After a couple minutes of silent staring, London asks, "Well what am I supposed to be doing out here? Why are we in a desert?"

Sun Ray didn't respond. The tension was cloud thick.
London knew he was missing something. He thought to himself.

"Will you please teach me to truly hear?"

Sun Ray immediately comes to life.

"There are many ways to observe something. Especially
something in motion; sight is but one. The problem is most rely too
heavily on sight. This reliance gives birth to a laziness to develop
one's other options."

London looks puzzled. Sun Ray walks closer to him and
smiles. He then swings as if to slap London but stops short of
making contact. London flinches.

"In the time it took you to react, I could have slapped you
twice! Other than sight, how did you know I made a move?"

London thought about it.

"I guess I could feel it."

"Yes, that is another option. However, it is the least
effective. It's actually the past. You felt the wind created by my

swing. But, that wind is being powered by a force. You need to detect that force before you feel the effect of its wind. That is far too late. In other words, by the time you feel the air, I've already slapped you! Yet, wind is the movement of air. And air, is the answer."

"Air?"

"Indeed. Close your eyes."

Sun Ray swung again. This time he swung past London's ear.

"I can hear the air!"

"Yes, the sound of the air's movement, or the air being moved. The bookend you threw at me was easy to avoid. When it hit the air, it flipped and twisted repeatedly. This drastically disturbed the natural movement of air."

"Okay listen I know English is probably not your first language, but can you try speaking it."

"Oh, okay I get it, short bus, well …"

"Short what, what did you say?"

"Stay focused. As I was saying, a trained ear can hear an object moving through the air."

London looked at Sun Ray side eyed. He subtly grinned.

"How do you train your ear to hear such a thing?"

"Sun Ray smiled. Your questions grow wiser."

He reaches behind his back and reveals a long black cloth.

"What's that?"

"It is to cover your eyes."

For the next eight months, Sun Ray familiarized London with the blind sounds of objects flying through the air. For the first two weeks, London would walk the desert blind folded for thirty minutes, then stand still for another thirty minutes. The desert was a complete vacuum. There was no sound or wind. He'd repeat this from sunup to sundown. The reason was simple; Sun Ray wanted London to recognize the sound of natural air movement. He wanted him to be able to distinguish between the sound when he's moving, and when he's still. The third week, Sun Ray began

throwing various objects through the air past London, as he

walked. He was careful not to throw anything too close to him.

He didn't want London to feel the wind. He wanted him to hear

the very parting of the air as the objects pierced through. Sun Ray

would repeat this every other day. After several days, London

began to take notice. Sun Ray kept with the same procedure for

several more weeks. London was getting good. He began to react

to almost everything. Most of what was being thrown were bulky

objects like sticks, and big rocks. Sun Ray decided that it was time

to step it up. He began throwing smaller more fine objects that

would cut through the air with more speed and less sound. These

objects included knives, darts, and arrows. After several months of

this, London mastered it. Sun Ray began to mix rocks and sticks,

with knives, and ninja stars. London flourished. He was able to

not only hear them; he was now able to dodge and avoid straight

shots. It was time to introduce him to the next level.

The next day, London went about his normal routine of

bathing with the well water, dressing, and eating. He stretches and

walks out the door. Even though he would normally have a five-minute walk before he met up with Sun Ray, he could always see him in the distance. Today was different. There is no sign of him. London kept walking until it was apparent that Sun Ray was nowhere to be found. He looks in every direction. The only thing visible is the cottage. He walks back wondering if his training is complete. As he re-enters the cottage, he feels he's missing something. At first, he can't figure what it is; then he sees it. The *other* door is ever so slightly ajar. He apprehensively approaches it, and peers through the small opening. What he sees is in no way possible! He looks again. Though he can't make much out, what he can see, is trees. He opens the door wider. Trees are everywhere. There is no sand. London slowly walks out. He walks for a few feet then turns around. Trees continue endlessly in all directions, even past the cottage. They are just as abundant as the sand is on the other side of the first door! Suddenly, there's a scream from above. It startles London. He looks up. A monkey jumps from one tree to the next! He was in a jungle. A light drizzle began to fall. There had been no rain on the desert side. London walked further into the jungle. The biggest difference on this wild side is the noise. There are animals, rain, birds, and some sounds he didn't recognize. It was chaos. Without warning, a spear pierces through a tree no more than two feet from London's head! By the time London had heard it, it was too late. He turns around. Sun Ray stands in the distance. London walks over and joins him.

"A few seasons ago, you asked why we were in the desert. The reason was because it was a controlled environment. There was no noise to interfere with the sensitizing of your hearing. You have completed that first stage of your training. This is the final stage of your exercise in sound. This rain forest will test you in ways the desert cannot. It's the unexpected, an uncontrolled environment. It represents the real world. You did well to hear the spear. You have been trained to react when you hear an object approaching. You will now be trained to react to multiple objects approaching in any and all directions, in a world of noise. This is truly *hearing*. May I have the spear?"

London turns in the direction of the spear.

"But its way back there, don't you have any..."

When London turns back to face his teacher, Sun Ray is gone. London knows immediately, his advanced level of training has now begun.

A wind begins to blow the trees around. There are many animal sounds. London cautiously walks through the jungle. He doesn't want his footsteps to add to the concert of noise. An hour passes. He walks down a hill and comes upon a flowing river. It is very loud. London realizes that his new level of training is going to be extremely difficult. He walks back up the hill. When he reaches the top, he looks around. What is he expected to do? As he wonders what is next. He abruptly receives his answer.

"AHH!"

London screams out in pain and falls to the ground. There is a sharp pain coming from his right leg. He looks down at it. There's a knife sticking out of his leg, and blood is flowing from the wound. He hadn't heard anything above or under the rain forest to alert him of an attack. Somehow, he summons the courage to wrap his hand around the handle of the knife and pull it out of his leg. Again, he screams out! He throws the knife to the side. As he does this, he notices that his bracelet once again shined. He remembers the bracelet is supposed to heal him of any wound. The thing he doesn't know is just how long it will take. He does his best not to panic. He has to re-focus. Sun Ray had made it a point to inform him that multiple weapons could be thrown at him, and from all directions. He has to get moving. Lying here he's an easy target. He digs his hands into the grass and mud and begins dragging himself off of the hill. The pain slowly melts away. He looks at his wound and discovers it is almost completely healed.

Standing over London Sun Ray asks, "Harder to hear, yes?"

Looking up, "Yes!"

"That's all for today."

The pain is now gone and there is no evidence that a wound has ever existed. London walks back to the cottage and prepares his mind for the next day of training.

Over the next five years, London endures many cuts, bruises, scrapes, bumps, and lacerations on the wild side of the house. True to its' purpose, the bracelet allows London to walk away from it all. He is mastering the art of unseen observation.

One particular morning, London walks out into the jungle for the day's next session of training. It isn't long before something catches his attention. It isn't a sound however, but a feeling. He turns around. There standing powerfully and undeniably is the 4th Corner.

"What now?"

"A message."

"Really? What is it?"

"Well done."

He touches London on the shoulder and the two of them disappear. The next thing London sees is the 4TH Corner disappearing alone. A horn blows. London looks and sees a taxicab with its' driver anxiously staring at him. London is standing in the doorway of his dorm house surrounded by his bags. He bends down grabs his things and races over to the cab. After closing the trunk, he jumps in.

"Where to?"

"The airport please."

London realizes that even though his training with Sun Ray had easily lasted over six years, no more than a few seconds had passed here at home.

Chapter Five:

Moment of Truth?

Where had he been? What kind of place could contain both a desert, and a rain forest? And how long was he really there? These and many more questions and thoughts raged in London's head as he stared out of the plane's window. Sun Ray was amazing! He felt honored to have met him, but most of all he couldn't believe what he could now do.

His destination is Houston where he'll catch a connecting flight to Cancun. John and the rest of the crew from Maryland should already be there. When his plane touched down, London was still thinking about sand, and trees. When he finally entered the Houston airport, all of that changed. The first faces he sees are John, Ronnie, Michael, and Warren. This was the first time the crew had been back together since high school. They were like kids again.

"Did you all eat yet? I'm starving?"

"We were waiting for you." Said John.

"There's a bar and grille we passed on the way to your gate." Says Ronnie.

"Cool, that'll work!"

The crew walked into the entrance of the restaurant. They waited to be seated. London was immediately attacked! It was an attack that not even his fabulously tuned hearing could sense. It was the aroma of food. It was sheer torture. The only food London had eaten in over a years was rice, fruit, vegetables, and oatmeal. His sense of smell was now being bombarded by the calling of: hamburgers with countless condiments, chicken fingers with various dipping sauces, juicy steaks, crispy fries, and not to mention the beverages. He could smell soft drinks of all kinds, and lemonade, and coffee, and…

"Hey, you alright over there, I think you're drooling!" Warren says.

London wipes his mouth and straightens up.

"Dude, I can hear your stomach all the way over here! Here, take my gum if it's that bad!"

The fellas all laughed.

"I just haven't eaten in a while."

"Excuse me miss, we need seats quickly. My friend here's about to go cannibal!"

The guys are taken to their seats and order drinks.

"I'm going to wash my hands."

Once London enters the bathroom, he locks the door. He splashes his face with water and stares in the mirror.

"Let's get it together London, let's get it together. It's just food; *great food*, but just food."

He dries his face and begins washing his hands, when someone struggles with the locked door trying to get in. He uses his foot to flush the toilet, then opens the door.

"Man, you in here stinking it up? That's what was wrong with you." Michael says.

"Hey, when you gotta go, you know the rest."

London rejoins the others. They have their drinks, and his is sitting waiting for him. He ordered a kiwi lemonade. There it was. Tall neon green glass of goodness! He wanted to snatch it and gorge himself! He resists. He sits and tries to continue catching up with his friends.

"Yeah, yeah I remember that; I still do that sometimes."

"Who can forget that?"

"Oh yeah!"

It was torture. Michael approached the table and seized everyone's attention.

"Hey, check out the girl in the blue shirt."

Everyone but London looked. He used the distraction to do just what he'd been fighting. He downed the lemonade like air!

London and the old crew ordered their food and ate heartily; especially London. And he was the picture of contentment. Everyone was all grins, until Warren brought up a topic that gave London pause.

"Hey, remember that day we all went out to the bike trail and London started crying about how late it was getting?"

Ronnie and Michael laughed.

"I wasn't crying."

"Yeah well anyway, when you and John bailed because you were scared of curfew, the rest of us stayed for at least another hour. You mama's boys missed out!"

"I hope you two left your curfews at home, cause it's a long swim back!" Ronnie says.

Everyone was laughing, London more so chuckling. The only exception is John. His mind is elsewhere. The guys pay their bill, leave a tip, and head for their gate. Most of the talk now has to do with sports. The last conversation in the bar and grille is all but forgotten; or so it seems. The groups of friends are now seated on the plane. Ronnie and Warren sit in the same row. Michael, John, and London sit together a few rows back. Michael immediately leans his seat back and closes his eyes. John pulls out his iPod. London turns on the television in the back of the seat he's facing. He hadn't watched a TV in forever. By the time the plane hit the air, everyone is asleep except John and London. Michael sits between them. John raises his head and looks at Michael. He's knocked out. John removes his earphones. He glances once more at Michael, then at London.

He whispers, "London. London."

London was gazing out of the window. In his perspective, just hours ago, he was entering a jungle, ready for more training, and now here he sits on a plane on his way to Spring break! He hears John whisper his name.

"London, we need to talk."

"What's up?"

"That day when we left the bike trail …"

London's insides froze! He wasn't prepared to have this conversation. Deep down he knew that someday it would come up, but he had hoped not. He was hoping that somehow John would've forgotten. But that wasn't being realistic. After all these years, it comes down to now, the moment of truth. What would he say?

"… The same day that Warren was talking about. What happened?"

London had to be smart. He had to be discreet. He knew he was being watched.

"Yeah, I remember that day. I would've gotten in serious trouble if I would've stayed."

"You know that's not what I'm talking about. I know we haven't talked about it since we were kids, but I think we need to."

"Alright, but if I recall correctly, we swore not to talk about it."

"What, man please we were like eight! I think the statute of limitations is up!"

London tries to stall, "statute of limitations? Man, that's dealing with crime. I think…"

"Yeah and I think the only crime here is the way you keep trying to play me!"

"Alright, alright what's on your mind?"

"I never really stopped thinking about that day."

London is stuck. Just how much does John remember?

"We saw something that we weren't supposed to see. What was it?"

"I don't know. *What did you see?*"

"What do you mean what did I see? I saw what you saw."

"I saw something."

"Yeah, a blue something!"

London tries to normalize it, "I think it was black."

"Black, no it wasn't, it was dark, but not that dark. It was blue."

"Are you sure? I'm thinking black."

"Well how many legs did you see?"

"How many legs?"

"LONDON!"

"Listen man, I don't know exactly what we saw, but there are reports every day of people seeing things they can't explain. Especially in remote woodland areas; think about it, are we those sorts of people who see the Loch Ness monster, or Bigfoot? Some people would say we just saw a bear. I'm not saying that's what we saw, but by chance it was that would be strange enough in and of itself. Whatever it was, it was definitely odd. Maybe it was some new species."

There is silence. London is satisfied with his explanation. He hadn't straight out lied to John. And at the same time, he was able to obey and keep the charge he'd been given. He raised possibilities that were scientific, and he also showed John that he too was baffled by that day. John thought about the things that London had said. He hadn't thought along those lines. But then, he remembered something else.

"What about the man?"

"The man?"

"Yeah, you know, the Men in black ninja. The one you said was able to disappear."

"Yeah, I don't know where he came from, but he outsmarted that thing and got me out of there. He must've been a ranger or something. I heard they sometimes patrol around there. I think I passed out, because when I came to, I was back in the neighborhood. I guess he put me in his jeep."

"How did he know where to take you?"

"He must've looked in my wallet. I had my I.D. on me."

John just sat there. London knew he was suspicious of his answers. But his answers were good enough to be real.

"What's up John, you're acting like you don't believe or something, like you don't trust me! What's up with the third degree?"

"It's just when Warren got to talking, I don't know, it just presented me with the means and the opportunity to confront you with my questions. I didn't mean to sound like I'm accusing you of anything, I'm just looking for answers."

"Yeah, I know that feeling."

"I guess I was kind of bugging out."

Michael started to stir between them. They waited until he was still again before continuing their conversation.

"It's cool man. Let's get some rest before we land."

"I'm with that."

London turns to his window and lets out a silent sigh of relief. He had survived a confrontation from the one person that had experienced some of what he'd experienced. Though it didn't compare to recent confrontations he'd had, London was still glad it was finally over; however, he still wasn't entirely comfortable with the situation. Although he didn't lie to his friend, he didn't reveal all that he knew, and couldn't. He just hoped today's events wouldn't someday come back to bite.

The plane landed and began a much-needed vacation for London. For the next two weeks, London and his friends enjoyed some serious R&R. The guys did some of everything. They went parasailing, snorkeling, played beach volleyball, and of course, did some clubbing. It was just what the doctor ordered. For the first time in a long time, London was at ease. He let loose. He was able to clear his mind and be a regular college student on Spring break.

The day comes to leave. London is very glad that the whole time they were in Cancun; John didn't bring up the taboo subject. The guys board the plane for home. Everyone is beat. The plane lands in Charlotte.

London parts with his friends, his final destination being different from theirs. He slaps his friends up and says his goodbyes before heading for his gate.

Later at BWI airport, London flags down a cab. He gets in the back and replays the entire vacation over in his mind. It's a relaxing ride back to his dorm.

Chapter Six:

Make him no more!

The cab stops in front of the dorm. The driver gets out and goes to the rear of the car to open the trunk. The driver takes London's bags out and sets them on the ground. London pays the fare plus a five-dollar tip. He climbs the stairs, walks down the hall and unlocks the door to his room. London drops his bags and looks around the room with a genuine smile on his face. He hadn't seen his room in years! He was glad to be back. As he looks around, a feeling comes over London, the familiar feeling of being watched. His smile fades. The last time he had this feeling, he had the misfortune of being introduced to the Dark Author. He carefully searches the room. He first looks under his bed and then under his roommate's. He looks in every crevice he could think of. He finds nothing. He'd saved the most obvious hiding place for last; the closets. London prepared himself. He grabs one of his basketball trophies and slowly walks toward his closet. He cocks it back with his right hand and reaches for the doorknob. Before his fingers made contact, "Bang, bang, bang". London swings the trophy wildly in response to the sound. He bashes the closet door ripping a chunk of wood off. It reminds him of the bookend he threw at Sun Ray. London calms himself as he realized that the banging was actually someone knocking at his room door. He starts toward the door then stops.

"Hold on a sec."

He returns to the closet door still clutching his trophy. He swings the door open with his other hand. The only greeting he receives is from the clothes that he'd chosen not to pack for vacation. Again, there is a knock at the door. London goes to the door and puts the trophy down. Upon opening it, he is immediately tackled to the ground! London rolls with his attacker and gains a quick advantage. He pins his attacker and reaches for his trophy, but just before he swings...

"London, London hold up it's me!"

London recognizes his attacker.

"Donald? *Boy you almost got yourself killed*!"

"You should've seen your face," he laughs.

"Yeah and you should've seen your face if I had swung!"

London stands then helps his brother to his feet. They slap each other and hug. They hadn't seen each other for some time.

"What are you doing here?"

"We wanted to surprise you."

"We?"

"Yes we," sounds a voice through the still open door.

James walks into London's room.

"Hello son."

London looks up at his father. A sharp pain stabs through London's chest. The last time he'd seen him was in the stands at his first college game. He hadn't seen him this close since the last time he'd visited California.

"Hey Dad." London walks to his father sticking his hand out to shake, the same thing he'd done in California. Once again, James ignores it and embraces his son. London reluctantly hugs back. It doesn't go unnoticed.

"So, what are you guys doing here?"

" Dad wanted to see you."

"The three of us haven't been together in years. It was time to do something about that."

James looks around the room and sees London's bags.

"You going somewhere?"

"No. Actually, I just got back."

"So perfect timing is what you're saying."

"Well how about we all go out for dinner, my treat."

"Okay, cool when do you want to go?"

"I was thinking now."

"Okay well let me get cleaned up really quick and we can go."

The three of them head out and London locks up. Just as they exit, the presence that London felt, emerges. The curtain moves aside. There atop the window seal, stands a creature about three feet tall. It resembles a wingless gargoyle. The creature jumps down, and then walks directly into the wall at the far corner of the room. But instead of colliding with the surface, the creature disappears into the shadow. It resurfaces in a nearby dark alley. It stops when someone steps into view. That someone speaks to the creature.

"What happened?"

The creature in turn speaks in a raspy voice.

"He was only there for a few moments, then others came, and he left with them."

"Very well. Wait for him to return. When he goes to sleep, unzip his skin!"

The creature disappears back into the alleyway shadows. Pat walks in the opposite direction. He enters a neighborhood park. A couple people out walking their dogs have no idea they've just brushed shoulders with the key figure in the planned annihilation of man; a plan that is not far from fruition. Pat stops at the foot of a large tree. There perched by twos and threes in every branch is a murder of crows. But something is very quaint about these crows. They are silent; and their eyes are fiery red; not to mention, they speak.

"I have discovered the mystery of the 4th Corner, the crows say in unison. It gives us a window in which to deal with this... London."

"What is it O Dark one, what is the mystery?"

"It is this, he has only six hours in each day in which he may place his feet on the Earth. The Earth is divided into four parts, or corners. Each corner has a gatekeeper. In a 24-hour period they each are allowed six hours. No more. This information is extremely valuable since this London has accepted his calling. It is not known how soon the 4th Corner's hour will come, but now is not an hour that his foot touches Earth. Find this London, before the 4th Corner returns. Make him no more. I want his soul torn! This is to be your only focus. Use every resource; everyone is at your disposal. Move quickly, for once the 4th Corner does appear; this London will undoubtedly complete The Knight's Birth. For now, he is only a threat, but soon he can become a thorn in the side of my larger plans. Go now, do my bidding, I await word."

The crows take flight. A cloud of black quickly moves through the air.

Though the Dark Author was indeed anxious at the opportunity, he had not placed all of his eggs in one basket. In the event that this London does complete The Knight's Birth, The Dark One has begun developing his own warrior.

Pat immediately made his way back to the alley where he met with the Shadow walker. He summons two more to join the first Shadow walker in wait for London. He then summons the six-legged beast Dozorn, who was able to roam freely and invisible, due to Pat's illusion ability, as long as he remains within a mile of Pat. Pat apprises him of the plan and the two go out and search for London.

Donald laughs … "No, that was just once!"

"Oh, so I guess you've gotten that all straightened out now (more laughing)."

"Of course, I was a kid then."

"A kid then; hate to bust your bubble son, but you're still a kid now."

It had been a long time since the three of them had gotten together like this. They laughed and visited for hours.

"Excuse me ma'am, where's the restroom?" Donald asks.

"It's just around the bar."

"Thank you. I'll be back."

"London."

Well here it comes, I guess we finally get to do this.

"You've been upset and holding a grudge against me for a very long time now son. You stopped coming for the summer, you don't call, and you ignore my calls. Hell, you don't even send me your game schedules anymore. London fidgets. I want you to know that I understand that you love your mother, and you should. Believe it or not I still love her in my own way. But son the time comes when a person has to move on in life. That's what your mother and I have done. The divorce was hard on all of us. But I feel like we've been lucky to make the best of it. And a few years ago, I met someone, Evelyn. She makes me happy son, that's all. I don't want her to replace or be a second mother to you and Donald. I would never do that to you boys. I just wanted the two most important people in my life to meet the person that's been making me smile when you guys aren't with me. I'm having fun again. She's got me eating things, and going places, and doing things that I never would have even tried. Can you understand that son?"

London sighs.

"It was hard meeting her, but I do understand Dad. You and Ma have been divorced for a long time now, and you deserve to be happy."

James smiles, "thank you son."

"But Dad my problem wasn't so much with you having a girlfriend. The part that I can't get over is how you can so happily go to Church with your Evelyn, when I can remember you refusing to go when Ma took us. And I remember that being the main thing that tore our family apart."

James doesn't know how to respond. He had it all wrong. He retreats to the shelter of silence. London lowers his head and does the same.

A full minute later, "I'm so sorry son. I didn't realize that this is what you were dealing with."

Donald returns and lightens the mood. "Ooo wee, London I think I need to come to school here when I graduate! The women around here are serious!"

"Yeah I know right. You should see them on game day."

James looks at his watch, "I have a nine A.M. meeting in South Jersey tomorrow."

"Yeah it's already after eleven, I haven't been to sleep yet I'm beat."

"Well what are you doing tomorrow London? Can I chill with you until Dad gets back from his meeting?"

"Yeah I don't see why not."

"Cool! But the pool in our hotel doesn't close until one tonight. Dad can you just bring me back here in the morning?"

"Yeah I can do that, but it'll be pretty early."

James asked for the check. Across the room beyond the other restaurant patrons, a man sits alone drinking coffee. He'd just recently entered. James pays the bill, while London goes to the restroom to clean up. The same man drinking coffee alone walks to the restroom door and stands in front of it. The man watches Donald as he approaches his father at the cashier. Donald turns at the sound of his name being called.

He sees London standing with two other guys.

"You and Dad go ahead; I'll call you back at the hotel. One of my boys will drop me off."

"Alright, I'll talk to you later." Donald says.

At the same time, the real London is drying his hands in the restroom. James and Donald leave the restaurant. London opens the restroom door and walks past the same guy that Donald had just been speaking to. The man never faces London. London approaches the table and looks around. Where was his family? He looks around for another minute, before figuring they must be waiting outside in the rental car. Pat watches him closely as he walks out of the restaurant. London knew where the car was parked but couldn't understand why there was an empty spot there now. He stands there.

"Oh, they think they're funny. Now he hollers out; *"Oh you all think you're funny!"*

He listens for a response, but there isn't one. None come. He looks around.

"I know you two are out there."

A strange voice speaks, "Indeed we are."

London feels a chill go down his spine. He slowly backs away from the parking spot.

"Who's there?"

"Look closer."

Dozorn, no longer cloaked, charges out of the darkness aiming for London. London runs toward the nearest car. He knows the only chance he has is to use his agility. He also knows that he needs open space to effectively use it. He jumps on the roof of the car. The second his feet hit the roof of the car; he springs into a double back flip clearing the now unbelievably close Dozorn. So close, that Dozorn crashes into and smashes the car that London jumped from. It is totaled! The beast is only slightly affected. It shakes its' head and roars before turning to re-pursue London. London runs at top speed in search of safety, but Dozorn's six-legged speed is inescapable. He makes up the distance London had created in no time. London turns his head and realizes that escape is hopeless. He has to make a stand. He runs to the middle of the street and turns to face the beast. As the beast charged, London jumps sideways performing a cartwheel. Dozorn easily topples a streetlight as he misses London. He turns back to where London stood, but his prey is no longer there. Dozorn frantically looks around. London is hiding on the other side of a parked car.

This would be a good time for the 4th Corner to appear, London thinks to himself.

He looks under the car to be sure of where the beast is. What he doesn't know, is Pat's is approaching from the same side of the street. Pat makes eye contact with Dozorn and alerts him of London's hiding place. London can see from under the car that Dozorn has stopped pacing and is very close to the vehicle. Has he found him? Just before he can fully contemplate the question, the car, which was serving as his safe haven, lifts off the ground and reveals the blue beast. He had picked the car up and thrown it! London immediately reacts jumping up off the ground, however Pat was expecting that. Just as London's feet leave the ground, Pat tackles him out of the air.

A customer at the restaurant sees someone being chased by something he can't explain!

"Hello 9-1-1, yeah I'm on South Elm St., I just saw a man being chased by some kind of … I don't know some weird looking animal of some sort! They're headed toward the University."

The authorities were planning to send Animal control, until they began receiving more calls for the same area. Each call got more and more disturbing. One involved an airborne car, another complained of a streetlight being knocked over, and another said a black bear was on the loose! Dispatch alerted a nearby patrol car to check it out.

Dozorn holds London down as Pat stands to speak.

"Your end has come mortal! The Dark Author offered you wisdom, but you chose death! We are here to deliver it. Prepare for ..."

Someone yells from behind "Nobody move! Keep your feet glued to the pavement!"

"Good Lord, what is that blue thing?!" The second cop asks.

Dozorn straightens up and turns toward the cops while still holding London down with the three limbs on his left side. The cops nervously step back.

"These affairs are none of your concern human! Leave now and you may keep your lives."

"It talks, sweet Jesus, it talks!"

"Shut up Jack! Okay, both of you, place your hands … feet, claws or whatever you have on the hood of that there vehicle. Do it now!"

Pat nods at Dozorn. The beast reaches with his other three limbs and shoves a nearby car sending it on a collision course with the officers. They take cover. The parked car turned projectile, smashes into the cop's squad car. As the beast reaches and shoves the car, he inadvertently loosens his grip on London. London kicks and twists trying to free himself from the clutch of the beast. The cops open fire. A few shotgun slugs are enough to get Dozorn's undivided attention. He is no longer focused on holding London. London frees himself and takes off running. A third shotgun slug blows Pat to the ground. Dozorn charges the officers. Pat slowly stands. He is now in his demon form. He realizes that in all the confusion, London has escaped.

"The boy is gone!"

Dozorn digs all six limbs into the street to stop, "WHAT!"

"Find him quickly!"

Dozorn lifts his nose in the air and sniffs. He knows London's scent. He's trying to determine in which direction the boy had gone. He turns around and runs in the opposite direction of the officers. Pat looks directly at the officers.

"If ever we meet again, that same day will be your last!"

He then runs after Dozorn. The officers run the other way while calling for back-up. London is out of sight, but not far. He spots a parked cab and makes a break for it. Dozorn picks up on his trail. London hears a loud crashing or crunching metal like noise. As he nears the cab he looks back. The beast's four legs are running powerfully towards him. He's using his arms, thought to be legs, to grip the sides of buildings and cars he passes, smashing them in the process, to further accelerate himself. The cab driver is dozing off awaiting his next fare. The noise makes him turn to his main rearview mirror. A young man is running toward his cab. But that's not all; he looks beyond the runner and sees something chasing the kid. Something that he was sure he'd never get out of his nightmares! He immediately starts the car and floors the accelerator. Dozorn is now close to striking distance.

"Wait, please, help me, I need … "

London is floored by the fist of the beast. Dozorn's momentum carries him past London. London lifts his head and sees Pat coming. Dozorn gathers himself and turns back to finish the job. At that very moment, the living rainbow waterfall that announces the arrival of the 4th Corner, cascades over an unaware London Bishop. There is however, a very big difference from his past appearances; two to be exact. There he stood with two magnificent wings outstretched in white glory! He flaps them several powerful times. But his purpose was not to get airborne, it was to create wind. He did just that; so much so, that it dramatically impedes Dozorn's approach.

Pat runs hard trying to catch up, "No!"

London sees Pat's anxiety and looks up, unaffected from the eye of the storm. The 4th Corner then lowers his wings covering London, and they disappear.

A few seconds later, London stands up on a rooftop.

"What took you so long?! They almost killed me like four different times! Listen, seriously what kind of warrior can I be; especially against enemies like these? How can I fight? Give me some wings or something! No, wait that would mean I'd have to die first wouldn't it?"

"The Dark Author has discovered my secret."

"What secret?"

"There is a certain six-hour window in which I may enter the Earth each day. I may watch, but the remaining eighteen hours I must stand my post."

"What, but why?"

"Twenty-four hours are evenly shared between all four Corners."

"Are you telling me there are other Corners, or Angels, or whatever?"

"There are."

"Well why wouldn't one of them help me!"

"Such is not their task."

"Whatever. This is all getting confusing. What happens when your six hours are up this time?"

"You shall be equipped, for The Knight's Birth shall be complete."

"Equipped with what?"

The 4th Corner places a hand on London's shoulder and once again, the two of them disappear.

Chapter Seven:

Knight Born

They reappear in a huge padded gym. It is furnished with the works: there are heavy bags, speed bags, weights, a boxing ring, mirrors, and more.

"Where am I now?"

"You shall be equipped. The Birth continues."

The 4th Corner then fades out of existence.

"What now?"

A voice speaks, "Step into the ring."

London steps in. A man joins him in the ring. The man throws London some protective head gear, body pads, and gloves. London puts them on as best he can before the man says just one word, kickboxing. He then dances and jumps around wearing fingerless padded gloves, and bottomless padded footwear. He wore no head gear. London puts his hands up and swallows hard. For the next thirty seconds, London feels like a tennis ball in the spin cycle. He is hit with punch after punch, and kick after kick. He uses the ropes to pick himself up off of the canvas.

The man looks London up and down, then says "Again!"

London throws his hands up in defense. The man does a series of side and head kicks topped off by a spinning back kick that once again floors London.

"Again!"

London is understandably frustrated. This is obviously another session of training. He is not altogether in favor of being thrown into the fire. Here he is the involuntary punching bag of a man with serious anger management issues.

London takes a second to get up. He contemplates his options. He stands. The man swings. London flips completely over him. The man turns around surprised. He gives London a nod of approval. London thinks to himself…

Yeah that's right, the kid has talent, the boy's got skills, I'm the… The man then does his own flip, sweeping London's legs out from under him and pounds him in the forehead with the back of his fist.

"Again!"

This goes on for another thirty minutes. London doesn't try anymore acrobatics. However, he does keep getting up. The last time he gets up, the man takes his gloves off.

"Enough. You have courage. The locker room is that way, the kitchens over there, and the blankets are in the closet. So are the towels. Your quarters are that way."

The man then exits the ring and hollers back ...

"The name is Brazen. I'll see you in the morning."

London showers and thanks to the bracelet, feels no ill effects from the pummeling he'd received. He dresses in sweats left for him in the locker room then walks around to survey the place. To his surprise, there is a full kitchen; and not only that, it's fully stocked; not just rice, fruit, and bread!

Training was different for London this time. His training with Sun Ray, while extremely valuable, was very tedious. Brazen however, is teaching him how to fight! He learns how to effectively punch, kick, use elbows, knees, and anything else he could think of. They also sparred every two days. Brazen even instructs London on incorporating his acrobatics into his attacks. London is extremely glad to be training to fight; especially after the most recent attacks. However, London begins to wonder about something.

"May I ask a couple questions before we begin?"

"You may."

"First off, what kind of name is Brazen?"

Brazen smiles. "Because I do what needs to be done, unapologetically."

London raises his eyebrows and nods.

On a serious note, I don't want you to think I'm unappreciative, but I have enemies that are much stronger than I. They're also large! How can I really hurt them?"

"You must be clever. Kick with both feet together. Propel yourself off of objects to lend more power to your blows. Use strategy. Brains win more fights than do brawn. You must be cunning."

It made sense. London internalizes everything that Brazen is imparting to him. They train long hours every day for two years. One morning, London comes into the gym and is surprised to see another man in the ring with Brazen. Brazen is a big man, but this new guy dwarfs him.

"Your training has gone well, very well. However, this is a test to tell whether or not you can put it all together. You must be able to think on your feet."

Brazen steps out of the ring and stands ringside. London stepped into the ring.

"Where's our protection?"

"Your skills are your protection. Now engage your opponent."

London and the behemoth of a man lock in combat. The man hits London with body jarring blow after blow. But London is far from a punching bag.

He dishes out a fair amount of punishment of his own. The fight rages for twenty minutes and seems to be a draw.

"A demon disciple will not allow *even* to pass. You must find a way to win. Either knock your opponent out or force him to surrender."

"What? How am I supposed to do that?"

Brazen is silent. Then, London has an idea.

"There are no rules, right?"

Brazen gives this some thought.

"There are two rules. One: you must win, Two: no weapons."

London unleashes a flurry of attacks. It wasn't to win the fight, he knew it wouldn't, it was part of a plan. The goliath swings repeatedly and fails to connect. London avoids him with a series of ducks, blocks, and flips. The goliath is now frustrated. London attacks again, and then flips out of the ring. The man follows. Brazen is intrigued. The man charges hard, but London expected this and does two back handsprings rapidly approaching the back wall. Just before he hits the wall, he does a cartwheel to the right. The man goliath runs headfirst into the wall and busts through trapping his head in the hole. He is motionless for a couple seconds, and then he pushes his hands against the wall and eventually frees his head. Dazed, he staggers and stumbles. He lifts his head, only to be met by two feet as one, violently making contact with his face. He falls unconscious. London looks down at the man, then up at Brazen. Brazen nods in approval. London sighs in relief. Brazen looks above London.

"He is ready."

London looks up and is immediately embraced by a huge set of wings. When the wings release him, London rubs his eyes and asks a pressing question.

"Hey listen. I forgot to ask before, but I've got to know. What's the deal with the wings?"

London looks around. Not only does he not see the 4th Corner, he doesn't see anything resembling his dorm room. He is standing in some sort of an outdoor arena filled with sand. He calls out. His voice echoes off of the high surrounding walls. There is a response. Even though it wasn't the voice he'd hoped to hear, it wasn't a disappointment either. The voice is a very pleasant one.

"Wings I do not have, but swords, I do."

It is a woman's voice. London looks in the direction of the voice. She is sitting on the sand against one of the far walls. She stands and walks confidently toward London. As she nears, London finds himself entranced. With every step, she grows more beautiful. She now stands directly in front of London. He is speechless.

"My name is Meika, and you are?"

London doesn't respond.

"Am I to believe you have no name?"

"Oh, I'm sorry my name is London."

"Well London, what do you know about swords?"

"I know yours seem to be invisible."

He had a slight smirk on his face. All of a sudden, her face turns deathly serious.

"Do- Not- Move."

She said it calmly, but she meant it. In a flash she pulls two swords, seemingly from her hair, from behind her and begins twirling them around London's body. She moves side to side, up and down, and in circles for about fifteen seconds. When she stops, she holds the swords up in front of her in the shape of an X. London stands stiff as starch. The only movement is his heart, which doubled its' beat!

"You may move."

She then sticks both swords into the sand blades first. London slowly lowers his head and sees that the sweat suit that he was wearing, is now a shredded short set.

"That's better. You'll be much more comfortable now. It gets hot here."

"Okay listen, it seems you're far and away the most talkative of all my trainers."

"I am a war maiden."

"Right, well I was wondering why I was brought here instead of home. When I finished my first session of training, I was taken home afterward. I didn't begin my next session for another two weeks."

Walking away from her swords, "Time is of the essence, especially your essence. Come London. The enemy was nearly successful in his attempt at taking your life this last time."

" Yeah, tell me about it!"

"These are the final stages of The Knight's Birth, which will culminate with you receiving your remaining gifts."

"While we're on that subject, what kind of gifts are we talking about?"

"The answer to that question is a mystery."

They stop at a black wooden chest. Meika opens it. She reaches in and reveals two wooden sword-like weapons.

"Catch. Defend yourself!"

Two hours later, London is being led out of the arena. He drags his wooden sword behind him leaving a trail in the sand. He is glad the bruises and soreness left by Meika's wooden sword are already healing. They stop about fifty feet away from the arena, at the foot of a tent.

"This is where you'll sleep. There's a brook just past those trees over there. There's a change of clothes and a blanket inside the tent. I will have food brought to you."

London looks around and considers his surroundings, as Meika walked back toward the arena.

Stopping and turning around, "One more thing, keep your weapon with you at all times. I'll see you in the morning."

Later that same day, London slowly walks past a group of trees with a feeling of contentment. He's wrapped in a towel and has just taken a much-needed bath in the brook. He re-enters the tent and allows himself to fall on top of the blanket left for him. The only thing on his mind is sleep. Suddenly, the tent violently swings open. London grabs his wooden sword. Two kids appear holding dishes of food. London puts the wooden sword down and thanks the children for the food. They run off laughing. Soon after

eating, London vacationed in dreamland. But, on this night, he

seemed to be the only one sleeping. The normal sounds of the

night did nothing to disturb London's sleep. He finds the sound of

trees blowing in the wind, and the occasional splash of an animal in

the brook, to be both peaceful and settling. But the sudden snap of

a tree branch, also snaps London out of his sleep. He raises his

head and yawns. He isn't suspicious, but his finely tuned ears

refuse to sleep. London drops his head back down convinced that

all is well. After all, he's in the middle of training. The 4th Corner,

and Meika for that matter, would make sure nothing interrupts his

training. Then, there is a sound that alarms London. It is subtle,

but it makes him react. The sound is that of the sand outside of his

tent moving. Someone or something is out there. He grabs his

wooden sword, and slowly slides it under the zipped opening of the

tent. He waits for the next sound of sand sifting, and then swings

his weapon upward. The motion forces the tent to open wide.

London explodes from the mouth of the tent. Two men armed with

real swords stand surprised. One of the men darts at London sword

first. London spins in a circle and steps to the right swinging his

weapon like a bat. His wooden sword connects with the back of his attacker's head. He's out cold. London slowly bends low and picks up the man's sword. He stands and drops his wooden practice sword to the sand. The problem is, he's holding the sword all wrong, and the second attacker knows it. It's apparent to him, that London can fight, but it's also obvious that London is new with a sword. He has the advantage. He takes up his sword and slashes through the air in a display of brilliance! London is in over his head and he knows it.

Think London, THINK!

Agility is his normal advantage, and as long as his attacker's skills are limited to the sword, it could still be his advantage. London puts on his own dazzling display, but with acrobatics. He knew that combined with the darkness; his summersaults would make him a hard target for a sword. The attacker must've thought the same. He helps his unconscious friend to his feet, and they flee. London breathes heavily as he looks around for Meika or the 4th Corner. He walks back to his wooden sword and picks it up. He's unsure of what just happened. He fights the urge to call Meika's name. Instead he keeps both the real and the wooden swords near his hands for the rest of the night. London's remaining sleep is feather light.

The next morning London wakes and goes to the brook. It's cold, but London's temper is hot. He gets dressed, eats, and then enters the arena. Meika is sitting on the sand. London spots her and wants answers.

"What was that last night? I'm supposed to be training! I'm supposed to be focused. I need rest in order to properly train. *Safety would be the ideal condition to do so!* I trained with Sun Ray and Brazen in safety. It wasn't always comfortable, but I wasn't in any danger!"

He finally notices Meika's eyes are closed. She's sitting with her legs crisscrossed meditating. When London stops his rant, she opens her eyes.

"That is precisely the point. You were too protected. You were in controlled environments; Too comfortable. You are being groomed to be the SoulKnight, not a pampered brat. When you return to your world, the enemy may attack at any given time. Not just in the mornings after you've had a meal. These matters are life and death. Fight and survive or perish without mercy."

Again, she closes her eyes. London takes the time to think about what Meika has said.

"So, my training is two-fold then, Sword play, and readiness. Please accept my apologies."

"Indeed. And with that said, on guard!"

For the next many months, London trains intensely. He learns conventional and unconventional grips, defensive vs. offensive sword handling, and more. He eventually earns the respect necessary from Meika, to receive an unsuspecting surprise. As any other morning, London approaches Meika as she meditates, and stands ready with his wooden sword. Meika would normally engage him in any variety of sword attacks upon his approach. Today is different. Meika sticks out her left-hand palm facing London. He apprehensively lowers his weapon. Meika stands.

"Follow me."

Meika leads him to one of the far walls of the arena. She turns and stands next to the two swords that she'd stuck in the sand almost a year ago. She motions for London to take one of the swords. He is honored. He drops the wooden sword and slowly pulls one of Meika's real ones from the sand. It is magnificent.

"Let us now train with steel."

London braved many cuts, punctures, and lacerations. Over time London began to give as well as he was receiving. Meika was impressed. The readiness portion of London's training advanced as well. It became more and more unpredictable. As did the amount of sleep he'd get. There were nights when London was attacked multiple times. There were also whole weeks when he was only attacked once.

In the second year of London's steel training, Meika stopped holding back and attacked London with her every talent and remarkable skill. It took London a couple of weeks to adjust. But in the third week he held his own. London was a fast learner, but it still took over two years of displaced time to make him into what he needed to become. A day of training had ended. Meika and London fell to the sand of the arena panting like dogs.

"You are a quick study."

"You are a good teacher."

"Go, bathe and get dressed. But do not eat."

Meika stands and walks across the arena.

"Don't eat?"

London did as he was told. He heard the approach of small feet to his tent. He knew it was the children who bring his meals. He opens the tent to inform them that he would not be eating tonight. But they held no baskets.

"Lady Meika requests your presence."

London stands and follows the two children. But after only a few steps he goes back for his sword. The second child smiles at London, then looks back at his friend.

"He has learned."

London follows the children around the arena. When they reach the other side, a regal tent three times the size of London's comes into view. The children hold open the entrance and London walks in. The children then enter behind him and walk around him. London looks around. The inside is even more beautiful than the outside. Thick Asian rugs line the floor of the tent. The walls are white and purple, two of which support paintings of men holding swords identical to the ones Meika wielded. And the fragrance inside is a sweet subtleness that London has never experienced. A flawless mahogany table stands in the middle of the tent. Torches are lit around the perimeter. Their light makes the gown that Meika is wearing at the other end of the table look alive. She stands up. Her hair reaches her waist. London has never seen a woman more magnificently beautiful.

"I was hoping you would join me for dinner."

"I will do whatever you ask."

Meika laughs. "Please sit."

London sits. The children bring in several baskets and platters and sits them on the gorgeous table.

"London will you give thanks for us?"

"Sure."

Meika bows her head and closes her eyes.

London bites his bottom lip.

The two children's heads are bowed, but they are looking directly at London. He hadn't given thanks before eating since he was a kid.

London bows his head, "Our God is great... You know our God is good. It is now that we must thank him, for this our food. Amen, and Jesus wept."

He hopes they don't laugh.

"That was really sweet London. Where did you get that?"

"Oh, that was just something that my brother and I grew up saying."

"Tell me more about your family and how you grew up."

While London and Meika ate, London told her all about his life with his family, the breakup, the repressed memories, sports, and his dealings with Pat. It was the first time he'd shared so openly every aspect of what he's been through. It felt amazing!

"London, there is something that you need to understand."

"What's that?"

"God is not the Dark Author's enemy."

"What do you mean, of course he is? Good vs. evil."

"No. They are far from equals. God has no rival."

"The Dark one is the enemy of man. And the SoulKnight is his rival."

"What are you saying?"

"I am saying that your life will never be the same. Your first priority is warring against the agenda of the Dark one. It will not be easy. There will be sacrifices, many of them. It will put a great strain on the life you once knew. It can be a very lonely road."

London thought over all that Meika had said. He had never realized the true depth of his decision.

"This is the first time I'm hearing this."

"Yes."

"But… he chose me."

The children look up at Meika.

"I will not betray his call."

"May thee be Knight born," Meika whispers.

"I'm sorry?"

Meika smiles.

"Can I see you again, after The Knight's Birth?"

"You will forget all about me London."

"I swear to you that will never happen."

"Thank you for supping with me London. Go now and rest. Tomorrow comes quickly."

The next morning, London entered the arena. Meika was not seated in meditation. She stood in the center of the arena. London approaches and then stops in front of the war maiden. They each hold a sword. Meika pulls a second sword from behind and through her hair. She now holds two to London's one.

"This final test will end your preparation."

"Thank the Lord!"

"Yes. Let him be blessed."

"Shall we begin?"

"To the death."

She attacks. London blocks her swords and backs away.

"What? What did you say?"

Meika spins around and swings a sword slicing London's right leg. He grabs his leg and holds his sword in a defensive stance. She is serious. London jumps and flips out of the range of Meika's swords.

"I don't think we serve the same God; mine said 'Thou shalt not kill!'"

"The same God that ordered the children of Israel to kill and leave none alive?!"

"That was war!"

"And you are now a Warrior!"

She charges London, he eludes her. Meika stops and points a sword. He turns to look. There's an hourglass sitting atop the wall.

"As you can see, the sand has begun to fall. When it runs out, so shall we."

"What are you saying?"

"Simply put, if I survive, you do not. My job is done. Your training is complete. The time has come for your purpose to be fulfilled; the purpose of The SoulKnight."

London looked at the hourglass, then back at Meika.

"This doesn't make sense! No. I won't do it!"

Meika twirls her swords and once again sticks them blades first into the sand. She walks toward London. A tear runs down his cheek. Meika kisses him and wipes the tear away. She then backs away and pulls her swords from the sand.

Whispering, "Defend yourself London."

He reluctantly raises his sword and breathes deeply. They begin battle. Their swords clash for what seems like eternity. It is remarkable. Both combatants suffer many wounds. One of London's abilities is to recover from exhaustion quickly. But it only activates when he has a few moments of time to be still. This war of swords has no such moment. They breathe so heavily, that their bodies bob up and down, their lungs burn. The two circle each other. Meika has one attack left that she had yet to attempt. It is primitive, but worth a chance. She stops in her tracks. In anticipation of her next attack, so does London. Meika slowly approaches. In these moments London is recharged. Meika swings both of her swords as one but stops in mid swing. London swings his sword to block, but when his sword receives no contact; his momentum carries and leaves his face open. Meika immediately flips backward purposely kicking sand into London's eyes. When she lands, London is blinded. He backs off in pain.

His eyes feel like they're being stabbed by a million tiny knives!

Meika then throws one sword at London's heart, and charges with

the other. London hears the sword slicing through the air. He slips

to the side and catches it by the handle on the back end. He hears

her feet quickly sifting through the sand. London traps her last

sword between the two blades he now holds. In the same motion,

he twists and disarms her. Before Meika's sword hits the ground,

London stabs with both his swords at her throat! Just before the

peak of his reach, a half inch from decapitating Meika, he holds

back. He can't see it, but he knows what he has kept himself from

doing.

Whispering, "I won't."

London feels Meika's hand touch his. Then a hand touches his

eyes. He blinks and the sand is gone. He can see. But Meika is

also gone. What he sees are the unmistakable eyes of the 4th

Corner. The two of them stand high on a dark rooftop. London

falls to his knees.

"I didn't, I couldn't have. Did I..."

"No. You did not. You displayed the one ability that could not be taught; Mercy."

Relieved, London closes his eyes and breathes deeply.

"You have proven worthy to receive the gifts previously spoken of."

London slowly stands. The 4th Corner's wings appear and unfold. He flaps them two powerful times and circles over London like a bird of prey. As he circles, the sky changes colors. It turns clear blue from black. The stars disappear. London looks down at his feet. He had been standing on a dark and damp rooftop; he is now standing on solid gold. He starts to look up again. His eyes climb an extremely wide staircase to the foot of what can only be a throne. Just before his eyes finished their climb, just before he discovers who it was that sat on the throne, a voice destroys the silence. The sheer weight of this voice throws London on his face. He recognizes it. A voice like unto many waters, it was the voice of the Almighty!

"WELL DONE. IT PLEASES ME TO BLESS YOU.
NOW STAND, AND DO NOT ATTEMPT TO LAY EYES
UPON ME. FOR NONE MAY DO SO AND LIVE. STEP
DOWN INTO THE WATER BEFORE ME."

London stands. He didn't know that the ground in front of
the staircase was water. It was impossibly still. It reflects the
stairs so perfectly that it just looks like more stairs! He keeps his
eyes down and enters the more than magnificent pool. It is wet, it
is indeed water. But it doesn't behave like water. Not once does it
ripple as London enters in. His very soul feels like it's breathing.
There are now others standing around the pool. There are men and
women in white. Some have wings. Judging by his recent
dealings with the 4th Corner, those without wings could have them
hidden. London knows where he is; it is clear.

"KNEEL AT THE BOTTOM AND INHALE THE
WATER SEVEN TIMES."

London allows himself to sink to the bottom of the pool.
He closes his eyes and kneels. Faith is a must. He inhales. With
each breath, a large portion of water disappears. By the time

London takes his seventh breath, the water is gone. Those that surround the pool speak one word in concert…

"Amen."

"GO NOW, AND SERVE THY KING, FOR YOUR BIRTH IS COMPLETE. THOU ART SOULKNIGHT."

Still on his knees, London opens his eyes. He is once again on a dark and damp rooftop. He looks up as the 4th Corner descends to the ground. The sky is dark again.

"Heaven! I was in heaven!"

"Stand now London son of James. London stands. The enemy has resorted to attacking in the sight of man. If thou must, thou may now engage them openly. But not as London, son of James, thou must conceal thy identity."

Now hear of the gifts that are thine: Thou can collapse matter. When both your fists are combined to punch as one, thou can cause boulders to crumble! Thou can even smash through metal. This gift shall give the impression of immense strength.

But this punch shall not kill. Thou may use it on the living, but the effect will only forcibly repel them.

Thou can make thyself completely void of weight. Thou can slow any fall, making thy landing as light as a feather. There are no limits to how thou can apply this gift.

Also, thou art given three hours of protection. Once sheltered, say these words, *Mercy upon me*, and you and any with thee, will have three hours of total peace and safety. Use them wisely, for this window of time comes once within a 24-hour period.

Now, in the book of the Genesis, these words are written: "… Therefore the Lord God sent him forth from the Garden of Eden, to till the ground from whence he was taken. So, he drove out the man; and he placed at the east end of the Garden of Eden cherubim, and *a flaming sword* which turned every way, to keep the way of the tree of life." Gen 3: 23-24.

As the 4th Corner spake these words, a sword of fire descended from the heavens. London's eyes and mouth open astonished. The sword lowers to the right hand of the 4th Corner. It blazes and crackles with red, white, and yellow fire.

"Take hold tightly, and do not let go!"

London steps forth and takes hold of the sword with both hands. He holds the sword away from his face as it burns brightly and sparks. The sword begins to shake violently. London struggles to keep his grip. The flame burns brighter. Then suddenly, it is still. Not only does the sword stop shaking, the fire also stops burning, and the light dims. London turns his face to the sword. What was, just seconds ago, a sword of fire, is now a red metal-looking blade.

"Behold the Eden Sword!"

London silently marvels.

"Do not underestimate. Though the blade appears to be metal, it is not so. This sword is a solid and inextinguishable flame. It will both burn like fire, and slice like the sharpest steel. Keep it enclosed in this."

He hands London a sheath.

"Won't it burn?"

"Neh, for this scabbard is made from wood from the tree of life."

London is fascinated as he sheathes the sword. Attached to the scabbard is a belt-like band to allow London to wear it on his back.

"It is also written, "To everything there is a season, and a time to every purpose under the heaven: A time to be born and a time to die; A time to plant and a time to pluck up that which is planted; *A time to kill* and a time to heal; A time to break down and a time to build up;" 3:1-3. Remember these words."

The 4th Corner then spread his previously unseen wings and let them carry him from the rooftop to the sky.

"Hold on, you still haven't told me about the wings!"

The 4th Corner doesn't respond. London looks down surprised to see that he is miraculously wearing the sweat suit that was cut to shreds by Meika's swords. It is now whole. He takes the sweatshirt off and wraps the sword up in it. London turns to look for the door to get into the building he now stands on top of. He walks towards it, before remembering his new gifts; especially one, weightlessness!

How do I use it? How do I use any of them for that matter? Okay wait. "Faith is the substance of things hoped for, the evidence of things not seen." Heb 11: 1. I believe I have this gift! (London pumps himself up), and since faith is dead without works, James 2:20. I have to put it to work!"

London places the sword underneath his left arm. He holds the section protruding in the front like a football. He takes a few steps backward as he eyes the edge of the rooftop. Even though it's dark out, London doesn't want to take any chances being seen; his plan is to jump down into the alley. He takes a deep breath and runs toward the edge. At the last moment he dives right arm first into a sea of blackness. Gravity seemed all too eager to force London to the bottom! London does a front summersault and is now right side up. He is not weightless! In fact, to him it seems that he's heavier! His acceleration is too much to handle. There's so much air blowing in his face that he is unable to see or breathe. To keep from suffocating, London holds his breath.

Immediately, he can open his eyes. The wind has stopped blowing. He looks down and sees why there is no more wind. He is no longer on a collision course with the pavement. London is no longer moving. He's suspended in midair, no more than twenty feet from the ground.

Is it my breath?

London slowly blows out some of the air he's holding in his lungs. He begins to descend at the same speed in which he blows the air out. He continues exhaling at this speed until his feet touch the ground, as soft as leaves fall in the autumn. London smiles. However, he has no idea that his eyes are perfectly imitating those of the 4th Corner.

London emerges out of the darkness of the alley, an expert in hand to hand combat, with powers designed by the omnipotent; and under his arm, he carries an unstoppable weapon. The Knight's Birth is complete.

London is anxious to get off of the street. Even though the Eden sword is wrapped up, it still looks like he's concealing a weapon, namely a gun. A car is parked up ahead, another cab.

London remembers not to run this time. But there's another problem. No cab driver in his right mind would ever give a ride to someone carrying a possible weapon; plus, it's the middle of the night. He has an idea. He quickly un-wraps the sword and ties his sweatshirt around his waist. He uses the sword as a cane and limps toward the cab. The driver is asleep. He wakes at the sound of the pretend cane, tapping the cement as London approaches. The driver looks and sees what appears to be a physically challenged man, laboring his way up the street. He calls to the man out of his window offering him a ride. London smiles and accepts.

Back home, London re-wraps the sword in his sweater and quickly climbs the stairs before running down the hall to his dorm room. Just before he unlocks the door, he realizes his roommate is more than likely asleep on the other side. He quietly opens the door. His roommate is in bed. He places the sword on his bed and walks toward the window. Just before reaching the window, his roommate calls his name.

"London? How was the trip?"

"Man, I thought you were sleep."

"I was, but I need to go to the bathroom."

So much has happened since London last saw Tommy; he'd forgotten that the last thing Tommy knew about was Spring break.

"It was perfect man, just what I needed."

"Cool."

Tommy opens the door and walks down the hall to the restroom. London still wanted to look out on the city he'd been away from for so long. He reaches for the curtain. The moment he pulls it back, the shadow walker that had been waiting on his return, pounces on him. A second shadow walker grabs one of his legs. Then a third grabs his other one. They'd come out of the shadows. London falls over knocking the first creature loose. He yells out! Then, he rolls toward Tommy's dresser and kicks his right leg against it jarring the second shadow walker loose. London swings a right connecting with the first creature, sending it flying across the room. He kicks the third creature with his free leg. It holds tight and bites his calf. Again, London cries out! London rolls to his bed and reaches up for the sword. The second shadow walker jumps at London. He swings the wrapped-up sword like a bat, knocking it several feet back. The third creature, still hanging on, is pounded with the sheathed sword before it finally releases its grip. London jumps to his feet and unleashes Eden in its' full glory! The second shadow walker attacks just as London drops the scabbard. London swings the powerful sword for the first time. The creature is cut in two! The blade which is actually fire burns through the shadow walker like a bolt of lightning! London spins around and swings the sword again; the third creature's head goes flying. The first shadow walker is just recovering from the trauma of London's punch. It looks around and sees the pieces of its partners scattered about. London stands confidently holding the red colored sword awaiting the last shadow walker. It bares its teeth and snarls at London before disappearing into a shadow. London slowly walks to the wall and carefully touches the spot where the creature vanished. The wall is solid. Unlike that day in the airport, this was no illusion.

Tommy is on his way back from the restroom still half sleep. He drags his feet up the hall. London hears him. The room is a mess! Papers lay everywhere, one dresser is moved from its' original spot, trophies on the ground, and pens are scattered. But the only concern London has is the mutilated bodies of miniature creatures! He grabs the scabbard sheaths the sword and slides it under his bed. He then throws the remains of both creatures on top of his bed. There is no blood. London wraps his top sheet around the bodies and rolls them into a ball. Tommy clumsily walks in. His face frowns up.

"What is that smell? He then looks around. And what happened in here?"

London lifts the balled-up sheet and darts for the door.

"I don't feel too good!"

"I guess not! But you could've opened a window!"

London makes like he's heading for the restroom. He looks back to his room and sees Tommy close the door; upon seeing this, he runs down the stairs outside and around back. He ties a knot in the sheet and throws it in the dumpster. By the time he makes it back to his room, he finds his roommate back in bed. London is glad he doesn't have to answer any questions about what just happened. He keeps his eye on the wall where the creature had disappeared, while he straightened the room up. London hears Tommy mumble something.

"Tommy, did you say something"

Tommy yarns "Yeah, I said you really have to stop drinking man."

As Tommy falls back asleep London laughs to himself. He knows he would think the same if he was in Tommy's place. London then eyes the spot of the creature's escape as he readies for bed. He figures he'll be sleeping like he did outside of the arena tonight. But then he remembers one of his gifts.

"Mercy upon me"

Three hours isn't much but he'll take it. London then gets on his knees and says his prayers for the first time since he was a kid. It certainly won't be the last

Shadow walkers can indeed do what their names suggest. They can enter and exit our world through shadows. However, they can only use vertical shadows. They cannot use a shadow more than once, so darkness must be in abundance. When they exit the world of man, they enter into the realm of the Dark Author, the Under.

The lone surviving shadow walker that fought with London kneels at the foot of the rotted tree throne. He tells the Dark one all that has occurred. The Dark Author sends word for Pat to meet him in the same park they'd met in before.

Pat enters the park and approaches the tree where the murder of crows had once perched. There is no sign of them. He sits on the bench. A minute later he feels a funny sensation on his legs. He looks down to an uncountable number of spiders climbing him. Each one has six tiny red eyes.

"The mortal has resurfaced."

"Has he been given the gifts?"

"He has, we do not yet know the full extent of them; however, he is no longer your concern. Refocus your attention on my larger plans. Let nothing deter you."

"Forgive me O Dark one, but if not mine, then whose concern shall he be?"

"I have made provisions for this contingency. They shall soon go into effect. Go now and do my bidding."

"Yes, my lord."

Chapter eight:

Accept the unexpected

The next morning, London wakes up very much on guard. He knows that he's slept beyond the three-hour window of protection. He takes a quick shower and gets dressed with his head on a swivel. Both Tommy and London have early morning classes. Just as they're getting ready to leave there's a knock at the door. Tommy answers it.

"Can I help you?"

"Yes, I'm looking for my brother, London Bishop."

London hears his brother's voice and comes to the door. "Donald?"

"Yeah, remember you said I could hang out with you today while Dad went to his meeting in Jersey."

London had totally forgotten. After all, from his perspective, much had happened since he'd made that promise. He was almost killed by Dozorn and Pat. He'd met and trained with

Brazen, met trained and fell for his potential first love in Meika, and been granted access into the presence of the Most-high! Not to mention he was given several unimaginable gifts.

"Tommy this is my brother Donald. Donald this is my roommate Tommy."

"Dude... my bad. I slept so hard I forgot all about it."

Tommy, who's standing behind his roommate, silently imitates a drunken London for only Donald to see.

"Don't worry about it. I think I can catch Dad before he gets too far."

"No, we're good! Come on, I'd love to have you chill for the day."

This was only partly true. London did indeed miss his brother, but he was silently praying that Pat and Dozorn wouldn't show themselves while he entertained Donald.

"You sure?"

"No doubt. Let's go."

"Cool."

"I'll catch you at later at practice," says Tommy. Good to meet you Donald."

"You too."

London was carrying two bags. He can't help but wonder whether he should've left the Eden sword under his bed. He has it wrapped up in another sweatshirt and is carrying it in his biggest gym bag. He zipped it up as much as it would go. Some of the sword pokes out, but that's okay.

"You need me to carry one of your bags?"

"Uh, yeah thanks."

London sets his gym bag down close to his feet and takes his backpack off and hands it to his brother.

"What's that; some kind of project or something?"

"Yeah, I guess you can say that."

The brothers enter Spencer Hall, where London's history class is. London leads Donald in and immediately takes a seat in

229

the back. Although there are closer seats, London doesn't want to risk drawing too much attention to the object sticking out of his bag. Much to his delight, the class goes on without a hitch. His last two classes for the day also go well. London and Donald go to the dining hall to get a bite to eat before practice.

"What time is it?"

"It's 12:15. What time is Dad supposed to be coming?"

"He sent me a text saying around 3:00."

"Cool, you'll be able to come to practice."

"So, what's up with you and Dad?"

London sighs, "Man… I just…"

"I tried to give you two a few minutes alone last night."

London had to think. He finally remembered talking to his father when Donald went to the restroom in the restaurant.

"Oh yeah, right."

"It wasn't the easiest thing to get used to, but Evelyn's alright, she really is."

"I'm not so upset about the whole Evelyn thing. I'm upset Dad was so eager for all of us to go to Church together. You're probably too young to remember, but he was never okay with going when Mom wanted him to. That's the main reason we're not all a family today. I just can't get over that."

"Wow. That's... crazy. You're right. I guess I was too young to remember. But I do remember He would never be there. Does he know this is why you're upset?"

"He does now."

"What did he say?"

"He said he was sorry. But listen, I don't really want to talk about that right now. I gotta get focused for practice. We have a pretty big game coming up. It determines whether or not we'll play in the post season. You ready?"

"Yeah cool let's do it, I'm ready."

London and Donald gather their things and head for the door.

"Hold on London. I just have to say this last thing. You have a right to be upset with Dad. I would be too. But give him a chance to explain. He misses you man, for real. You're his first born... his first. He's always talking about you. He loves you London, he loves you. And at the end of the day that's our Dad man. You have to honor him. It's like a commandment bro."

London swallows hard and nods. He was just schooled by his younger brother. He was speechless.

"Now let me see how college has your game looking!"

London takes Donald into the locker room and introduces him to the team and the coaches. Donald sits in the bleachers and watches while practice goes on. London made sure to show out a little more than usual for his little brother to see. Donald covers his mouth and does his best to calm his excitement. He's glad to see his brother is still the man on the court!

After practice London and Donald waited outside of London's dorm for their father. James pulls up fifteen minutes later. Donald and London dap each other up and give hugs.

Donald opens the door and gets in. London then walks around to his father's side of the car. James lets his window down.

"I got this for you."

James opens the envelope. It was London's game schedule for next season's home games. James looked up at his son and bit his lip. He wouldn't risk trying to talk. He knew his voice would betray him. Donald looks at his brother and smiles widely.

"Hope to see you at a game."

James looks back at the schedule. He can't stop nodding his head.

"You Bishop men be safe out there."

"You too son."

The first step had been taken. Both sides felt new life in a part of their hearts that had died long ago.

Chapter Nine:

A Public Debut

The next morning London hesitantly leaves the Eden sword behind. Twice before he makes it to class, he almost goes back for it. For the second straight day classes go smoothly. He eats lunch and goes to practice like yesterday. When the coach finally decided to end practice, London and his teammates decided to go out for pizza. Things are actually feeling normal. The way a college student's normal should look; no demonic interruptions, no heavenly ones either for that matter. London's mind is far away from his new Knight status; plus, he was no longer dragging the Eden sword around. The next day is just as smooth. As is Wednesday. By the time Friday rolls around, London wonders whether his enemies have somehow forgotten about him.

What does a warrior do with his down time? The newly crowned Knight had been enjoying himself the last few days by being the regular old London Bishop. But this can't last. He knows how important the *new him* has become. He decides to be proactive. That night, he begins walking the streets looking for anything out of the ordinary. He has no idea what to look for. It's not like Pat and Dozorn will just be hanging out on a corner somewhere. They always find him. That's when he realizes he's the bait. He revisits every place he's encountered the Demon Disciple and his enforcer. First, he stages himself outside of the diner. When that doesn't work, he walks the streets he'd gotten lost on when he came face to face with The Dark Author. He retraces these steps the entire weekend. His bait catches no fish. Monday and Tuesday London continues his patrols. By Wednesday he feels like a fool. He hasn't seen anything. He hasn't even lured any of the small aggressive creatures out of hiding to take a shot at him. The fruitless patrols have taken their toll. London decides to instead to focus his energy on keeping his skills sharp. He begins with his super sensitive hearing, riding the subway wearing dark sunglasses with his eyes closed. He pretends to be blind and reacts to the many sounds of the city. He also continues to borrow the keys to the school's gym in order to practice his acrobatics, incorporating his gift of weightlessness. London even kept up with his fighting skills, and sword play. All gift and no responsibility was how it seemed. Then one day, he spots a familiar face.

Classes have just ended, and London is eager to get to his dorm. He isn't happy about the ton of reading that he'd received for homework. It's Friday and all he can think about is his ruined weekend. There's a party or two that he'd hoped to attend. He sighs and tells himself that this is what being an adult feels like. There are dozens of people walking around and about, nothing unusual about that. But the one guy, who favors Pat, snatches London's attention away from his homework woes. He stops in his tracks. The man is walking up the street toward the intersection. London follows. It can't be Pat! It wouldn't make sense. Pat has the ability to disguise himself as a human, why would he continue to use the same face? London keeps following, all the while debating with himself. Before reaching the intersection, the man stops at a parked car. He's holding a briefcase in one hand and reaches in his pocket with the other. London ducks, thinking he's grabbing a weapon. But the man pulls out a set of keys. He opens the door and turns to get in. Just then, London gets a good look at the man. It is indeed Pat! He drives the rest of the way to the intersection and turns right. London places his backpack on both shoulders and pulls the hood of his windbreaker over his head. He looks around. No one is watching. He explodes with speed! He runs in the direction that Pat had driven. When he hits the corner, London decides it's time to hit high gear. He takes a deep breath. Although he didn't pierce the sound barrier, he put any and all world class sprinters to shame! The car is in range in no time. But what he doesn't know is his eyes burn a magnificent blue, and shimmer all the while. London zips past several bystanders leaving them awe struck. Two of which see his eyes.

"Whoa, what was that?" Says the old man.

"I don't know, but did you see his eyes?"

"He was wearing those contacts that light up."

"What contacts that light up?"

"You know, the one's that the kids are wearing now."

"Okay but how do you explain how fast he was going?"

"He was on one of those hover things."

"What? You mean the hover boards?

"Yeah the things that people keep falling on!"

"He wasn't on any hover board! And for that matter he wasn't wearing any contacts either!"

"Well what are you saying just happened?"

"I'm just saying, why don't you just admit that you don't know, and you're just as confused as I am?"

"I am not... well umm... yeah let's get out of here."

London is right on Pat's heels, when he notices something in one of the windows that he's blazing by. He turns to see what it is, and exhales; thus, dramatically slowing his speed. He comes to a complete stop. London stares at his own reflection in the window of a corner business. More specifically, he's looking at his eyes. He is in shock. No one told him about this part of the agreement.

Then he remembers.

"Pat!"

London turns and looks for Pat's car. There is no sign of it. By this time, he's attracting attention. People have seen him drop out of his warp-like speed. When he notices all the eyes, he once again holds his breath and darts away. He turns a corner and runs behind a building. He takes his windbreaker off and stuffs it into his backpack. Subtly, London walks back into the open. He looks around to make sure that no one recognizes him. He keeps his head down.

Pat has gotten away, and London's directly to blame. He heads for the dorm. Suddenly, he hears something large rapidly approaching from behind. He turns around just in time to dodge a violent charge from the six-legged blue demon! The beast crashes into a parked SUV. It's completely totaled. London quickly snatches his backpack off and digs his windbreaker out. He rams his right arm through just before Dozorn mounted another attack. His other arm gets stuck. This time when he attempts to dodge, Dozorn anticipates it. The beast charges as he did the first time, but when London jumps, he jumps with him. The beast grabs London by the jammed-up arm in jacket. Before touching ground, Dozorn slams him into the side of a building! London slides to the ground. He's hurt. Two women across the street scream as they witness the unbelievable sight. Dozorn hears the screams and looks their way. Instantly, their screams hush. Several people who hear the screams come out to see what was going on. Upon seeing what the women were staring at, everyone is frozen with fear. Their hearts skip a beat. The beast roars. The pain of his bellow reanimates everyone, and they all run. A few people have to pick themselves up off of the ground. While all of this is going on, London's bracelet does its work. He finally gets his left arm through and tightens his hood around his head. When Dozorn turns his attention back to him, London is rising to his feet. He is focused and poised for combat. His eyes burn blue. Sirens are in the background. This time it is London who charges. Dozorn rushes to meet his arrogant attacker. London swings with both fists and connects with the beast head on! Dozorn is repelled a half of a block backward! London runs in pursuit. Before the beast can re-gather itself, London hops on top of a car and uses it as a springboard to jump high into the air. Then, just before gravity can take hold, as his momentum ends, he holds his breath, thus pausing in midair. Several on-lookers have dared to remain, they are amazed. Dozorn shakes his head trying to clear it. He stands up on his six legs and frantically looks around for London. The source of the sirens came into view. Four police cars race from around the corner. Dozorn stops underneath London, who is hovering in air. London exhales all of the air from his lungs and shouts...

"Up here!"

As the beast looks up, London uses gravity to deliver a ferocious double footed kick to the face of the creature! Dozorn falls like a bag of rocks!

Upon seeing the blue six-legged creature, all four cop cars come to a screeching stop in near unison. Rumors of a couple burnt out officers who had reported seeing such a sight had been circulating in their precinct. The jokes, they themselves, had made and had laughed at, were words that they were now eating! When London landed the kick, they got out of their cars and drew weapons.

"You there, put your hands-on top of your head and get on your knees!"

When London turns around, the cops react to the sight of his eyes.

"Whoa, do you see his eyes?!" The second cop says.

London raises his hands to show that he has no weapons. Then Dozorn stands up. He attempts to balance himself. The cops nervously point their guns at the creature.

"What in God's name is that?"

"You know what it is. They say it's supposed to be bulletproof!"

Another cop speaks, "They also said it can speak!"

When Dozorn finally rights himself, his eyes focuses on London.

"Your death will be slow torture. It will be eternal legend in the deepest depths of hell!"

"It is written, to everything there is a season, and a time to every purpose…, to die is not mine, for my purpose is at hand beast!"

This enrages the demon Enforcer. He steps forward and roars. Terrified, the cops open fire. London does a couple handsprings and takes cover. The effect on Dozorn is like that of a cold wind. It simply causes him to turn his head and squint his eyes while using a hand to block part of the annoying spray of bullets. Angered, Dozorn takes hold of a station wagon and throws it at the cops! London quickly springs into action putting himself in between the cops and the on-coming car. He swings both fists forward and smashes the station wagon in two! The vehicle was no longer recognizable. Back-up arrives on the scene at the same time that London destroys the thrown car. They abruptly stop their squad cars! A few of the officers run to the aide of their fellow officers. The others fire their weapons at London and especially Dozorn. London jumps behind a truck where he can still see the beast. Once again, Dozorn is unharmed by the bullets. In the midst of the chaos, London sees something very strange. A group of rats run across the street in front of Dozorn. However, just before passing the creature, each one pauses. The beast also sees the rats. He looks directly at them. As they scurry away, Dozorn runs off in the opposite direction. He smashes a couple more cars and leaves them as roadblocks to keep anyone from following him. London is the only target that remains.

"He's behind the truck!"

Upon hearing this, London decided to do what the beast did. The police gave chase and radioed the direction of the two fugitives' escape. London dodged the many sounds of bullets being fired his way. He then manipulates his gift of weightlessness in a way he had never done before. He didn't know what inspired it; without thought he dove straight ahead and held his breath. It resulted in what everyone who saw perceived as flight! His speed increased ten-fold. The cops stopped shooting and stared in awe. Though his speed was remarkable, he was only about six to seven feet off the ground. London didn't care. He was astonished! It didn't take long for him to build a safe distance. This was good because he was so excited that his adrenaline made it hard to hold his breath for long. London slowly exhales and lands running. His eyes return to normal. Trying to look inconspicuous, he jogs into a nearby deli. He asks where the restrooms are and quickly enters. He takes the wind breaker off and throws it in the garbage. Next, he takes all things identifying himself out of his backpack and dumps it. His energy returns as he stood still. He then exits the restroom and calmly walks out the building's back door.

Minutes earlier, back at the scene of the battle, just as London was doing his impression of flight, no one noticed a middle-aged man who stood by watching the impossible happenings. As London made his escape, the man walked away and zipped up his jacket.

About thirty minutes later, the police were trying to calm the panic. T.V. reporters were now on the scene interviewing witnesses. London made it to his dorm room. Although there were more important aspects of his latest encounter, the only thing he could currently think about was his brand of flying! He looks under his bed to make sure the Eden sword is still there. He grabs it. Had he taken it with him that morning, he could possibly have one less demon to worry about. Tommy storms in putting London on the defensive. Using the still concealed sword, London sweeps his roommates' feet from under him. Tommy falls backward with a loud thud.

"What the hell! What is your problem?!"

"My bad man, I've had a wild day." London helps his roommate to his feet. "You scared me coming in like that."

"What's really going on? You've been acting strange for a while now!"

"Yeah, you're right. To tell you the truth, I've been going through some personal stuff. But I'm getting it together."

"Now I get it, that's why you've been drinking."

"No Tommy. I have not been drinking."

"No drinking?"

"No Tommy! No drinking."

"You sure you're not in denial."

"It's family drama man, that and some spiritual stuff."

"Oh wow, sorry bro. Yeah, I can relate. You have to find a way to relax man. Something that works for you. That's the key."

London thought to himself; *if you only knew.*

"Yeah, I'll keep that in mind. Why were you busting in here like that anyway?"

"Oh yeah, turn the T.V. to channel four!"

London presses the power button on the remote as he slides the concealed sword back under his bed. He turns the station to four and sits on his bed.

"…witnesses are terrified! They say the creature was the size of a van or a small truck. And that's not all; this thing was described as having six legs! This lady says she saw the creature. What did you see?"

"It was horrible! A real life monster! It was huge; it was blue with enormous teeth! And that roar!"

"This man says he also saw the creature, but he said there's more. What else did you see sir?"

"There was a fight going on, and I don't mean with the police. I'm talking before the cops arrived. The creature was fighting with someone who looked like a man."

"You say he looked like a man?"

"No man can do the things he did!"

"What kind of things are you talking about?"

"He punched a car in half! Then when police tried to apprehend him, he flew!"

"What do you mean he flew?"

"I mean he was flying!"

"And his eyes," says a witness in the rear.

"Yeah, his eyes were creepy."

"What was creepy?"

"They glowed blue!"

The reporter turns back to the camera.

"There are several witnesses here with the same story Bob."

"What do the police have to say about the incident?"

"They had no comment, but I've been told that the commissioner is planning to give an official statement."

"So obviously, there's something to this story?"

"No question Bob, and we're going stick around here and learn as much as we can. Back to you."

"Can you believe this," Tommy turns the TV off.

"Do you?"

"It's on the news right, it has to be real!"

"I don't know, maybe it's an escaped bear from the zoo or something."

"Bear, I think they know what a bear looks like, and they didn't describe one!"

Meanwhile, a man wearing sunglasses and a cap walks into the lobby of channel two news. He approaches the information desk.

"May I help you?"

"Yes, I need to speak with a producer, or whoever's in charge."

"Do you have an appointment?"

"No, but believe me, they will want to see me."

"What did you say your name was?"

"Look, just get on your phone and tell your bosses that there's a man down here with video footage of the six-legged blue creature fighting the man with the eyes."

The receptionist grabs the phone and does just that. Not even two minutes later, three anxious looking men and a woman in a dress suit step off the elevator.

"Hello sir, I'm Sarah Arnold the executive Vice President of the station." She sticks her hand out. "I can't efficiently express our excitement in the fact that you chose to bring your video to us."

The man shakes her hand. *"Oh, I'm sure you can."*

"So, what's your name sir?"

"No names."

"Okay, that's no problem. If you don't mind, we can go talk in one of our board rooms."

"Yeah, let's do that."

They take the elevator up and enter a board room.

"Can we get you anything?"

"No, I'm fine."

"Alright then, what is it that you want?"

"Fifty thousand dollars. And I want it in cash."

"Fifty thousand dollars, sir that's outrageous!"

"Yeah, so is this footage; just be glad I'm not asking for a cool mill!"

"Sir we can't pay you that much, only the President could authorize such an amount and he…"

The man unzips his jacket and pulls out his cell phone. He pushes a button and begins watching the footage.

"Oh well, I guess channel seven will be the first to show the world then. Ooh, wait 'til the public sees this."

He begins walking out.

"Sir wait; we haven't even seen what it is that you want us to buy."

"I suppose I can give you a sample. But not you, let one of your assistants come and take a look."

The VP makes eye contact with one of her assistants. The man holds tightly to his phone while he allows his footage to be seen.

"Sam, what do you see?"

"Oh my God! We have to be the first ones to air this."

The man turns his phone off.

"Fifty thousand"

Sarah Arnold pulls out her phone and turns her back as she walks to the far end of the room. Sixty seconds later...

"You'll have your money in one hour."

"Works for me; I'm just going to need it in writing."

"Sam, make it happen. Sir, may I see now."

"Be my guest."

She reaches for the man's phone and presses play. "*Dear God!*"

London stopped trying to suggest logical explanations to his roommate. After all, there was no logical explanation. This was the supernatural.

"Who knows what really went down?"

"It sounds like some alien type stuff to me. They even said one of them was flying."

London covers his smile.

"This is too much for me to deal with right now. I think I'll take your advice and try to relax. I'm going to the mall to pick up a CD."

"A CD? London, what are you talking about? Are you hearing what I'm saying?"

"Yeah and it's nuts! I'm not trying to add E.T. to the list of what I already have going on if you don't mind."

"Alright, but you see what's going on out there, watch yourself... *And step your game up and get some iTunes or something from present times!*"

London silences his phone. He doesn't want to hear from anyone. He waits at the bus stop for about 15 minutes. The bus is half full. Thankfully the ride is a quiet one. When London walks into the mall he is in deep thought. This is the first chance he's had to think about what has happened. Everything had started with him trying to catch up to Pat. He's still pretending to be a man! He's up to something; But what? London knew he had to find out. He just doesn't know how he's going to do it. He walks into the music shop. He needed something to help him relax. His father always said jazz was the perfect cure for stress. Today he was going to find out. He didn't know where to start. But what he did know was the name Miles Davis. He was supposed to be so cool. That's what he needed. The cashier was in to jazz, and suggested Miles Davis' Kind of blue CD. London bought it and headed out. On his way to exit the mall he passes an electronics store. A bunch of people are gathered at the window. London backs up to see what the commotion's about. They're all watching the TV screens in the electronics store's display. Each screen is showing the news.

"What's going on?"

"Shh," says several people.

London didn't need to ask again. There in high definition, he sees himself destroying an airborne car. Then he sees Dozorn. It has begun. London reaches into his bag and pulls out the CD. He uses a key to open it. He loads it into his father's old Walkman and puts his earphones on. The first song title on the list read, *So what*.

"My thoughts exactly"

Chapter TEN:

The Response

London pressed play and walked to the bus stop. Under the circumstances, he enjoys the ride home. No professor giving piles of work, no coaches yelling out plays, no need to hide anything from his roommate, and above all, no hell born threats! It was just him and Miles, miles away from everything. He should've listened to his father long ago. This was escapism at its best. The bus ride was only twenty minutes, but it served as a mini vacation. London's stop comes, and he strolls off as if he hasn't a care in the world. It's comfortable outside and the stars are shining brightly. Traffic is low, and the wind is calm. Most everything is still. He walks the stairs temporarily content with life. He stops just before opening his room door. He presses stop and pulls out the CD case. London looks at the cover and smiles before putting it away. He looks up and whispers thank you. He knows the peace he'd just experienced was only a brief fix. London takes a deep breath; he knows as soon as he opens the door, the sky is going to fall.

He unlocks the door to find his roommate frantic.

"London, where have you been? You think things were crazy before, wait 'til the news comes back on. Wait... here it is."

Of course, it was the footage that London had seen a piece of in the mall. He knew that he needed to show both concern and emotion. Anything less would alarm Tommy.

"What the... What is that?"

"I told you it was real!"

"What are they saying?"

"They've been talking to experts... "

Yeah right, experts London thought.

"... and they're all in agreement."

"About what?"

"That these are aliens, both the blue thing, and the one with the eyes."

"Oh really? How can they be sure"?

"Yes really, what else could they be? And Before I forget, your mom and Dad called. And some friend of yours keeps calling."

"Friend, What friend?"

"His name was John. He said it's an emergency."

This gave London pause. He decided to change the subject.

"Are you still going to that party tonight?"

"Party? Are you crazy? Who can think about...? Wait a minute. This maybe our last chance to party. For all we know the world may be about to end."

"Don't you think you're going a bit overboard?"

"No. No, I don't! Take a look at the TV screen my dude! Aliens have officially invaded the Earth. *Freaking aliens London*!"

"We don't know what's going on."

"Well I'll tell you this; I'm going to get my last groove on. What are you going to do?"

"Professor Ian and Dr. Hill gave the longest assignments. I need to get some work done."

"Get some work done… Are you serious?"

"Yeah man."

"Alright, well I'm out of here."

London listens to the messages from his family, and then texts them letting them know that he just fine. He then refocuses. He paces the room considering how he might track Pat down. Where was he coming from, and where was he going? He was on Elmwood. What's on Elmwood? London figured he was going to have to do some investigating. The TV was still on and they were showing the footage again. London sits down and watches. He sees the rats. He had forgotten the weird behavior they had displayed. He waits another ten minutes, knowing they'd be re-showing the footage all night. He pays close attention to the interaction between Dozorn and the rats.

"They're communicating!"

London continued trying to put things together. He hadn't seen either Pat or Dozorn in weeks. They seemed to be unconcerned with him. Now all of a sudden, he encounters both of them. But they weren't after him. At least Pat wasn't.

"Hold on… That's it! The beast attacked because I was following Pat. What is he up to?"

The phone rings. London answers it.

"Hello."

"London, didn't you get my message?"

It was John.

"I was just about to… "

"I know you saw the news!"

"Yeah, I've been bugging out, this is crazy."

"Tell me about it! Everything is exactly as I said it was, blue with six legs. You remember, now don't you?"

"I believe I do," London wished he hadn't answered the phone.

"And what about the man? That was him wasn't it?"

"Oh, well I didn't say all that. I'm not sure if..."

"Come on London, who else could it be? I think you're in denial, big time. Get with it man this is serious!"

"It does all seem to be related."

"You think?! What are we going to do?"

"Do?"

"Yes. We have to tell somebody."

"Tell somebody what?"

"We were the first ones to see these aliens. The authorities should know that they've been here long before now."

261

"John think about it. Why would they believe us? They get reports about UFO'S and what not all the time! I'm sure many of those people are calling with I told you so statements!"

John got quiet.

"The humanoid one is obviously the good guy. If you notice, in the footage he's saving the cops."

"Who's to say he's saving them? He's running, excuse me, flying away from the cops!"

"I know I hope he comes out on top. Because it's apparent that that other thing is the aggressor."

"I guess."

"Listen, I don't mean to cut this short, but I have a ton of homework to… "

"Homework! Are you serious? The world as we know it has just ended and you're thinking about due dates?!"

"You sound like my roommate. Man, you don't know my professors."

"Whatever London, but whether you like it or not we're a part of this. Both of us, click!"

London hangs the phone up, "No, just one of us."

Tommy returned hours later. He finds London asleep at his desk, face in his books. He wakes him and convinces him to get in the bed. Needless to say, London had just ended an extremely eventful day. He didn't wake until early Saturday afternoon. He slowly got himself together and walked down the hallway to the bathroom to shower. When he returns to his room, he turns the television on. He decides to clear his desk off when the show he's watching is interrupted by a special report. There's a podium in front of a blue set with a United States Presidential seal. There is also an American flag. The president steps to the microphone.

"My fellow American's, by now I'm sure that everyone has seen the amateur video shot yesterday in Philadelphia. We're all concerned, and some of us are afraid. After viewing the footage, it is obvious that these visitors to our planet are hostile. In effort to effectively ascertain this threat, I am assembling a special team to investigate, detain, and if need be, terminate this threat. I encourage you to continue living your lives as you always have. However, stay watchful and under no circumstances should you attempt to engage these newcomers, which can only be described as aliens. We will find out where they come from and more importantly, what they want. I ask for your patience, and I ask for cooperation. Together we can… "

London turns the television off. Of course, the president was talking about him, and ordinarily that would be a big deal. But London had just recently met The Almighty! So, he wasn't too affected by the commander and chief speaking about him. And as for the team being assembled to find him, well London had also met the Dark Author. And he was a bit more menacing than Special Forces.

London gets dressed and leaves the dorm. He figures there'll be more public brawls in his future, so he's going to need a disguise. He has a bus pass and a credit card, he's on a mission. The first costume shop is a bust, too colorful. The next one was worse, too gothic. London tries a couple more shops and finally decides to gamble on a few masks. He's just about to leave the store when he hears the all too familiar sound of dead silence come down. He turns around and gazes upon what is a collection of living humans, frozen in time. Pat can't do this.

"Well, well, look who decided to pay us a visit," he says without actually laying eyes on him.

"Greetings London son of James".

"You here to help me pick out a costume?"

"You are wise in searching for a disguise."

"Which one do you think is the best?"

"Not much is needed. Any addition to your disguise need only be subtle."

"Any addition, that implies that I already have a disguise."

"Quickly you forget."

"What am I forgetting?"

London thought about it.

"You mean my eyes. Is that why they're like yours"?

"What is in a man shows through his eyes. There is much inside of you."

"I guess eyes really are the soul."

"The soul of a man is eternal, the very breath of God… "

"It was just a joke. But listen, how do I make them… light up?"

"Whenever you use a given gift, your eyes will quicken. They will sleep when you determine the evil is past."

"Okay. I can see that. But I have more questions. First, how am I supposed to find Pat? I know he's up to something."

"You must find a way."

"I knew you'd say that. Well since he can create illusions, why does he keep using the same human form?"

"That is his only human form."

"Excellent! Now what's going on with the rats and Dozorn? Can Pat assume animal form?"

"No. That was the Dark Author. He walks the Earth in the shape of many different life forms. However, he may only do so in multiple numbers. He cannot walk the Earth in his true demonic form; the form that you witnessed."

"Now it all makes sense," London replays the scene in his head, he ordered Dozorn to flee because Pat had gotten away. The beast had an agenda! "I hadn't seen either one of them since the night you took me to Sun- Ray. It's clear they have bigger plans now. Don't leave yet! I know how you like to just disappear. What exactly is this?" He holds his left arm out.

"You have been told."

"I know what it does, yes. But what is it? How does it do what it does?"

"Well spoken. It is torn from the hem of the Holy robe."

"Holy robe, what Holy robe?"

"Your spirit speaks the answer."

London looks at his wrist. "You mean the one that the woman with the issue of blood touched?!"

"More questions?"

"Umm, oh yeah what's up with the wings?"

The 4th Corner disappears without answering the question.

"That's cold."

"The wings are on the back wall."

London turned around. The clerk was back to life, as were the rest of the customers.

"Oh. Yeah thanks. Listen, I'm sorry to have to do this, but I need to return these masks and get my money back."

"Well, I'm sorry to have to tell you, that Hell has not yet gotten a wind chill."

"Excuse me?"

The man points to the wall behind him. There's a sign that reads, *Refunds when Hell freezes over*!

"Great. It figures."

Later on the bus, London sat across from a mother with three kids. When his stop came, he gave them the masks.

London walks to his room. There's a note on his desk from his roommate: *London I'm going to visit my brother; I'll be back sometime on Tuesday.* London welcomed the privacy. This would give him time to focus on the things that were most pressing. Number one on that list is Pat.

Little did London know, but the Dark Author had a multifaceted plan. Pat, while responsible for the most important part of the plan, was only part of the whole. Dozorn, along with the shadow walkers, were now tasked with keeping London off of Pat's trail. But there were other stages to the plan that were now taking shape. At the foot of the rotted tree throne, kneeled one such stage; A new disciple. But this one is unlike the others. Though all of his predecessors were charged with killing London, they all had expertise in some other area. Pat's was deception. Dozorn's was to inspire fear, and panic as an enforcer. The Shadow walkers' expertise is surveillance, and sheer numbers. The latest disciple was also charged with bringing London to an untimely end; however, his expertise was the very act of assassination, the actual kill.

"Alas, my weapon of choice is complete. Your charge is simple. Seek and destroy! Bring this Knight's existence to end. He is strong, but you shall break him. Arise and cause the mortal to fall."

The demon assassin stands and whispers, *Blood is my sport O Dark One. Blood is my sport.*

"And so, shall your name be … Bloodsport."

Earlier that same day, before the nation was addressed by the president, The Philadelphia police department was briefed by N.S.A. Police headquarters was abuzz with activity. Every cop not on patrol at the time was ordered to attend the briefing. The atmosphere was anxious and unsure. The commissioner stepped to the podium. The crowd started to hush.

"Settle down please, everyone please settle down. In response to the events on yesterday, the federal government has acted quickly. The President will be addressing the country shortly, but National Security is here now to brief the department. Let's give General Morris our undivided attention."

"Thank you, commissioner, … What happened on yesterday was to say the least; shocking. It was proof positive. Hard evidence of what many have speculated for decades, maybe even centuries. We do not inhabit this universe alone. Unfortunately, what is also evident is the fact that we were not prepared. These beings displayed unbelievable abilities. We do not know the complete nature of this threat. But with such hostilities shown, it is wise to assume that their intentions are not for our good. The President wants you all to know that the safety of Philadelphia is our priority. We know how consuming your responsibilities can ordinarily be. We also know these responsibilities are not going to disappear just because of recent happenings. A special division of the National Security Agency is being assembled as we speak. They will be known as E.S.A.D. - Extreme Security and Detainment. They will be armed with prototype weapons and other technology. They are militarily trained on the highest levels. They will deal with this threat. E.S.A.D. will be here in a matter of days. In the event that you come across these beings, you will be given our frequency. Contact us immediately. Evacuate the area, and under no circumstances are you to play hero. At this time, I will take questions."

The crowd erupted. It took the commissioner over a minute to put things back in order. One by one the officers stood and asked obvious questions. Sergeant Jessica Walker had her own questions. She and her partner were the first cops on the scene yesterday. They'd seen more than the others. Walker felt that there was one critical fact that was being overlooked. She stood and was recognized.

"Gen. Morris, my partner and I were the first ones on the scene yesterday. I'm not sure of how clear it was on the video, but what was apparent to us was the fact that if it wasn't for the humanoid alien, a number of us officers wouldn't be here right now! He fought against the blue creature."

Many officers agreed in their commotion.

"Well let me first say that we appreciate your point of view. Although, we can't be sure of what motivated him to act in such a way. We need to be sure. They need to be detained for everyone's sake, for if we misinterpret his actions, we'll be guilty of dropping a very heavy ball."

More commotion from the room in agreement with the General. Walker understood the concern, but she didn't feel that the humanoid alien was really a threat.

Gen. Morris answered a dozen or so more questions.

"If there are no more questions, I want to thank you all, and wish us all good luck."

Most of the officers huddled up and voiced their many displeasures with the government's plans. Sgt. Walker remained seated in deep thought. While she indeed felt the same as her blue brethren, she also knew they were missing something, they all were. But she was uncertain of what exactly that was. Jessica Walker wasn't sure how she'd do it, but she was determined to find out more.

Chapter Eleven:

Scene of the crime

It was Saturday night, and London still had no idea of what Pat was up to. He decided to return to the last place he'd seen him. He needed answers. London waited for the sun to set to investigate, the darker the better. He suits up in all black and tightens his boots. London looks in the mirror. He feels he needs to add something, something subtle. Although he'd given the masks away, he did keep one item. He reaches into the drawer and pulls out a container of eye black, and then dresses his face like a soldier on the field of battle. London then reaches under his bed and un-wraps the Eden sword. He straps it on his back, turns the light off, and walks to the window. There is no one was in sight. He opens the window and effortlessly dives out; leaving *London* behind. Holding his breath, the Knight smoothly descends to the ground, unaffected by gravity. Standing on the side of the building, he walks to the front and checks for bystanders. The coast is clear. He springs into action! The Knight raced up the street unimpeded. A figure comes into view. It's an older gentleman mailing a couple of letters in a corner mailbox. He has his back to the un-coming momentum of power that is God's SoulKnight. The gentleman walks passed the mailbox. The new London jumps on top of the mailbox, using it as a springboard. The man hears the impact and turns around to see what had made the noise. He doesn't see anything. As he continued to search for the source of the noise, the Knight ascended toward a rooftop on the other side of the street. He slowly exhaled and landed on top with a soft two step.

"Sweet!"

The Knight reminisces on his escape from the cops. He decides to repeat the maneuver. He holds his breath and runs toward the edge of the roof diving across. As the new London continues this dance from rooftop to rooftop, he realizes that as the SoulKnight, he would not have to worry about a vehicle. The new London stops the dance on top of a building in the vicinity of where he'd last seen Pat. He looks down to the street. It's late and no one is around. He steps off and plunges into the alley. A couple seconds later the Knight pierces the darkness and walks to the front. He tightens his hood. This is where he lost Pat. He's reassured when he sees his water-like eyes burning blue in the same window as before. He retraces his steps. The Knight has no idea of what he's looking for. He then walks to the street where he first spotted Pat and looks around. There are various buildings and businesses; and from the top of one, he is closely being watched. There's a coffee shop, a bank, and a post office; along with a couple of fast food spots. He takes a mental note, and then proceeds toward the scene of his fight with Dozorn. The Knight glides swiftly and silently over the sidewalk. As he approaches, he spots someone bent low in the middle of the street. He exhales and hides before the figure sees him. He isn't close enough to make out a face, but the stranger seems to be searching for something. It can't be Pat? That would be too easy. The Knight carefully moves closer, but just as he moves, so too does the unknown figure. The stranger turns around suddenly. The new London was already out of sight.

"Who's there?"

The figure takes hold of a weapon and runs. The Knight bursts into speed! He jumps sideways onto a wall and springs off.

The stranger looks back and screams at the sight of the unearthly attacker, complete with glowing blue eyes, giving chase; by flight no less! The stranger dives to the ground. The Knight flies clear over the figure's head. He exhales, twists, and flips to his feet to face the stranger. It was a woman. She rises to her feet and fires her weapon. The Knight's finely tuned ears allows him to react to the shots with precision. In the time it takes the woman to fire three more shots, the Knight dodges, makes up the distance between them and unsheathes the Eden sword. He swings it and burns the handgun in two. The woman falls to the ground. When she looks up, there is a sword aimed at her throat. She can feel heat radiating from the red colored blade.

"Please, don't kill me! I don't know if you can understand me, but I'm a cop."

The Knight considers this for a moment, and then pulls the Eden sword away from the woman's throat.

"May I stand?"

The blue eyed being nods. The woman pulls out her badge.

"My name is Sgt. Jessica Walker."

The Knight turns around and re-sheathes the Eden sword. He walks away.

"Right, you probably don't care. Wait, this is where you fought that blue creature."

Walker runs after the humanoid alien.

"I was one of the officers whose lives you saved. I'd like to thank you."

The being nods.

"Where are you from?"

The being hesitates, but then points up to the sky.

"Would I be correct in assuming that you come in peace?"

Once again, the being nods.

"I won't ask the same question about that beast."

"Dozorn."

This startles Walker.

"You can speak our language?"

"I can."

"How long have you studied us?"

All my life, The Knight thinks to himself. "Long."

"Are there more of you?"

"Not of my kind. But Dozorn is not alone."

"You're telling me that thing has friends! Oh, I'm sorry for yelling."

"You need not be sorry. I must depart."

"Umm listen, is it asking too much to meet with you again?"

The Knight carefully considers her question. He was going to need some help finding Pat, and this woman is a police officer. She knows how to find people.

"Tomorrow night, same time, same place. Tell no one."

"No one, you have my word!"

Sirens sounded. Walker looks toward the sound.

"Someone must've called in the gunshots. You should… "

Walker turned back and saw no sign of the humanoid alien. She scrambles to pick up the shells and the pieces of her gun, and then runs to her car. She opens her car door and pretends to be the first cop on the scene. Several emergency vehicles pull up on the scene. Walker shows her badge.

The same eyes that watched the Knight from a rooftop before his meeting with Walker are still watchful. Standing high, and looking low, is Bloodsport. Though he isn't readying an attack on this night, he would soon make his move.

The new London glides back through his window and becomes the old London. He turns to close the window, and whispers to himself, *good night*. As he says this, he sees his image in the reflection of the window.

"Goodnight. Good, Knight. *That's it*! My name will be Good Knight, Sir Good Knight!"

London knew he had taken a chance in talking with a cop, but she may be able to help his cause. He isn't sure why, but he feels he can trust her. He needs something to finally break in his favor.

The next morning, London's alarm clock goes off at 8:00 a.m. He's decided to go to church this morning; and not the campus chapel services that he'd visited a couple times. He wanted to visit a service that reminded him of his home church. But he had no idea where he'd find the right one. But then he remembers that Pastor DuBois had given him a name and address. London opens his junk drawer and finds the card. He takes a shower and calls the campus shuttle.

When London walks into the Church, he's immediately reassured that he's made the right decision. There's a feeling that radiates from his chest to the rest of his body. He sits in the middle of the congregation. It's a midsized Church, just like home. The choir sings the roof off! London can't keep from standing. He claps and sways to the beat, just as he did as a kid. He can see himself and Donald perfectly. When the Pastor stands up to preach, London says to himself; *The main course*. The Sermon is phenomenal! After the service, London waits in line to shake hands with the Pastor. He introduces himself and tells the Pastor how much he's enjoyed himself. The Pastor recognizes his name and tells London that Rev. DuBois has spoken to him on his behalf. The Pastor invites London to his office and the two speak for a half hour. London leaves Church feeling the best he's felt in very long time. He told the Pastor that it will not be his last time visiting.

The campus shuttle picked London up, and took him back to the dorm. As he heads toward the entrance, he fails to notice the line of all black vans, and two huge trucks that roll by. Their windows are dark tinted. The passengers can't be seen, but in all they numbered fifty, fifty highly trained and serious men. The walls of the vans are lined with high tech weaponry. The trucks carry special prototype vehicles. They pass the scene of the fight between the two aliens. They consider it a tactical location and code it, *The Encounter point*. The destination of the Agents of E.S.A.D, is an abandoned warehouse two miles away. It will serve as headquarters. Any and all trespassing is strictly forbidden.

The specially commissioned force arrives at their new base of operations. They have two superior officers; Gen. Morris, and Col. Charles Foster.

"Col. Foster"

"Yes General?"

"Send a couple of Agents to the Encounter point to set up the motion detectors."

London takes a shower and changes his clothes. He's starving. He gathers his menus and tries to decide on what to order. After his taste buds imagined what topping he should experiment with on his pizza, pineapples are the unanimous winner. Just as he reaches for the phone, it rings.

"Please don't let it be John. (He takes a deep breath) Hello."

It was Rodney; a teammate of London's who lives in the same building.

"A few of us are ordering eats and Quincy brought his movies over. What's up with you?"

"I was just about to order something. When are you starting the first movie?"

"If you're coming, we'll wait 'til you get here."

"I'm on my way!"

London grabs his money, locks up, and jogs down the hall.

When the food arrives, London's appetite goes into overdrive. Not only is there pizza, there's also chicken fingers, wings, soda, and shrimp. They have a ball! The movies they watch are all classics; Coming to America, Bad boys, and Dumb and dumber. It had been a while since London had hung out and had some real fun. Anytime he could relax and get his mind off of things was a good time. It was getting late. One of the guys asks the time. Rodney calls out 11:30. London nearly forgot that he was meeting Sgt. Walker at midnight. He plays it cool.

"It's about that time for me fellas."

"You sure, I was going to break out the cards."

"Aww man, well next time I'm in. I'll see you guys at practice."

London rushes to his room. Once again, he suits up in all black and goes to the window. This begins a series of déjà vu. He exhales his way to ground level. Again, he creeps to the front and checks for human traffic. Amazingly, the same guy from last night is once again out and about. This time he's walking a small dog. He seems fidgety. The man approaches the same mailbox. So, the self-proclaimed *Sir Good Knight*, stays true to the sequel like atmosphere and takes off running. He once again uses the box as a springboard and glides out of sight. The man is even more startled than before. He was actually on the lookout for who or whatever had snuck up on him the previous night! The man frantically looked around and hollers out…

"Who's out there?! I've got my pocket knife, and my dog bites!"

The man looked up at the dorm building and concluded that college students had been throwing things to fool around with him these past two nights. He waves his fist and yells, "*Arrogant little shits!*"

Sir Good Knight proceeded to perform his rooftop dive and dance until he came to the same location as before. He looked at his watch; it was two minutes to 12:00 am. He decided he'd stay up high and wait for Sgt. Walker. Minutes later, a car rounds the corner, blinks its lights, and parks in darkness. Sir Good Knight is just about to jump down; when a faint noise catches the attention of his sensitive ears. In under a second, he spins around Eden sword in hand, ready for battle! He was alone. He listens closely and hears the noise again. It was dark, so he knew someone, or something could be hiding. Then, the source of the noise ends the suspense. A dozen or so flying insects come into the light. Sir Good Knight isn't sure of the species, but he isn't concerned. He re-sheaths the Eden sword then turns and jumps down. The locusts multiply greatly in number. What was just seconds ago only a dozen was now well over two hundred.

Sgt. Walker stepped out of the car. She puts her hands in her pockets and slowly walks to the middle of the street. Her right hand grips her nine-millimeter. Even though she mostly trusts the alien being, she is no fool. She feels a cool breeze and decides to go back for her jacket. As she turns back to the car, she stops in her tracks. She was no more than ten feet away from her vehicle and had never heard the Knight arrive. He was standing on top of her car.

Walker grips tighter on her weapon, "I didn't think you were coming."

"Follow me" Sir Good Knight jumps down.

Walker reluctantly follows. Sir Good Knight walks to the corner, stops and points.

"A few blocks down, there's a bank, a couple of restaurants, and a post office."

"Yeah, Chase Manhattan bank, Taco Bell, and Wendy's are all down that way. Wait a minute; How are you so familiar with our culture? How long have you been studying us"?

Sir Good Knight wanted to say, *all my life*, but he knew better.

"Long enough, now listen, I told you the beast Dozorn has friends; I spotted one, Pat, coming from that immediate area.

Dozorn attacked me that day to keep me off of his partner's trail. He's up to something, I need to find out what."

"Pat... that's it? He doesn't have some creepy name like Dozorn?"

Sir Good Knight describes Pat's abilities to Walker.

"I need your help to find out what building he was in, and more importantly, what he was doing there."

Walker thought about the request.

"This is an opportunity to be a part of something more important than you can ever imagine."

That was all the coaxing she needed.

"*I'm in.* Oh, and by the way, what do I call you?"

"Sir Good Knight."

Her eyes widen, "I like that."

Meanwhile, at E.S.A.D.'S new headquarters, an Agent sits at one of the monitor stations.

"Col. Foster."

"What is it?"

"I'm picking up movement at the Encounter Point."

"How many?"

"Looks like two."

"What time is it?

"00:15 hours."

"Send a Unit to check it out."

Sir Good Knight described the outfit that Pat was wearing the day he was last seen.

"I'll try to get a look at their security tapes."

Walker waves her hand in front of her face. "What are these, grasshoppers"? No, I believe those are locusts.

Sir Good Knight realizes that these are the same bugs from the roof.

"Something's wrong."

"What do you mean?"

The Locusts fly to the middle of the street. A small swarm forms.

"What's going on?"

"Take cover!"

The locusts unite and form into the shape of a humanoid. Walker runs to her car. Sir Good Knight grabs the Eden sword and prepares for battle. The figure stands eight feet tall, even taller than Pat in his true form. His body is covered in some sort of armor. It was dark in color, most likely black. There are also various lines of red. His face, which seems to be a kind of mask, has red tiger-like stripes. There are air holes in the area that you would expect to see a mouth. The demon's ears are like those of a fox. There's a long ponytail that extending from the center of his head. His eyes are white on the outside like a human's, but in the center they're deep red.

"Dark Author?"

He answers in a whisper, "No."

"Then who?"

"Bloodsport. And *your* blood… is my sport."

At the moment he whispers his last word, he pulls something from behind his back. It's long, skinny and cylindrical. He holds it to his mouth and seemed to blow into it. Two-disc shaped projectiles spinning rapidly, shoot toward Sir Good Knight. The Knight jumps and flips backward avoiding the discs. But just as he lands, they circle back and once again threaten. Sir Good Knight runs up a wall flips off and swings the Eden sword. Both discs are burned in two.

Walker looks on from behind her car holding her gun tightly. Again, Bloodsport blows into his device sending another two discs spinning; but this time, he simultaneously reaches behind his back with the other hand and reveals a pitchfork like weapon. He charges behind the projectiles. Sir Good Knight jumps to his left and swings his sword at the first projectile. The second one goes high. He ducks and burns the second disc all while attempting to elude Bloodsport. He is unsuccessful. Swinging his trident, the demon assassin smacks Sir Good Knight like a baseball. He is sent flying and lands a third of a block away face down on the concrete. Sir Good Knight lies dazed by the blow. There's a deep gash in his shoulder from a sharp point on the trident. Bloodsport positions his weapon upside down and holds it over his head with both hands as he approaches the Knight.

BOOM!

A large hole appears in Bloodsport's torso. It originates in his back. The force of the shot blows Bloodsport frontwards over Sir Good Knight, and through a display window. Walker stands behind the Demon assassin holding her police issued pump shotgun. Smoke rapidly rises from the barrel. Walker rushes to the side of her new partner.

"Are you okay?"

The Knight pushes up off the ground as his wound begins healing. Walker helps him to his feet and away from the broken window. Just then, the Philadelphia night air reveals two aircrafts, never before seen by civilian eyes. Two hovering platforms with automatic cannons mounted on each side, rocket toward the three combatants. They are piloted by two men in body armor.

E.S.A.D. Agents. Bloodsport stands and steps out of the display window. Locusts fly into the cavity in his torso. His body becomes whole again.

"Did you see that?"

"I did."

Just before Bloodsport could mount another attack…

"Nobody move, you will all be detained by E.S.A.D. under the authority of N.S.A."

"Not M-E!"

The Knight holds his breath and dives laterally. One of the Agents speeds after him and fires his cannons. As Bloodsport bends to pick up his trident, the second Agent fires a small hand-held device. A spray discharges from the device and becomes an electronic net that entraps the demon. The assassin separates into hundreds of locusts and escapes through the net's holes. The locusts reunite immediately on the other side of the net reforming Bloodsport. He pulls his blow gun from behind once more and blows into it. The Agent tries to dodge the projectiles, but one makes contact. The aircraft the Agent stands upon is easily penetrated and ripped apart. The Agent and the two halves of his aircraft fall to the ground. The disc returns to the assassin's blow gun. The Agent is obviously well trained, as he avoids injury by performing a tactical roll instead of a hard fall. He pulls out a gun and is able to get off a single shot, before his hand is sliced clean off by another one of Bloodsport's projectiles. The assassin deflects the shot fired with his trident. He then raises it in a throwing motion with designs on finishing the job. But before he can release his weapon, he is surrounded by E.S.A.D reinforcements. They had been monitoring the scene ever since the first two Agents were deployed. Walker is also surrounded. She pulls out her badge and runs to the side of the maimed E.S.A.D. Agent. Bloodsport searches for The Knight. He is nowhere to be found so Bloodsport bursts into locusts and flies off. The reinforcement Agent's jaws drop.

Meanwhile, Sir Good Knight is many blocks away dodging shots and working hard to keep a safe distance from the Agent in pursuit. He is tiring he needs to think of something. He jumps into the second floor of a multi-level parking lot. The Agent follows not far behind. Sir Good Knight knew the Agent, though well trained, was no match for him; but he doesn't want to hurt him. He has an idea. He makes a sharp right and temporarily disappears out of the sight of the Agent. The Agent attempts the same maneuver and meets with a blade of fire that separates the top of his craft from the bottom. Before the Agent can hit the ground, he is snatched backward by his uniform. He is sat involuntarily down on the ground, and other than a little whiplash, is unharmed. The Agent reaches for his weapon and spins around. He is alone. He surveys the area and radios for help.

Back at the scene only a few E.S.A.D. Agents remain. They were among city police, reporters, and the worried public desperately trying to see and hear. E.S.A.D. are investigating, the police were only there to keep the crowd and media back. The rest of the Agents had returned to headquarters. The man who lost his hand was receiving medical treatment on the same grounds. The facility is self-sufficient. A prisoner is being escorted to a room in the rear. A door opens, and the prisoner is told to sit. Sgt. Jessica Walker is left alone as the door is closed and obviously locked. Other than the chair and table where she sits, the room is empty.

The light is very bright. The room is cold. Walker's hands are cuffed to the table. The walls and ceiling are lined with asbestos and the room smells sour. She's been sitting there for almost an hour. Sgt. Walker had assisted on the other side of this situation enough times to know what was going on. This was an interrogation room. The door finally opens. Gen. Morris walks in carrying a chair. He sits on the other side of the table.

"Well, well, Sgt. Jessica Walker. Why am I not surprised?"

"Why am I being held here?"

"I don't think we'll need these. (Morris unlocks the cuffs) I'd hoped the briefing we gave would've been successful in explaining our roles."

"When it comes to enforcing the law in *this city*, that role is mine!"

"Enforcing the law? Is that what the Philadelphia police department calls it? I'd call it obstructing justice!"

"Obstructing justice? Read the job description General, Protect and Serve!"

"And who were you serving by conspiring with the enemy?!"

"I was questioning a suspect."

"You have no jurisdiction in this matter. He is ours to question. Besides, you're not equipped to confront such a threat. You could've gotten yourself killed!"

Walker sits back in her chair and sighs.

"Only one of the alien beings was hostile. The humanoid is the reason I'm still alive. He's not the enemy."

"And how can you be sure?"

"This is the second time that he's saved my life."

Gen. Morris sat silently, pondering.

"Did he speak?"

"He did."

"And?"

"And you can't keep me here without due process. You need to …"

"If you know nothing about N.S.A. Sgt. Walker, allow me to share this bit of knowledge. In the interest of National security, we can do anything! (He pounds the table as he made his point, then sits back and adjusts his uniform). It's that whole "needs of the many outweighing the needs of the few" thing. And you Sgt. Walker, are that few."

This frightened Walker, but she refused to show it.

"I'm a highly respected and well-known officer. There are many who would ..."

"Relax Sgt. Walker. We don't intend to erase you."

"Erase?"

"Yes, I think that's a more pleasant word, don't you? But let's get back to the matter at hand. What did he say?"

"He said he came in peace."

"*Peace*? Is that what you call his activities, *peace*?"

"He's here to deal with the others. He's harmed no human."

"Whether he's harmed a human or not, is not the issue. The issue is, hostile beings have decided to wage their war on our planet. In our country, your city no less! How long do you think it will take before a human is hurt; or even killed?"

He had a point. Walker didn't know what to say. Gen. Morris stands up and looks in the mirror. Col. Foster and two other Agents watch from the other side. They were observing the interrogation.

"What else did he say?"

Walker didn't want to mention anything specifically. Sir Good Knight had confided in her.

"He said the beast has friends, but he's here alone. He's on our side."

Morris turns to face Walker, "This isn't a Spielberg movie. *We're* the ones on your side! He gathers himself before continuing. What's his name?"

"What?"

"What did he say his name is?"

"He didn't."

"And I suppose he didn't tell you where he's hiding either?"

"Of course not!"

"How did the two of you become so buddy, buddy? When did you set up this meeting?"

"It happened by chance. I went to the scene to look for clues. I guess he had the same thing in mind. We sort of bumped into each other. When it was apparent that he meant me no harm, I told him who I was, and thanked him for saving my life and the lives of my fellow officers. It surprised me when he spoke, but he said he's been studying us for years."

"Studying us? Why, what is he looking for?"

"He didn't say."

"Really; Did you ever consider the possibility that he could be playing you?"

"Yes, as a matter of fact I did."

"And?"

"I have since eliminated that as a possibility."

"Where did he say the so-called others are hiding?"

"He's also searching for them."

"How many others are there?"

"He didn't say; Look, I've told you everything I know. Can I leave now?"

"One last question, when are you meeting again?"

"There is no again. It was a chance meeting!"

Again, Morris sits down.

"Okay Sgt., You're free to go. We know where to find you if we need you."

An Agent opens the door from the other side. Walker stands and walks to the door.

"How am I getting home?"

"We'll have an Agent assist you."

Walker follows an Agent out of the room. Col. Foster joins Gen. Morris.

"Tail her?"

"Indeed. The next time they meet we'll hit him with everything."

Gen. Morris exits the room. Another Agent approaches Col. Foster.

"May I have a word with you sir?"

"Yes, what is it?"

"I pursued the humanoid alien when he fled."

"And you lost him."

"Yes sir I did, but, sir he could've easily taken me out. When he disabled my Hover-form he sat me down unharmed. Not only did he not attack, but he made sure I didn't crash with my craft."

"What are you saying?"

"Nothing sir, I just thought you should know."

As the Agent walked off, Foster considered the information.

Chapter Twelve:

Unseen

It was Monday morning. London had overslept. He was rushing to get ready. It wasn't working. He plops back down on his bed and decides that anyone who's responsible for saving innocents from demons deserves a day off! Besides, there was now a new and improved demon assassin trying to kill him; As if there wasn't enough already. Yeah, he was staying home today.

Sgt. Walker was used to extra-long nights. She was up without hesitation. She wanted to get to the precinct nice and early. She has a lot to explain to her Captain. Investigating while off duty is pretty serious. Especially when the case belongs exclusively to N.S.A. Gen Morris had most certainly reported her. Walker is facing nothing less than a suspension. She could even be fired. She only hopes her reputation works in her favor. Walker enters the precinct. Everyone is busy. No one really even notices her. She isn't exactly anxious to get her head chewed off, so she goes straight to her desk. Twenty minutes pass; nothing. And Then...

"Everyone listen up," the Captain calls for everyone's attention.

"*Please no*, he's going to do it all out in the open like this?"

"I'm sure some of you already know, E.S.A.D. has arrived and have officially taken over the Alien investigation. We will continue to operate as we always have. Any officer, who finds this difficult to understand, will face disciplinary actions and possible charges!"

"Charges?" Walker hadn't considered that.

"Last night there was another encounter. This time there was bloodshed. An E.S.A.D. Agent got his hand chopped off. There is commotion. If the press questions you about it, tell them Gen. Morris of the E.S.A.D. will answer all inquiries. That's all people, go protect and serve."

The captain returned to his office. Walker seemed to be in the clear. Her relief lasts for all of five minutes. Walker is just about to go out on patrol, when she hears the words she was hoping to avoid.

"Walker, the captain wants to see you in his office."

She knew it was too good to be true. Walker enters the Captain's office.

"You wanted to see me sir?"

"Sgt. Jessica Walker… come in and shut the door. Have a seat. The commissioner has gotten wind of your activities."

Jessica's heart sank.

"He feels, and I concur, that you no longer deserve to be a Sgt. In this department. I'll need your badge."

Once again Walker refuses to show emotion. But as she hands over her badge, inside she's falling apart. The captain stands.

"It hurts to have to see you go, but you brought this on yourself."

He hands her a small box. She opens it and sees gold; a gold badge. The captain sticks out his hand.

"Congratulations, the whole department is proud of you."

This time Walker cannot contain her emotions. She tears up. She is caught totally off guard.

"Thank you very much sir!"

"If anyone deserves it, it's you."

Walker steps out of the office and is met with a thunderous round of applause. There are even refreshments. Tears stream down her face. It was the first time any of her fellow officers had seen her cry.

An hour later, the newly promoted Detective Jessica Walker, is introduced to her new partner; Detective David Owens. They are given their first assignment as a team. This is the day that Walker had always dreamed of.

London awoke hours later. The clock read 3:15pm. The last game of the season starts at 4:30. He rolls out of bed and jumps in the shower. By 3:45 he's running out of his building. He makes sure to pack the Eden sword. In the game, London is so preoccupied, that he finally seemed normal. He doesn't play well. He was always careful to keep his true abilities a bit modest, but this was the first time that he seemed to be totally off. It doesn't go unnoticed.

"London. London come here a second. Frank go in for London."

"Yeah coach?"

"You alright son?"

"Yeah, I'm alright."

"I've never seen you like this. You sure you're not coming down with something?"

"I just have some things on my mind."

"Well they must be pretty heavy; cause they're weighing your whole game down!"

"Heavy is an understatement."

"This is for postseason play, London. We need you son. Take a breather and get ready to go back out there."

London sits on the bench. All he can do is picture Bloodsport. This was a new threat. Dozorn is strong, but he can outmaneuver the beast. The Shadow creatures were cunning, but small. Up until now, Pat was the most formidable. But this new one; He's all of the others wrapped into one! Plus, he has weapons.

London returns to the game, but his game doesn't return to him. His team loses. He uses his frustration for what he's facing from the Dark Author and company, to express his sorrow to his teammates and coaching staff for his performance.

After meeting with his team, London walks home alone. For the first time he actually feels bad about the game. But the feeling is short lived as he realizes that he's been too preoccupied with his new tormentor. He rubs both hands over his face and takes a deep breath. He stops in the middle of the sidewalk and looks up into a darkening sky. He tells himself to refocus. Pat is first and foremost. He has to be found.

London is on his way to his dorm when it starts to rain. Once again, he is being watched. As he nears the street, an object shoots his way. Fifteen feet from decapitation, London hears its approach and ducks. It was a close call. He instantly knew what was happening. He frantically looks around but doesn't see his attacker, only people. There are too many bystanders around for him to engage the new demon. London walks fast searching all the while. The rain picks up; it makes him comfortable enough to use his incredible foot speed. He takes off. The rain comes down harder. London looks back. He's being pursued by a swiftly moving black cloud of locusts. Bystanders are running to get out of the rain, so London doesn't attract much attention. He looks back again and is shocked to see that Bloodsport, in Locust form, is effectively gaining on him. He's doesn't realize he isn't manipulating his gift of weightlessness. Fleeing is no longer an option; he has to make a stand. London holds his breath and jumps in the air. He pulls his body into a tight tuck ripping through an endless sea of rain. In the midst of his acrobatics, he pulls the Eden sword from his bag and releases his body from its' tucked position. He finishes his aerial display with a full twist to face his attacker. The exact moment his feet touch the ground, the storm's first thunder and lightning roar. Sir Good Knight stands eyes blazing alive and blue, holding the Eden sword dripping with rain. The swarm of locusts gathers more tightly and begin to unite. Sir Good Knight charges forward leading with his sword. He stabs through the demon's just formed torso. Bloodsport growls in pain, then shoves Sir Good Knight so hard that he and the sword fly almost twenty feet back and to the street. Once again locusts fill in the hole in the demon's chest and make him whole. The rain is now full. Solid walls of water fall one after the other. Visibility is no more than three feet. Sir Good Knight stands and shakes his head to clear the water from his face. A second bolt of lightning flashes. He can see Bloodsport. A third flash, Sir Good Knight is knocked backward. He lies on the ground tucked in a ball. He can't breathe. The wind was knocked out of him with a kick to the mid-section. As he gradually catches his breath, Sir Good Knight realizes that the Eden sword had been knocked from his hand. He looks up from the ground. He doesn't see anything, but he hears something shooting through the air and water. Sir Good Knight

popped up off the ground as fast as he can. A razor-sharp disc rips

into the street where The Knight was just lying. He holds his

breath and slowly descends. As he lands, he wonders, *how can*

Bloodsport see him? Visibility is virtually nonexistent, and yet he

had just nearly shot one of his discs through him! Suddenly, Sir

Good Knight faintly sees something through the rain. There it was

again, two small red dots moving in sync.

"His eyes!"

Sir Good Knight understands how the demon is seeing

him. He immediately covers his eyes. Then he hears something, a

sizzling sound. Shielding his eyes, he looks in the direction of the

noise. He sees the red blade of the Eden sword. Steam is rising

from it. The sound he was hearing, was the instant evaporation as

the rain landed on the blade of fire. Sir Good Knight stays low and

crawls toward his weapon. A split second from reaching the

sword, lightning flashes. Bloodsport looks directly at him. The

Knight grabs the sword and quickly rolls away. The demon comes

within inches of impaling him with his trident. Bloodsport can still

see Sir Good Knight moving. He quickly grabs his blow gun and

312

blows into it. Two discs race toward the Knight. He hears the projectiles and emerges from his ground roll shooting straight up. As he ascends, he swings the sword destroying the first disc. He exhales forcing all of the air out of his lungs, dropping himself quickly to the ground. This well-timed maneuver allows him to elude the second disc. As he lands, he hears fast approaching footsteps. Red eyes accompanied them. The Knight swings the sword. It connects with something that is resistant to its' heat; Bloodsport's trident. The Knight can only see the eyes of the demon. Not enough to have a swordfight! As they struggle, he uses the sword to push against the demon's trident and propels himself to the right, out of Bloodsport's range. Bloodsport charges through the endless wall of rain. Sir Good Knight runs, bad idea. He makes it ten feet before slamming into a parked car. He drops the sword and falls to the ground. The demon's trident smashes through the window of the car. Sir Good Knight squints his eyes and quickly crawls away from the car. Bloodsport stands over it looking for either the Knight's eyes or the red blade of the Eden sword. From the ground, Sir Good Knight can see the sword lying underneath the car. He decides to leave it for now. Bloodsport will have a harder time seeing him. He realizes he now has an advantage. The Knight closes his eyes. A safe distance from the demon assassin, he stands and listens. Outside of the rain he can't hear anything. He takes a chance and looks through his fingers; like a kid watching a horror movie. He sees Bloodsport's eyes panning from side to side. The Knight explodes with breathless speed! He still uses his left hand to cover his eyes. Lightning flashes. Bloodsport sees Sir Good Knight, but it's too late. He thrusts both fists forward knocking the demon backward and separating him from his trident. Sir Good Knight reaches under the car and recovers the sword. He immediately re-sheathes it. Bloodsport pulls himself from the ground. He stood twenty feet from the spot where he was hit. The demon carefully looks around. He sees nothing. Somehow his opponent has adapted to the conditions and gained the upper hand. Sir Good Knight waits patiently to see the demon's beady red eyes; upon seeing them, he again speeds silently toward him. He swings his fists as one and once again sends the assassin in reverse. The demon lands even harder this time. He is furious! It was clear, his target was defeating him. He can't turn the tide. Bloodsport bursts into locusts and flies off. Sir Good Knight sees the demon's eyes disappear and hears a pop. He knows the sound. The locust's

314

wings flap hard in the monsoon-like rain. Sir Good Knight listens closely to make sure the demon has truly retreated. He sighs in relief. He's won this round; the score was one to one.

This was crazy. Who had ever seen rain like this? It was totally unmanageable. Walker and her new partner, Detective David Owens, were contemplating returning to the station. But they can't see well enough to safely drive; they have to park. They decide to use the time to get to know each other a little better. Owens had transferred from D.C. He had only been in Philadelphia for a month. He was also a well decorated Marine. After about forty minutes, the rain starts to let up.

"Finally! I can actually see. Does it rain like that regularly here?"

"No, that was crazy for me too. I don't know what to tell you."

"Are you hungry, I think we earned a sandwich break."

"Definitely. Where do you want to go?"

"I was thinking Taco Bell or something like that."

Taco Bell, Walker remembers what she and Sir Good Knight had talked about.

"I know a good one. There's one on Urban Blvd, plus there's a Chase Manhattan across the street. If you don't mind, I need to run in."

"No problem."

A few minutes later, Walker and Owens pull into the parking lot of Chase Manhattan Bank.

"I won't be long."

"Take your time Detective."

Walker smiles. She liked the sound of that. She also liked driving around in a car without permanent red lights on top. She pulls her coat over her head and walks into the bank. Walker heads for the customer service desk. She wastes no time; with badge in hand...

"My name is Detective Jessica Walker I need to see the manager immediately."

Though insistent, Walker was able to keep the bank customers unaware of the presence of an officer. She didn't want to draw attention. A manager came quickly.

"I'm the manager. Is there a problem?"

"Where can we talk?

"Umm, follow me."

As Walker follows, she is relieved to see that the line is long. This way if her partner gets impatient and looks in, he'll see the wait. Walker is led to an office in the rear.

"We at the department have reason to believe that a high priority fugitive has recently visited your bank."

"I'm afraid you're mistaken. We've had no disturbance of any kind."

"I didn't mean to insinuate that he created one. We simply believe he may have done some banking here. He was seen in this immediate area."

"I see, well what can we do?"

"I'd like to take a look at your video surveillance footage from last Friday."

"Sure, we can handle that. I'll take you to security."

Walker digs for her phone and calls Owens. She tells him she has to meet with a manager and will be a little longer.

Moments later "This footage is taken from the entrance. Anyone who entered on Last Friday, will be in this video."

Walker shares the description of Pat that she'd received from Sir Good Knight. She and the manager view the footage on fast forward and pause. But one by one, each person is ruled out. Walker thanks the manager for his help and heads out. But before she exits, she grabs a loan application so as not to come out empty handed. The rain has stopped. Walker approaches the passenger side of the car with the application purposely in plain sight.

"Owens I'm so sorry. The wait was much longer than I expected."

"It wasn't that long, I'm fine."

"Are you sure, I felt like I was wasting your time."

"No, I'm fine."

"Well if I can persuade you into letting me run into the post office, tacos are on me."

"Say no more! I need to make a call anyway."

"I promise I won't be long."

Walker is unaware that she's crossed paths with her new partner before today. However, Walker's inability to recognize Owens is by no means a knock on her observational skills. Many factors contributed to this circumstance. For one, he was in the air. Second, he was moving fast and wearing a uniform. Not to mention the fact that while she was running to the aid of an injured E.S.A.D. Agent; Owens was chasing after Sir Good Knight.

Owens watches closely as Walker enters the post office. He then pulls a small device out of his jacket pocket.

"Owens to Col. Foster. Come in Col. Foster."

"Foster here, report."

"Nothing unusual yet sir. We've made a few routine stops and investigation follow ups."

"Where are you now?"

"Parked outside of a post office. Walker's inside."

"Have you mentioned the aliens?"

"No."

"Good. Don't initiate, let her bring it up. I've read her file. She's no fool."

"Yes sir."

"How does she feel about her promotion?"

"She's on cloud nine! No matter how good of a cop she is, her judgment has to be a little off."

"Even so, don't press the issue."

"Yes sir."

"Keep me informed. Foster out."

One person is ahead of Detective Walker in line. Once the customer is finished, Jessica walks to the counter and takes out her gold badge. She had to resist the urge to smile when it shined.

"I need to see the manager."

The clerk quickly locates his supervisor and follows him back to the front counter.

"How can I help you officer?"

"We have evidence that a dangerous fugitive was recently in this area. We have reason to believe that he visited this postal facility. I need to view your video surveillance from last Friday.

"Certainly. Come right this way."

They begin viewing the footage. Two minutes later …

"Wait, pause the video. Walker can feel it; The guy in the over coat, that's him!"

He wasn't facing the camera, but he fit the description that Sir Good Knight had given her. She looks closer.

"Isn't that clerk in the video the same one that's in the front now?"

"Yes. That is him."

They keep watching. According to the video, Pat stayed in the facility for over fifteen minutes. He never faces the camera.

"What is that he's filling out?"

"I don't know, but I think we know who does."

The manager picks up the phone and calls the front desk. He tells the clerk to lock the front door and come to them in the back.

"This video is from last Friday. As you can see, you're on it. What business did this man have?" Walker asks.

The clerk stares closely at the footage.

"Yeah I remember. He was picking up his passport."

"Passport?! Where's he going?"

"I don't know exactly, but he did mention something about mountains in Asia somewhere. He's a climber."

"You mean the Himalayans?"

"He didn't say."

"Did he say when he was leaving?"

"Next week."

"By any chance did he mention anything else, anything at all?"

"No. No that was all."

"If you think of anything give me a call, handing her cards out. Thanks for your help."

"Code three! Owens whispers as he conceals his communicator."

Again, Walker comes to the car with paperwork in her hands. It's just a sheet of stamps, but it does the trick. Neither detective can see through the others' smoke screen.

"Was that long?"

"No, not at all. Besides, I was relaxing. But I can't wait for those tacos!" "Amen to that."

Chapter Thirteen:

The Woman and the Warrior

The rain has stopped. Sir Good Knight conceals the Eden sword and grabs his bag. He takes out his newest windbreaker and puts it on tying the hood. He then quickly runs around the corner to get out of sight. Even though he is only two and a half blocks away from his dorm, London decides to take the long way home in case anyone recognizes him as the one who was being chased.

After twenty out of the way minutes, London finally makes it home. He expects to be greeted by his roommate, then remembers Tommy wouldn't be back until tomorrow. He gets out of his wet clothes and takes a shower. His pains and bruises from his latest skirmish have long since disappeared. London is just happy to clean up and relax. He again tries to focus on Pat. As dangerous as Bloodsport was, and he is obviously the most lethal of demons, he too is just a distraction. Finding Pat is now even more urgent. Walker had given him her card. London pulls out his drawer and empties it out on his bed. He rummages around the contents and finds it.

Walker finished her paperwork and was online viewing the most popular mountains in Asia. She was giving particular attention to Mt. Everest. Her phone rings. It's London, Sir Good Knight to her.

"Sgt. Jessica Walker?"

"This is she."

"What of Pat?"

Walker sits up straight and gives her undivided attention to The Knight. Her demeanor, however, causes another to give his undivided attention. Walker talks low.

"Can you hear me?"

"Yes."

"I have some information, but I can't discuss it now."

"We need to meet."

"Where?"

London pauses. He almost suggests *The Encounter point*, until he thinks about their last meeting there.

"The harbor in one hour."

"One hour."

Owens knows something is up. Walker doesn't see him advancing toward her desk until he is just six feet away. She hangs up the phone.

"Hey Walker, you mind if I refer to your notes?"

As he says this, he looks at her monitor and sees what occupied her attention before her phone call.

"I didn't know you were into mountain climbing. Is that Everest?"

Walker quickly switches screens. "Oh no, I was just bored. Here, I'll email you my notes. You should have them in a second. Listen, I have to take care of something. I'll see you tomorrow."

"Is everything alright? You want me to come along?"

"No, no it's nothing like that. It's just a personal matter."

"Oh okay, well have a good night."

"You too."

Owens has no doubt that Walker is up to something. And he suspects it to somehow involve the humanoid alien. He waits for her to exit the building, and then attempts to follow her. But just before he makes it out of the building ...

"Hey Owens, calls another detective, I don't mean to pry, but you don't want to find out what the captain is like if your report isn't on his desk in the morning."

"Thanks a lot, I don't know what I was thinking."

"Don't mention it, just a heads up."

Owens hurries back to his desk and pulls up his email. He then rushes to finish his own report and sends it to the captain. He then does his best to appear nonchalant while exiting the precinct, and then sprints to his car. It was obvious that Walker was long gone. But Owens wasn't as upset as he should've been. As he gets into his vehicle, the reason comes to light. He reaches into his glove compartment and pulls out a tracking device. He had bugged Walker's car. He starts the car and follows the coordinates.

Twenty minutes passed. Walker pulls up in her driveway. She runs to her front door and hurries in. After a five-minute shower, Walker dresses in dark clothes and a baseball cap. Half a block away, a car parks and turns it's lights out. E.S.A.D. Agent David Owens conceals the remote and gets out of the car. He puts his hands in his pockets and turns the collar of his jacket up. He walks in the direction of Walker's house. Her car is in the driveway, but the house is dark. Owens doesn't see any light at all. Suddenly, the front door swings open. Owens reacts by calmly taking the car keys out of his pocket and climbing the stairs of the nearest porch. Walker runs down the stairs zipping her jacket. She looks to her right, then to her left. The coast is clear. The only person in sight is a man walking up the stairs at the Spencer's home four houses down. Walker glances at her watch, it was 9:28, she has thirty-two minutes to get to the harbor. Owens remains on the porch until Walker's car speeds off. He then jumps off the porch and runs to his car.

"Owens to Col. Foster, Owens to Col. Foster!"

"Foster here, report."

Owens gets in the car and peels off, "I'm tailing her now!" I believe she's in route to meet with the humanoid alien. I tracked her home, and she's changed her clothes. Now she's speeding down 5th street!"

"I'm dispatching two units to assist you. They'll track your communicator. Keep me informed."

"Yes sir."

Walker was making good time. She wanted to get to the harbor early, so she could check it out. Suddenly, it occurs to her; the Spencer's are out of town. They were visiting their son in Buffalo. They wouldn't be back until Friday. Even if they were home, everyone who knew them would know that the Spencer's are in bed no later than 9:30pm. It was 9:28pm when she saw the stranger on their steps. Something wasn't right. But she had no idea that it had to do with her.

Walker parks in the lot of the waterfront. She's ten minutes early. As she gets out of the car she realizes, she and Sir Good Knight neglected to say exactly where they would meet. The detective walks toward the water. There are plenty of boats, water skis, and yachts docked. When she doesn't see the SoulKnight, she quickens her pace.

The SoulKnight was not far off. He'd been watching since Walker arrived. He waited to be sure she was alone before signaling her. He then unsheathes the Eden sword and twirls it in a dazzling display, allowing the tip of the blade to touch the surface of the water. This caused the water to both sizzle and subtlety splash. Walker hears the noise and walks in that direction. She walks to the edge of the pier and stands motionless. Her eyes witness a more magnificent sight than her memory could ever recall. There in total blackness, in the middle of nothing, Sir Good Knight is running toward her, on top of the water! He was swinging a red sword in semi-circles side to side. Drops of water and steam rise from the surface and try but fail to touch and keep up with the SoulKnight. They simply testify of the place where he once stepped. Just before reaching the pier, Sir Good Knight explodes off of the surface of the water like a trampoline. As he nears the pier, he performs a triple front tuck landing two feet in front of Detective Jessica Walker. She doesn't know whether to clap or grovel! She settles for exhaling. This was the closest she'd ever been to the SoulKnight's blazing blue water motion eyes.

"Hello Sgt. Walker, and thank you for coming."

"Wow! She takes a breath. Umm, actually I got a promotion since last we met. It's *Detective* Jessica Walker now."

"Congratulations Detective."

"Thank you very much. They begin walking. I have some news, but I'm afraid it's incomplete."

"What have you learned?"

"When you saw Pat, he was coming from the post office. He was picking up a passport. The clerk said that he'd be traveling to someplace in Asia next week. He's going mountain climbing."

"Mountain climbing? Where, and why?"

"That's all the clerk knew. But the Himalayan Mountains make the most sense."

"Mt. Everest."

"Yeah, that's what I was thinking. I can check out any Americans connected to Himalayan expeditions for next week."

Sir Good Knight ponders this new information. He can't make any sense out of it. Time was of the essence, he needed specifics. He is so thrown off by this info, that in his confusion he tunes Walker out. Several minutes pass.

So… "What do you think?"

"Forgive me, yes that would be most appreciated; as are your efforts at the post office."

"Don't mention it. I'm anxious to see these, she pauses before saying aliens, not wanting to offend Sir Good Knight; *criminals* properly dealt with and brought to justice."

"I have a source that I too will consult. What can you tell me of the ones that tried to capture me?"

"They're called E.S.A.D, Extreme Security and Detainment. They're a branch of the National Security Agency. They've been commissioned to deal with you and the others."

A car parks in the darkness of the street outside of the harbor. The driver purposely keeps the lights off. Just seconds later, four E.S.A.D. Agents, two units, pierce the black night and join David Owens. Two of the four Agents are on Hover-forms. The other two are on some kind of two wheeled vehicle. It resembles a motorcycle, but not quite. It's very low to the ground, and the top half of the operator's body is encased. The legs are kneeled on top of two fixture supports that also conceal a row of in line tires. On each side of the front of the vehicle, protruded the barrel of automatic guns. They're built for speed and silence. One of the Agents on the Hover-forms speaks with Owens.

"Col. Foster wants you to remain out of sight."

"Out of sight, why?"

"He says in case we're unsuccessful, you can continue with your surveillance."

"I can still assist you. All I have to do is… "

"Those are the orders Owens."

The lead Agent turns to the others, "Units split up, Body cycles east, Hover-forms west. If anyone lays eyes on the humanoid, call for back up immediately."

Furious, Owens kicks his door shut as the units disperse. But he obeys orders.

As Sir Good Knight and Walker continued trying to figure things, the Knight's sensitive ears hear a faint noise. The Body cycle unit is close to spotting them. Walker doesn't hear anything, but notices Sir Good Knight's attention is suddenly elsewhere.

"What is it?"

The Knight turns to the detective and puts his finger to his lips. He then throws her over his shoulder! He doesn't know who, but someone is fast approaching; very fast. Sir Good Knight jumps over the railing down to the water. Walker does all she can not to make a sound. She is over the shoulder of an alien, and now seeing the surface of a black sea rushing to swallow them! Walker squeezes her eyes shut as tightly as she can. She expects to feel an ice-cold crash, but for some reason it was taking too long. She opens her eyes, holding her breath (*as is he*), the water is no longer rushing to meet them. It is ground level and racing away from them. Sir Good Knight is once again running on top of the water, this time with Walker. All this without making a splash. They aren't even wet! The water walking miracle ends at a buoy in the midst of the sea. The Knight lowers Walker onto the buoy. He then exhales and allowed the lower half of his body to submerge while he hangs onto the buoy.

"I saw movement. Follow me," says the Body Cycle Agent.

The Body cycle unit speeds to the area where one of them thinks he saw something. They stop in the spot where the woman and the warrior had just leaped from. The Agents turn headlights on and slowly patrol the area.

"I know I saw something."

Sir Good Knight and Detective Walker can see the searchlights from the water. But they're a safe distance away. The E.S.A.D. Agent that saw movement pulls his Body cycle up to the railing and shines his light out over the water. Nothing.

"Hey, if they're out here I don't think they came to swim."

The unit speeds off. But it's apparent that they're not about to stop searching. They know Detective Jessica Walker is somewhere in the harbor. And they believe she has company.

"They must've tailed me somehow. My car, they had to have bugged it!"

Each unit, which consists of two Agents, is now separated in an effort to cover more ground. Every couple of minutes, a headlight appears and searches another area. Then, a welcome sound whispers in the ears of Sir Good Knight. A humming sound. He looks in the direction of the sound with a smirk on his face.

"What is it? Why are you smiling?"

Walker looks in the same direction. Two minutes later she can hear it. And then she sees it. It appears to be a small yacht. Sir Good Knight is fixed on his target. He has to time it just right. He waits until there are no lights shining from E.S.A.D. Agents, then shoots out of the water and once again throws Walker over his shoulder. Sir Good Knight sprints, hoping to secretly rendezvous with the vessel. It approached from the left. The challenge is to intersect with the rear of the boat, and board it without attracting attention from the sailor, or E.S.A.D. As the front of the yacht passed, the Knight jumps from the surface of the water and into the back of the boat. There is absolutely no noise made. He exhales.

The sailor of the yacht is totally oblivious. Walker finally opens her eyes to find that she and Sir Good Knight have solid footing.

"Owens, this is Unit leader, come in."

"Owens here."

"We have yet to locate Jessica Walker and the humanoid. I spoke with Col. Foster, he said that you are to continue with your undercover operations immediately."

Owens is fuming. He hops in his car and peels off. He's doing all the work, and yet he's neither being consulted nor involved in the detainment faze. Meanwhile, Sir Good Knight and Detective Walker are more or less enjoying a moonlit boat ride. They're now a considerable distance from where they'd boarded the yacht. The Knight is satisfied, so for the third time he hoists the detective over his shoulder and performs a miracle.

"What the hell was that?"

"What was what?"

"Something just jumped off the back of the boat."

"Now I know why they tell you not to drink the water, he laughs. Just tell me when you see the Loch Ness monster!"

"See, that's why I don't tell you nothing!"

The two E.S.A.D. units' re-group in the harbor's parking lot.

"There's no one out here!"

"Her car's here, we're just missing something. This is what we're going to do, Cycle unit... "

"Someone's coming."

A woman was approaching from the opposite direction of the harbor. Both units rush to confront her.

"Can I help you?"

"What were you doing in the harbor?"

"What are you talking about, the harbor's been closed since ten o'clock."

"Don't play coy with me detective, your car's right over there!"

338

Walker continues toward her car, almost ignoring E.S.A.D. Well if you were perceptive enough to notice that, then how did you not notice the fact that I'm coming from the opposite direction? By the way, I didn't know they were equipping harbor security so well these days."

"We can throw you in a hole so deep that you wouldn't remember the sight of daylight!"

"Hmm, I didn't know taking a walk was a matter of National security; she opens her car door, or harbor security for that matter."

Walker calmly drives off. The unit leader radios Col. Foster and reports the situation.

She's clever, but don't worry she'll slip up. And when she does, we'll make sure she falls. Return to base.

Chapter Fourteen:

Intelligence

Sir Good Knight was nearly home. Two things were on his mind; the most pressing of which is hoping that Bloodsport isn't awaiting him. The other is finding a new place to live. His enemies know all too well where to find him. It seems he was walking into a trap every time he goes home. He isn't up for a fight tonight; he's relieved to make it home without incident. He immediately prays the prayer of three-hour protection. He hadn't been using it much, but now it seems essential. Although he has the ability to recover quickly from physical fatigue, he has no such ability to recover from mental fatigue. His blazing water blue eyes stop shimmering and turn back to their normal, still brown. London stashes the Eden sword and crashes. Before he knows it, he is asleep. Three hours pass, then all of a sudden London wakes. He sits up and looks toward the windows. The shade is open, so he could see that there are no Shadow walkers perched. He looks at the door, nothing. Then, he looks up. There is a very colorful and familiar disturbance.

"Greetings London son of James."

"Just the man… or angel… or whatever you are; that I need to see. What can you tell me about Mt. Everest?"

"It is the highest point on the Earth."

"Yeah I know that much, but why is it important to Pat?"

"By whose testimony is it important to Pat?"

"Uh well, I have information that he'll be traveling there next week. Are we wrong?"

"Again, you ask the wrong question."

London stops to think, "I've learned that Pat is going to Asia next week to mountain climb. We assumed it would have to be Mt. Everest. But if not; then where, what mountain; and why?"

The 4th Corner nods his approval, "The Lord is pleased with your diligence. He will allow me to answer one of your questions. *The where* is Turkey."

"Turkey! Why?! What could be so important about a mountain in Turkey?"

"The rest you must discover."

"Turkey. How am I supposed to get to Turkey?"

"You must find a way."

London sighs, "There's something else I need."

"And that is?"

"A hide out. Bloodsport is becoming too big of a distraction; not to mention I'd like to avoid his ambushes. Every demon the Dark Author has, knows where I live."

"I cannot provide you with a safe haven, but you are free to figure something; and figure something, you must."

"I'm sure you know that even the government is after me now."

"Indeed."

Then London has an epiphany. "Why hasn't Pat informed them of my identity?"

"The Lord hath given The Dark One certain parameters in which he may engage you."

"Are you saying, *they can't tell?*"

"I am saying, they *will* not."

"Wait, I don't understand. We're talking about The Dark Author, Satan, Lucifer, the actual Devil! If he was thrown out of heaven for acting up, why wouldn't he disobey now?"

"Because the *All sovereign one* has informed him of the consequences should he and his forces do so."

"Consequences?" London says sarcastically. "*You mean like being thrown in a lake of fire?*"

"No. I mean erasing his creation."

"Altogether?"

"Utterly."

"But if he's willing to do such a thing, it seems that he would have done it way before now!"

"The Lord has allowed him to tempt and threaten man. He serves a purpose. Man can prove himself strong, and worthy of the Kingdom if he can resist the wiles of the Sin Father."

"So, you're saying, he'd do that, just for me"?

"He is the same God that gave his son for you! What will he not do?!"

It was the first time that the 4th Corner had displayed emotion. Guilt overcomes London.

"Forgive me, London son of James." He hangs his head.

"There's no need to apologize. You're more than right."

"I will make amends. I give you my word, he disappears.

London goes back to sleep, secure in believing the 4th Corner would watch over him since three hours had passed. He has a morning errand to run soon as the sun comes up; well, maybe not as soon as.

Tuesday morning, Detective Walker enters the station with determination. She decides that this is the day that she will find the glue that makes all of the clues stick together. It's obvious that someone has been watching her closely. She is sure that it's someone from the station. E.S.A.D. has a mole inside of police headquarters. Walker looks around slowly at the various officers coming and going. They are her friends. Some of which had saved her life. Others she has saved. But what about Owens? The only info she has on him is word of mouth. He approaches and hands her a cup of coffee.

"Good morning. How did last night go?"

"Last night, what do you mean?"

"You left abruptly; you said you had something to take care of."

"Oh yeah, yeah things went well. How was your night?"

"I didn't do much. I saw a couple friends."

Neither believes the other.

"What are you working on?"

"I'm following up on a couple of leads on that bank robbery."

"I have one or two potential leads. I'm preparing a line-up; I'll keep you informed."

Ironically, both detectives are actually doing their duty. Owens has been in touch with a witness, and Walker along with the line-up, is expecting to meet with a local snitch. She makes a phone call. Owens' desk is too far away to hear who or what she is talking about. She's talking to a travel Agent. Walker is inquiring about any packages being offered to visit the Himalayan Mountains. In particular Mt. Everest. The travel Agent informs her of the packages that will take you to the region; however, the arrangements for climbing have to be made once you arrive. Walker then identifies herself as a detective and asks how many, if any, Americans have booked such a vacation for next week. There aren't any. Walker, trying to cover all bases, asks if the agency has any affiliates whose files they could check. The travel Agent does what he can to help, recommending other Agents and such. Then finally, Walker finds an agency that Pat may've contacted.

Even though there is a lot of commotion in the precinct, Owens is able to read a few words that are repeated in Walker's conversations, *Mt. Everest, next week.* Owens approaches his partner. She sees him coming and immediately ends her call.

"Hey, I'm going out to meet with the witness that I told you about."

"You want me to tag along?"

"No need, I first want to see what he has to offer. If it sounds solid, I'll bring him in."

"I'll be here if you need me."

Walker feels this is just the opportunity she needs. Owens feels he's seized the opportunity. He jumps in his car and heads straight for E.S.A.D. headquarters. He is sure he has something this time, something big. When he arrives, he immediately locates Col. Foster.

"I think we've got him!"

Foster pulls his attention from another Agent, "How's that?"

"Something big is going down next week."

"Tell me more."

"I don't know the specific date, but the where is the most interesting thing; Mt Everest."

"Mt. Everest?"

"Jessica Walker has been looking for information on Everest for the last couple of days. I overheard her on the phone speak of meeting someone there. Plus, she's conducting every conversation in secrecy."

He sighs as he sits. "That's on the other side of the world."

"Yes sir, on the frontier of Nepal and Tibet. I feel very strongly about this Colonel."

"I need to contact the general on this one, but let me ask you this; if this comes down to a judgment call, how secure are you with the knowledge that at least half of our Agents would be thousands of miles away from the only known place these beings have be seen?"

"Sir, if the decision were mine, the order would already be given."

Foster slowly nods. "Continue your surveillance. I will speak with the General."

"Sir, if I may, I request to be sent, if a team is deployed."

"Your request is noted."

Walker felt free to research now. She is reading information she'd just pulled up on her computer screen, when an officer approaches her desk.

"Detective"

Walker quickly switches to another screen.

"Very funny. I may have a gold badge, but you can still call me Jessica, Danny."

"And that's why we love you Jess. Hey before I forget, a package came for you this morning."

"A package, from whom?"

"The guy didn't say. I just made sure it wasn't ticking."

She giggles, "What company was it that delivered the package?"

"He wore no uniform. He was a young guy, hat, glasses, and turtleneck under a jacket."

"Wow!"

"That's right; you're not the only one who's ready to be a detective."

The two laughed. Walker wasn't expecting any deliveries. It was a rectangular shaped box with her name on it. A small envelope is taped to the top. She opens it. There's a note inside that says, *don't open the box until you're alone*. Walker secures her computer (with her research) and takes the box to the restroom. There's no one inside, she opens the box. There's an old two-way device inside that allows messaging. The number is written inside the box. She skeptically picks it up and sends a message.

"Hello, who are you?"

"*Are you alone?*"

The immediate response startles Walker.

"Yes. Yes, I am, now who is this?"

"I think you know. I'm sort of unique. We have a special relationship."

Walker didn't notice the stall door behind her slowly open.

"Texting your boo from work huh? Yeah girl, you have to keep him connected."

Walker reaches for her firearm. The woman doesn't notice.

The receptionist washes her hands, "I wish my boyfriend would do things like that. She walks out, you've got a good one there, hold on to him girl!"

"Is everything alright, are you still there?"

Walker checks the other stalls.

"I'm here, I'm okay. I think I like this idea."

"I thought you would. I have some info. Pat is indeed interested in a mountain in Asia, but that mountain is not Everest. Pat's going to Turkey."

"Turkey? What could be so significant about a mountain in Turkey?"

"That I don't know; my source told me all he could."

"When I think about it, the clerk at the post office never mentioned the Himalayans, I was the one who assumed that Mt. Everest was his destination."

"I would've made the same assumption."

"I'll do some research on Turkey, I owe you that much."

"I am very grateful for your help, but you don't owe me anything."

"What's the plan? Are we to follow him to Turkey? Will you allow me to be a passenger on your craft?"

Remembering that Walker still believes him to be an alien, Sir Good Knight answers her, *"I will figure something."*

"Gotta go, I'll contact you when I have something."

"I'm truly grateful."

Col. Foster immediately contacts Gen. Morris and reports the situation.

Morris didn't spend much time at headquarters, he's more of a politician. He spends a lot of time in Langley (Langley, VA CIA headquarters) and in D.C. Morris is the one who secures authorization for E.S.A.D.'s missions. Though, since they are a chapter of N.S.A., they pretty much have a green light. Morris keeps them abreast. All this being said, the general is an ex special forces marine. He is far from the average politician. In all, Morris has been involved in classified governmental operations for over twenty years.

Col. Foster is part of a small pool of people that Morris trusts. They'd worked together in the past. When Morris was chosen to lead E.S.A.D., he was given authority to assemble his own team. The first person he thought of was Foster.

"... One last thing, Owens has requested to join any effort sent to Everest."

"Brief everyone, E.S.A.D will indeed travel to the Himalayas." Half will remain to monitor the city. I'll speak with Owens when I arrive later this week."

London's first class is cancelled, and Tommy had left a message saying he'd be back around three. London decides to use the extra time to search for some kind of safe haven. He has no idea where to start. All he knows is, he needs a new living arrangement. Off campus apartments are the beginning of his search. Some have a lot of potential, but he needs something more reclusive, something off radar; But what? After two hours of riding around and looking through the paper, London gets on the bus and heads for his dorm. It's 2:05 and he wants to be home when his roommate returns. Staring out the window daydreaming, London is brought back to reality, when the very thing he is looking for, passes before his eyes. He alerts the driver to stop, and then jumps off. London stops in his tracks. He looks around. Has he been followed? Probably not, he'd been on so many buses and seen so many places in the last couple hours that anyone following would've gotten lost in the shuffle. The object of his attention is a sign, *Fallout shelter*. Ironically, it's in an old abandoned church. He wedges open a boarded-up door and enters in. *This has to be destiny!* There are several different exits, perfect in case of emergency. The fallout shelter is on the lowest level. It's behind a wall sized reinforced steel door. London reaches for it, it's unlocked. He walks in. It's empty inside, and huge. London sees endless possibilities. It needs some cleaning and minor maintenance, but nothing that he can't handle. He feels a vibration. It's his two way. He grabs it.

"Are you alone?"

"I am."

"There's not much info on mountains in Turkey. In fact, the only significant find is a biblical reference."

This piques London's interest like never before.

"What does it refer to?"

"It speaks of the mountains of Ararat. Supposedly, this is where Noah's Ark came to rest when the flood waters receded from the Earth." Gen 8:4.

London falls silent. He can't believe what he is hearing; Pat is after the Ark of Noah! But why? What could he do with it?

"Are you still there?"

"Yes. I'm trying to figure what Pat could want with such a thing."

"Yeah, I guess no one told him that's just a story. What's he going to do when he finds nothing up there? I say we let him go."

It is then that London realizes. Detective Jessica Walker is not a believer.

"He cannot be allowed to do as he pleases."

"Are we assuming that Pat is searching for Noah's Ark?!"

"We won't discount anything, and whatever his plan is, we can't let him fulfill it."

"*I guess*. Well, I'll keep searching just in case it turns out to be something else."

London is sure that the Ark is Pat's target; Even though it doesn't seem to make sense. He looks at his watch. It is 3:15. London closes the thick metal door and exits the church. He flags down a cab. The time is 3:40 when London walks into his dorm room. He frantically begins cleaning the mess he'd made while his roommate was away. Five minutes later…

"Well, I see you had fun while I was away."

Chapter Fifteen:

A will and A way

London helps Tommy with his bags. For the next ten minutes, London listens while his roommate details his weekend. As Tommy talks, London is trying to come up with a way to break the news that he'll be moving. He couldn't come up with much. It was almost 4:00pm. Tommy presses the button on the phone to check the messages. There are five: two advertisements, a bill collector, a hang up, and the last one, a voice that London used to be happy to hear from; but things were different now.

"LB, what's going on, haven't talked to you in a while. It was John. Listen, I need you to give me a call, it's important. In the meantime, make sure you catch today's episode of The Dorian Shelton show. Later."

"Yeah I heard that it was going to be a good one today."

"What channel and what time?"

"I think it's 5:30 on channel four."

London isn't sure of what this all means, but he's sure it won't bring a smile to his face. Five thirty rolls around. London and Tommy are glued to the television screen. London quietly wishes he had listened to the messages before Tommy had returned. The show begins. As London suspected, it has to do with the *Alien Invasion*. Three so-called experts are being interviewed. Then, things take a turn for the worse.

"My next guest claims to have escaped an attack from the same six-legged beast that was caught on video fighting with Philadelphia's finest. But here's the kicker, he says this was over eleven years ago! London's heart sinks. Please welcome John *Raeburn,* last name is really Reilly, to the show."

"Is that your? ..."

"Yeah."

"Let's get right to it. John tell us about your encounter when you were only eight years old."

"Well, I was bike riding with a group of friends. We had snuck out of the neighborhood and found our way to a popular dirt bike trail."

John went on to recount the entire experience from his and London's childhood, only, he tells the story with he and London in each other's places.

"…you're helpless, you're in the middle of nowhere, you're facing certain doom."

"Without a doubt."

"We'll be right back to hear the rest of John Raeburn's account of terror and escape. Stay with us. You don't want to miss this."

"Wow, this is crazy! Tommy pauses and looks at London, Uh, London, you're the friend that he's talking about, aren't you?"

London has to be careful. If he acts rash, this can all blow up in his face.

"I was with him alright, but we weren't being chased by aliens! We didn't know exactly what it was. I said it was a bear. But that was so long ago! We were so young."

He laughs, "So that's why you never seem too excited to talk to him."

"Something like that."

After a few commercials, John, and Dorian Shelton are back on the screen.

"John, when we left, you and your best friend, who shall remain nameless, were running late for curfew after a day of bike riding, when an unknown creature began to give chase. What did you think he'd do?"

"He was so close we could see his teeth! It was clear, this was it. We were prey! Then, out of nowhere, the humanoid alien appeared."

"The same one from … "

"Same one. He appeared in between the beast and my friend and I…"

London knows not to let his true feelings show, but he is heated.

"They started fighting. My friend wisely sped off, but I couldn't. It's like I was in a state of shock. My friend called for me to follow, but it was no use. The humanoid alien got the upper hand on the beast. Then... "

John continues telling his altered story to Dorian Shelton. It was one-part truth, one part false.

"That's an incredible story! So, what did you think when you saw the beings were back and continuing their war?"

"I didn't know what to think. I just knew I had to tell someone!"

"What does your friend think?"

"He's scared. He wants to forget about it and pretend that there's a logical explanation."

"Even now?"

"He accepts what's going on now, but not the fact that we've encountered them before."

London turns the television off.

"He's embarrassing himself on national television!"

"Does he just want to be on T.V.?"

"I don't know what he thinks he's doing, but I don't want anything to do with it. He quickly changes the subject, So, finish telling me about your trip."

Wednesday morning, the phone rings. Detective David Owens answers ... Walker glances over from her desk. Owens hangs up. He gets up in a hurry and walks over to her.

"I'll be back in about an hour; you need me to check on anything while I'm out?"

"Umm, no I think I'm good. Where are you going?"

"I may have something. I'm not one hundred percent sure, but it's worth checking on. I won't be long."

Walker no longer trusts Owens. She decides to tail him. Owens is visibly anxious as he leaves the station. It causes him to be careless. Walker notices and takes full advantage. She simply walks out of the station quietly, twenty-five feet behind Owens. He jumps into the vehicle he and Walker are assigned and speeds off. Walker quickly follows in her personal vehicle. Even though her partner is off his game, she is still wise to stay at a safe distance. He never spots her, and she never loses sight of him. Owens finally stops at an abandoned building. Walker recognizes the building.

"He's E.S.A.D.!"

Owens gets out and disappears into the warehouse. Walker heads back to headquarters. She is furious. She doesn't need to investigate; she knows why he's undercover.

Owens finds Col. Foster and is taken to Gen. Morris. Owens is surprised that Foster has contacted him so soon after they'd last met. And he is even more surprised to be meeting with the General. He stands at attention.

"At ease. Have a seat. Col. Foster has updated me on your progress. You've been doing good work."

"Thank you sir."

"He also told me of your request. Your work monitoring Detective Jessica Walker has been very valuable. It is the reason that making this decision has been so difficult. But I have decided to grant your request."

This was the best news that David Owens had received in what seemed like a long while. He tried hard to contain his excitement. After all, this was the General.

"Thank you, sir. Thank you very much!"

The General stands from his seat. "One more thing. (Owens stood up) You're going to lead this mission. Begin your preparations."

Owens wasn't expecting a promotion, but he wasn't going to decline.

" I won't disappoint you sir."

London's two early classes are over, and he is extremely anxious to leave school. Reason being an announcement that his first class' professor had made. He said a friend of his that heads up a regional volunteer service that assists the Peace Corps is looking for two volunteers to join them on a humanitarian mission to Iraq. The only catch was you had to already have a passport. London couldn't believe his ears. This was fate. No. As he thought about it, this was God himself making a way! The professor put the contact information on the board and said they'd be leaving next Tuesday. All London knew was, Iraq borders Turkey, and his passport is in his closet!

London's cab stops in front of the Peace Corps offices. He enters and asks for Dr. Bolden. He's told to have a seat and that Dr. Bolden will be with him shortly. After a brief wait, a distinguished middle-aged man enters the lobby from the rear. The receptionist motions in London's direction. London stands as the man approaches. He introduces himself and explains how he'd heard of the opportunity. Dr. Bolden takes London to an office in the rear.

"So, Mr. Bishop, tell me what makes you an ideal candidate to join our team."

London showers Dr. Bolden with reasons as to why he's the perfect candidate to join the efforts in Iraq. He starts with learning and helping, to supporting our troops, to gaining a life changing experience. He goes on for three straight minutes. He easily wins the man over. Besides, there weren't many other college students, or anyone else for that matter, who are willing to travel to the extremely dangerous war-torn nation. Dr. Bolden congratulates London and introduces him to the Peace Corps group members. London is given a bunch of literature about the Peace Corps, and about Iraq. His stay lasts three hours.

"London did you drive here?"

"No, I caught a cab."

"I'll have one of my associate's drive you home."

"Thank you, I really appreciate it."

"Don't mention it, you're helping us. Oh, and by the way, you'll need to be here tomorrow at 10:00 a.m. We'll be tying up any loose ends and receiving our immunizations."

"I'll be here," London hates needles.

"See you then."

London and his ride are almost at the dorm when he feels a vibration. He quickly grabs the two way.

"*Allow me ten minutes.*"

After being dropped off, London gets settled in and contacts Walker.

"*Can we meet; I have a couple of pressing matters.*" She types.

"*Yes, but It needs to be somewhere where no one would think to look. Do you know the cemetery on Sugar Rd.?*"

"*Of course.*"

"*What time can you meet me there?*"

"*Whatever time works for you.*"

"How's midnight?"

Every horror movie Walker had ever seen comes to mind.

"Uh, sure I guess."

"What's wrong?"

"No, I'm fine. It's just being at a cemetery at midnight is asking for trouble."

"There's already a scary movie going on, and this one's a true story."

"Yeah, you're right. Twelve it is."

Back at headquarters, Walker behaves normally around her partner. She does, however, watch his every move. Before leaving for the night, Owens comes to Walkers desk.

"How's it going detective?"

"It's going great now that it's the end of the day."

"Definitely."

Walker wonders how much he knows. How deep has he been digging? What conclusions has he drawn?

"Want me to walk you to your car?"

"No. I have a gun; I think I'll be alright."

Owens laughs and exits the building. Walker's smile quickly fades as she goes to the window to watch him go. She leaves the building only after she's sure that Owens is gone. Once Walker approached her neighborhood, she parks around the corner to hide the fact that she's home. She enters her home from a neighbor's yard and uses her flashlight to get around. Walker takes a much-needed nap before heading back out. Her alarm wakes her at 11:30pm. The detective gathers her things and creeps out the back door. Little does she know; Owens is no longer watching. He has bigger fish to fry.

Chapter Sixteen:

Fight of fists and fire

Detective Walker parks on a side road and hops a short fence to enter into the cemetery. Upon taking her first few steps, Walker realizes that once again, she and Sir Good Knight had failed to designate a specific spot to meet. As she reaches for her radio, a sudden movement catches her eye. Already uneasy about being alone in a dark cemetery, Walker draws her weapon. Sir Good Knight descends from the darkness of the sky, in slow motion. The wind blew, and leaves fell from the surrounding trees with a greater velocity than did he. Walker holsters her weapon.

"My apologies Detective Walker."

"I'm beginning to get used to it.

"Why don't we move away from the road."

"Good idea."

The Woman and the Warrior walk deeper into the cemetery.

"I will be going to Turkey shortly. I can use your expertise here in Philadelphia."

"I wouldn't take me overseas to mess things up either."

"I assure you; I do not believe that you will be a hindrance to me. It's just … "

"No, you don't understand. Unfortunately, it seems that E.S.A.D. is well on the right track."

"How so?"

Walker lowers her head and sighs.

"What is it?"

"I'm embarrassed to say it. They've been using me as their pawn!"

"What happened?"

"My partner, Detective David Owens, or so I thought detective, is an undercover E.S.A.D. Agent! They've been following and investigating me all this time. They're hoping I lead them to you. You trusted me, and I've repaid you with carelessness! I'm so sorry."

"You owe me no apologies; how could you have known?"

"I should be able to read people better than that."

"Do they know you're on to them?"

"No. I don't think so."

"Then your pawn has the advantage. (Walker smiles) What do they know?"

"Even though I was discreet, I can't be certain. They may know everything."

"Not much is known to us, so don't get too down on yourself."

Walker supposed he was right but couldn't help feeling like she'd dropped the ball.

"May I ask you a question?"

"What do you wish to know?"

"Why this planet? And where do you all hide your ships? Are they visible?"

"That was three questions?"

"Too many?"

The Knight smiles. He thinks to himself. This was as good a time as any.

"I have always lived here, on this planet. The others are more complicated."

"Okay, you have always lived here, but where do you come from; Originally."

"What I'm about to say, will be difficult for you to accept."

Walker listens intensely.

"Contrary to what you have been led to believe, I am not an alien."

"I apologize; I guess that word is a bit offensive. What do they call your kind where you're from?"

"We're called many things: people, humans, man, Americans."

"*Right*. I think, maybe you've been among us too long."

Sir Good Knight stops. Walker stops with him. He puts his hands together and gathers himself.

"I am not from another planet. Neither are the others for that matter; though we are from different ... realities."

"Different realities? The people from the planet that I'm from, can't do the things that you can do! And as for that other one... "

"The others as I have said are complicated."

"Wait, what exactly are you saying?"

The SoulKnight slowly begins walking again. "What do you know about Samson, Elijah, and Solomon?"

"Samson, Elijah, and Solomon?"

"The Judge, the Prophet, and the King."

"Are you talking about Bible characters?"

"Samson was endowed with extraordinary strength, more than any man before or after, Judges 14:6. Elijah ran faster than storm winds, 1st Kings 18:46. King Solomon was, and still is, wiser than any man who's ever lived, 2nd Chronicles 1:11-12. All three were given these gifts. They were all human."

"*Fictional humans.* Now what do they have to do with you?"

"They were all ordinary people, who were given extraordinary gifts for a purpose… As am I."

"You can't seriously expect me to believe that."

"All that I have said, is true."

"Oh really? So, what mad scientist gave you your abilities?"

"The same one that gave the Judge, the Prophet, and the King theirs."

Jessica squints her eyes. *"Who, God"?!* Are you saying that God gave you your abilities?"

Sir Good Knight looks Walker squarely in the eye.

"You've gotta be kidding me! The night we first met, I asked where you were from. You pointed to the cosmos."

"I pointed to the Heavens."

"Hold on, just give me a minute, you're freaking me out right now!"

He allows Walker time to compose herself.

"Why is this so difficult to accept? You had no such difficulty in believing that I was from a distant planet complete with flying saucers? The only truth that is real, is God. Man's refusal to believe is what gave birth to such imaginations as your alien theory."

They continued to walk. Walker was silent in deep thought. Sir Good Knight had stomped her, and he knew it. After several minutes, Walker breaks her silence.

"If you're from God, and on the side of good, then what about the beast, and the friends you say it has? You said they're more complicated?"

"You are a detective, Jessica Walker. And the answer that you seek can easily be found by reading between the lines."

"The devil? Are you saying there's a devil; a devil in hell, and evil?"

"There is indeed."

"You're just saying this because of my research. All the Noah's Ark stuff."

"I am not."

"Well, how are you travelling to Turkey without a spacecraft?"

"I have made necessary arrangements."

"So, you really think that Pat is after Noah's Ark?"

"I'm not yet sure, but I believe he is."

"Okay, let's say he is after the Ark. What could he want with it?"

"I do not know."

Walker grabs her head in frustration. Sir Good Knight wanted to ease her mind. He knew that this was a lot to take in, especially for a non-believer. He decides to change the subject.

"Are there any other new developments? Detective Walker?"

"Oh, I'm sorry, snapping out of her daze. No. Is there any new information that *I* should know?"

"Yes, drawing his sword, Duck!"

Walker dives to the ground just as two Shadow walkers dropped from the trees. Sir Good Knight swings the Eden sword dividing one of the creatures in two. The other plants a double-footed kick to the top half of the Knight's back. He manages to turn it into a diving roll. When the creature lands its hit by three burning hot slugs from Jessica Walker's nine-millimeter Glock. Before they could thank each other, the cemetery erupts with Shadow walkers!

"Behind you!"

Walker turns just in time to elude an attack. She quickly puts two holes in the demon's head.

"Run!"

The Knight jumps into the air spinning his body while swinging the sword. By the time his feet touch the ground, a dozen Shadow walkers lay with sizzling severed arms, legs, and heads. Others are in half. But this acrobatic assault does little to dent the number of Shadow walkers still spilling out from the darkness. Walker was headed for the short fence she'd hopped to enter the cemetery, when an arm appears out of a shadow on the ground and trips her. When she hits the ground, her gun is jarred from her hand. Five Shadow walkers surround her. Her gun is out of reach. One of the demons pounces. Walker kicks it in midair sending it tumbling. She reaches and grabs her flashlight, using it to smack the creature that follows the attack of the first. The impact turns the flashlight on. The light shines directly on a third shadow walker. The demon screams in pain as the light disintegrates everybody part it illuminated! When Walker realizes what has happened, she turns the light on a fourth Shadow walker. The effect is the same. She shines the flashlight on every Shadow walker within range. She then locates her gun and stands.

Sir Good Knight is still covering Walker's escape, by jumping, running, gliding, flipping, and slicing! Piles of limbs, and dead bodies of Shadow walkers lay everywhere. Just before the Knight readied to mount another attack, he hears screams. He looks in the direction of the screams and sees a beam of light race from side to side. He then sees Jessica Walker wielding a flashlight. A flashlight that seems to be every bit as effective as his sword.

"Let's get out of here!" She yells.

Sir Good Knight sheaths the Eden sword, runs to Walker, and throws her over his shoulder. Holding his breath, he runs toward the road where Jessica's car is parked. The creatures continue to emerge and pursue. However, Walker now covers their escape by shining her flashlight from over the Knight's shoulder. They reach the road and are happy to be greeted by a series of streetlights. The Shadow walkers are forced to stop their pursuit. Sir Good Knight sets Walker down. She pulls her keys out as they trot to her car. Five feet from the car, both the front and rear windshields are suddenly smashed out! A metal disc spins through the glass and returns to its source.

"Bloodsport! Get in the car and drive off."

"I'm not just going to leave you!"

"Go!"

He opens the driver's side door and pushes Walker inside. He closes the door an instant before having to duck another spinning projectile.

"Go!"

Walker reluctantly floors the gas pedal. The car peels off.

"Your time is at an end." The demon assassin whispers.

Sir Good Knight's water-like eyes shimmer violently. He pulls the Eden sword from its scabbard.

"Death will not make my acquaintance on this night!"

Then with power and speed unaffected by gravity, Sir Good Knight unleashes an amazing acrobatic attack on Bloodsport.

The Knight's attack is so sudden and skillful, that Bloodsport is caught completely off guard. The demon is separated from his trident, his blowing device is burned in two, and his torso is sliced diagonally in half. The entire attack lasts only two and half seconds. Sir Good Knight lands kneeling several feet behind the assassin. Even though the locusts Bloodsport is made up of made him whole again, he is enraged! Sir Good Knight has beaten him to the punch and disarmed him! Not to mention, he had defeated him last they met. Sir Good Knight puts ten additional feet of distance between himself and the demon. Bloodsport squeezes his fingers together and crosses his arms. He bends low, and then quickly straightens and spins around while throwing his arms forward and opens his fingers. Six fire lit darts shoot out from between the assassin's fingers. Sir Good Knight quickly reacts. He explodes into a frenzy of somersaults that would turn an Olympic gymnast green. However, having engaged the Knight twice before, Bloodsport was prepared for his acrobatics. He directed his fire darts, two at a time, to go beyond the spot where the Knight was standing. The demon aimed the darts at varied heights. Two of the darts hit trees and set fires. Two darts stick in the ground. But the last two darts pierce Sir Good Knight's chest!

He crashes to the ground and lays face up with his eyes closed and teeth barred. Bloodsport picks up his trident and approaches his mark. The two trees that were unintended victims of the assassin's darts are fully ablaze. With each step the demon assassin takes, the fire darts in the Knight's chest dig deeper. Sir Good Knight cries out so loud, that Walker hears him through her now half convertible car two blocks away. The moment Bloodsport takes his last step now standing over the SoulKnight, the fire darts complete their burrowing and are now entirely submerged in the Knight's chest. His body starts to shake, and then it seizes up. Finally, it releases. He lay motionless. Not one to assume, Bloodsport raises the trident over his head, and thrusts it down at the lifeless body of the Knight. But before contact is made, Sir Good Knight's eyes open wide and two beams of shimmering blue light blast out! Both the demon and his weapon are hurled over thirty feet up and backward! The hell fire that fueled the darts was shot out along with the Knight's own inner energy. Sir Good Knight rolls over coughing. He locates the Eden sword and climbs to his feet. A car screeches to a stop right in front of him. The passenger door flies open.

"Get in!"

Sir Good Knight doesn't hesitate. Walker buckles her seatbelt and speeds off. Minutes later, sirens scream as fire apparatus and police arrive on the scene. Someone had called 9-1-1 after hearing gunshots coming from the cemetery. Countless trees alongside the road are now on fire. But within the cemetery gates, there is an even more unbelievable sight. Not only are there broken tombstones and tree branches, but there are piles of dismembered gargoyle-like creatures everywhere! The only thing they didn't find was Bloodsport.

Walker was running lights and fishtailing around corners, but Sir Good Knight is silently staring out of his window. He's trying to figure out what had just happened.

"Are you okay?"

"Yes. Yes, I believe so. Although confused, he is indeed fully recovered.

"I heard you cry out. Or at least I thought it was you. That's when I decided to turn around. But before I got there, I saw a blue light shine in the sky. What happened?"

"It appeared that my time truly was at an end. But I was somehow able to overcome him."

"You mean he's dead?"

"I don't know."

"Well what was that light?"

"That's what I would like to know." Again, he stares out the window.

Walker slows the car down to a more manageable speed. She is just about to ask another question when Sir Good Knight rises up and motions for her to remain silent.

"It's him."

"What's him? What are you talking about?"

Walker looks in her rearview mirror and sees a black cloud rapidly approaching. She floors the pedal and tries to lose the swarm, but it's no use. Duck and hit the brakes the SoulKnight says. Locusts enter the car through the rear and materialize into Bloodsport. The car immediately drops low and scrapes the ground causing sparks. The top half of the demon's body is in the back seat while the lower half of his huge frame lay on the trunk of the car.

"Duck and Hit the brakes!"

Walker does just that. Both Bloodsport and Sir Good Knight fly out of the front windowless windshield. Neither has a chance to react. Sir Good Knight counted on the demon being thrown out of the car but didn't count on the demon colliding into him and taking him along for the ride! They hit the ground rolling. Walker was glad she was wearing her seatbelt. The Knight and the Assassin end up ten feet from each other, and twenty-five feet from the car. Both combatants are shook up. It takes them several seconds before climbing to their feet. Sir Good Knight realizes that he'd lost the Eden sword in the collision. The assassin gives him no opportunity to search for it as he launches his fiercest attack yet. He'd salvaged part of his blowing device. He blows into it sending two discs spinning, followed by six fire darts. The demon charges behind them twirling his trident with one hand! The Knight jumps backward into three handsprings then shoots directly up. He smashes through an eighth story window of a twenty-one-story building. Bloodsport's arsenal destroys the first-floor glass entrance of the same building. The alarm sounds. The demon separates into Locusts and pursues the Knight through the eighth story window.

Walker pops her trunk and jumps out of the car. She grabs her assault rifle, cocks it and straps on her vest. She heads for the now wide-open entrance of the building where the fight had advanced to, when something catches her eye. It's the Eden sword. She picks it up and runs into the building.

Meanwhile, at the cemetery, the area is now a crime scene. The fire department has put out the fires, and E.S.A.D. is there investigating. As they shine their lighting on the *alien body parts*, they are shocked to see the limbs, heads, and bodies quickly disintegrate. By the time they figure that it's the light that's causing it, and turn them off, only nine dismembered bodies are left. Col. Foster is approached by one of his team.

"Sir, we intercepted a police call about an alarm going off at an office building not far from here."

"Send a Body cycle unit to rendezvous with the police."

Meanwhile, the SoulKnight knew the Demon Assassin would not be far behind. He takes cover as soon as he finds a spot. The sound of beating locust wings fill the hall close to where the Knight is hidden. He carefully peaks from his corner and sees the menacing silhouette of Bloodsport. But something is different. The sound of beating Locust wings is still in the air. Sir Good Knight risks taking a closer look. He is surprised to see locusts flying around the demon. Normally, they only appear when Bloodsport is healing, or disassembling. Then, Bloodsport turns with his back to Sir Good Knight. Now the effect of the Knight's mysterious lifesaving eye blast is known. Two gaping holes, one through the upper right torso, and the other through the right shoulder have hobbled the demon assassin. Locusts hover around and fly through the wounds in attempts to make the assassin whole. But it is in vain. He is badly hurt.

Walker runs through the first floor looking for the elevator. But when she finds it, she reconsiders. Both Sir Good Knight and Bloodsport have the ability to smash through the elevator doors! *She'd be safer on the stairs.* She searches for the staircase and sees a series of cameras. Walker has an idea. She runs around until she finds a door marked *Security*. She kicks it in. There are dozens of monitors. Jessica closes the door and carefully watches them all. The very last monitor is broadcasting her show. Bloodsport is the featured star. She pulls out her phone and sends Sir Good Knight a message. He is now behind a water cooler. His two-way sounds. Bloodsport sends two spinning discs in the direction of the noise. Sir Good Knight runs down an intersecting hall and switches his two-way to vibrate. The discs rip through the water cooler splashing water through the hall. Sir Good Knight finds a closet and waits for the assassin to pass by. He grabs a mop and silently unscrews the mop head. Three minutes pass, and the Knight is still waiting on the demon. Something is wrong. His two-way vibrates. He takes it out of his pocket and reads the texts in order.

> 1) *I'm on the first floor in the security room watching you on the cameras. I have your sword, what should I do with it?*

But it was the second text that ended the suspense.

2) *He's setting the whole floor on fire with his darts*!

The sprinklers come on. Sir Good Knight hears them from inside of the closet. He slowly cracks the door to take a look. It creaks. Instantly, six darts are shot into the door and it begins to burn. The Knight dives out. Bloodsport separates into locusts and gives chase. Sir Good Knight runs around a corner and spots a door marked stairs. Still running he throws the mop stick in the air and thrusts both fists forward, pulverizing the door! He then throws his left hand backward and catches the stick as he crosses the threshold. He explodes down the stairs like flood waters. His momentum carries him past the seventh floor. The locusts still pursued. Sir Good Knight adjusts and smashes through the sixth-floor door. He turns to face his attacker, who is now only six feet behind. Sir Good Knight swings the mop stick back and forth through the swarm keeping them from forming Bloodsport. The swarm scatters in attempts to find space to form into the demon. Wasting no time, Sir Good Knight glides down a huge hall and finds himself in a cafeteria. He hides behind a wide-open door and sends a text to Walker.

The detective is closely watching the monitors as Sir Good Knight dashes for the cafeteria. No longer able to just stand by, Walker stands and turns to the door. Before she makes it out of the doorway, she stops. Her peripheral vision sees something. Police cars! The monitors she was facing, were for the front of the building. Four squad cars and two E.S.A.D. Agents had just arrived on the scene. She doesn't notice at the time, but her car is nowhere in sight. Walker's phone vibrates. Before reading the message, she realizes she can't allow the authorities to locate Sir Good Knight the same way that she had. Shooting the monitors would certainly be heard and draw too much attention. Then, she looks down at the Eden sword. She picks it up and swings it. It burns through the monitors. Walker is amazed at how easily it cuts through the metal and glass. Sparks shoot everywhere. Walker makes for the stairs. Just as she goes through the door leading to the staircase, a Body cycle unit sped into the building. Now two flights up, she is tiring. After all, she's carrying a rifle, and a huge sword! Walker reads her message. *Bring the sword to the fifth floor and hide*! She runs as fast as she can.

Bloodsport enters the cafeteria. Flames roar behind him. He passes by the door that the Knight is hidden behind. The two gaping holes made by the SoulKnight's surprising defense are still visible, and he's limping. The demon ransacks the place! He overturns tables, chairs, and garbage cans. Bloodsport approaches the serving area, twenty feet beyond Sir Good Knight. The Knight slides from behind the door and throws the mop stick strategically, so that it twirls sideways. As the assassin takes his next step, the mop stick flies between his legs and trips him to the ground. Once again Sir Good Knight makes for the stairs; he hopes Walker has gotten his message. He quickly glides down the next flight of stairs ahead of an ever-growing fire, and shoots through an opening fifth floor door colliding with Detective Jessica Walker. They both hit the ground. Before either can speak, the sound of beating locust wings is upon them. The sword is in reach. Sir Good Knight immediately grabs it and blocks Bloodsport's trident, which was coming down over them! Walker grabs her rifle and rolls away from the two titans. She aims at Bloodsport but can't get a clear shot with the two struggling. As she tries to maneuver to get a better shot, a large chunk of ceiling and debris fall directly on top of her! Walker is knocked to the ground. Piece by piece, flaming ceiling fragments continue to fall. The sixth floor, along with the two floors above it, are an inferno! The fifth floor was now feeling the effects. The two warriors clash. Bloodsport gets the upper hand and pins Sir Good Knight to the wall while gripping his neck. Locusts still buzz around trying to heal the demon assassin's wounds. As the Knight struggles to breathe, their weapons are interlocked. Walker emerges from under the ceiling fragments, and searches for her rifle. Unable to find it quick enough, she reaches for her handgun. Her movements catch the eye of the assassin. He turns his head taking his attention off of the Knight. It was just the distraction Sir Good Knight needed. He kicks both his feet to the body of Bloodsport jarring the demon's hand from around his neck. The same moment Sir Good Knight's feet touch the ground; he swings the Eden sword burning through the right arm of the assassin. The trident hits the ground with his arm. Before the locusts have a chance to act, Walker shoots the demon three times in the body. Already injured, the shots knock him back a few feet and to the ground. Walker runs to Sir Good Knight's side as he catches his breath. The locusts reform Bloodsport's arm and fill in his gunshot wounds. More fire and ceiling fragments rain down. The demon assassin opens his right hand and the trident flies into it. He stands. Sir Good Knight sees that the demon is breathing very hard. He labors to blow into his device. Two spinning discs shoot out. Walker backs to the wall dodging the first one as it smashes through a window, and Sir Good Knight destroys the second one.

Outside, the authorities await word from the E.S.A.D. unit that is currently searching the building. Firefighters had raised aerial ladders to contend with the sixth-floor fire now visible from the outside. All of a sudden, a metallic disc comes flying out of one of the lower story windows. They watch in awe, as it returns from whence it had come. The ranking officer on the scene immediately contacts the Body cycle unit inside and informs them of what has just happened on the fifth floor.

Still breathing heavily, Bloodsport charges! Sir Good Knight charges back. They clash. Holding the Eden sword with both hands, the Knight swings against the demon's trident, which he's holding with only one hand, causing his arm to go out wide exposing his wounds. In the same motion, Sir Good Knight spins in a tight left circle, at the end of which brings him closer to Bloodsport. He then shoves the Eden sword through the hole in the assassin's upper left torso. The Knight yanks the sword down diagonally burning through over half of the demon's body. Bloodsport staggers backward and drops his trident. Sir Good Knight remembers the scriptural words spoken to him by the 4th Corner, on a rooftop. (*To everything there is a season,* Sir Good Knight jumps up in the air and wields the Eden sword over his head, *...and a time to every purpose under the heaven: A time to be born, and a time to die; ...* The Knight swings the sword down and through his enemy's right shoulder and side, *... a time to plant, and a time to pluck up that which is planted; A TIME TO KILL, ...* Eccl. 3. 1-3, the right section of the demon's body slides to the floor. The Locusts do not attempt to heal him. Sir Good Knight swings the Eden sword at the waist of the demon assassin, burning clean through and separating the top half of his body from the bottom. Bloodsport's body shakes violently. The demon steps toward Sir Good Knight. As his heal touches the floor, his massive body falls apart. What remains of his torso, drops to the right and to the ground, followed by his legs. Bloodsport's mutilated body lay in four pieces. All four sections of his body glows bright red and then burst into locusts. They come together as one swarm and fly directly into one of the many fires that the ceiling fragments had set. Fire continues to fall. Sir Good Knight and Detective Jessica Walker seem oblivious, as they make eye contact and share a smile of relief. But victory is short lived, as a Body cycle unit shoots through the stairway door! Almost in sync, a Hover-form unit smashes through the windows. Sir Good Knight raises the Eden sword in defense. Walker pulls her badge out hoping to give the E.S.A.D. Agents pause. The attack never comes.

Chapter Seventeen:

Peaks and Valleys

Walker's jaw drops as she stares at the frozen E.S.A.D. Agents. "How did you do that?"

Sir Good Knight re-sheathes the Eden sword. I don't possess that type of power."

"Well who does?"

Looking up, "He does."

Walker looks up and flinches. The 4th Corner slowly descends to the floor. Frozen flames are his backdrop.

"The Father is well pleased."

"*His eyes are like yours!*"

"We're on the same side."

"But I thought you were the only one that …"

"It's complicated; turning to the 4th Corner, Though, I do have a question about the eyes."

"First, let us leave this place."

"Walker come join us."

The 4th Corner places a hand on each of their shoulders. Everything goes white; then the three of them are all standing on a rooftop. Walker steps back.

"What just happened? And who is he?"

"Take it easy, this is …"

"Guardian of the Fourth Corner of the Earth."

"I guess you can say, he's my liaison."

"Liaison to what?"

The Knight simply stares at the Detective.

Once again, the 4th Corner answered her question. "The Alpha, and the Omega, the beginning, and the end, the first and the last, The Almighty."

"Amen."

"I need a drink! *Oh, will I go to hell for that?*"

Meanwhile, the Body cycles land, and the Hover-forms fly in amidst a rainstorm of fire.

"Where'd they go?!"

They were just here they couldn't have just disappeared!"

"My career is over. There's probably a warrant out there with my name on it."

"You have nothing to fear, you were not seen."

"How can you be sure?"

"It was I who made sure."

"But they had to have seen my car."

Sir Good Knight stands on the edge of the building. "You mean that car?"

He motions to the alley. Walker walks over and looks down. She then looks up at Sir Good Knight, and then back at the 4th Corner.

"You have nothing to fear."

"Walker if you don't mind, I need to speak to the 4th Corner."

"Yeah no problem, she says sarcastically, I'll just wait over by the *air conditioners*".

She turns and walks in that direction. Her phone vibrates.

"This thing is brand new, why is it acting up?"

Walker looks at the screen of her phone. *I'll get in touch with you same time tomorrow. Be careful around your partner.*

She turns to face the Knight. "When did you ..."

Jessica Walker is alone. It is also darker than it was a few seconds ago. She turns back around and sees that the air conditioners are not where they were supposed to be. But what is most surprising is, the fact that her car is parked where the A.C.'s had just been! Unbeknownst to her, the 4th Corner had frozen her in time, and transported her into the alley. Walker looks up. As she does so, she somewhat realizes what must have happened; no matter how unbelievable it is. Walker gets in her car and tries to make sense of all that had happened tonight. It was a task that was easier said than done.

"My eyes! What was that?! What happened?"

"Your given energy was defending you."

"My given energy? It almost destroyed Bloodsport on its own! How do I use it?"

"You don't use it."

"Well, how do I control it?"

"You can no more control it than you can control your own heartbeat."

"Okay, how does it work?"

"That was the correct question. In the event that you are unable to defend yourself, your given energy will be your defense."

"A custom-made defense mechanism?"

"In a manner of speaking, yes."

"Whoa! And what about Bloodsport? Is he dead?"

"He is defeated."

"Good, one down." The SoulKnight bends at the waist and supports his weight on his knees. "Though, all it took to defeat him, it should count for more. He looks up; Is Pat after Noah's Ark?"

"He is."

"But why?"

"It is essential to his master's plan."

"How?"

"His goal is to make the Almighty a liar and take his place as God."

"*Okay*. Umm, how does that tie into him searching for the Ark?"

"I can tell you no more."

"Well am I on the right track? Am I going to the right mountain? Come on, you've gotta tell me that!"

While fading from sight, "You are indeed."

Thursday morning, London skips class. He wants to be early and show enthusiasm. The orientation is rather lengthy, but the people are pretty nice. The only thing that he doesn't welcome, are the immunizations. London hates needles.

Undercover E.S.A.D. Agent David Owens skips work as a Detective. For the first time in a long while, he is alongside his fellow Agents. They're in headquarters loading weapons and being briefed. They await pickup via military helicopters. They're heading to the nearest base, final destination… Tibet, Mt. Everest!

Walker sits at her desk at police headquarters. She gets situated and sips on her cup of coffee. After looking over a couple files, she takes a look around. Owens is not at his desk. In fact, he is nowhere in sight. Walker is worried. She reaches for her phone and begins to send a text, when she is interrupted.

"Detective, the Captain wants to see you in his office."

Jessica Walker enters the Captains office. "Close the door and have a seat Detective. Owens won't be with us today. His assistance has been requested by his former Captain. They need his input on an old case of his that's getting ready to be prosecuted. *Very convenient*, Walker thinks to herself. If you need any assistance in the field, I'll assign someone."

"Thanks Cap." Walker heads for the door"

"Detective. There is one other thing. She turns and sits back down. I've heard some rumors."

"Sir?"

"As crazy as it sounds, I'm hearing that you're in cahoots with one of the alien beings. Not only that, but they're also saying you're purposely hindering E.S.A.D.'s investigation efforts."

Walker breathes and tries to remain calm. "What am I supposedly doing?"

"They believe you have intimate knowledge and are unwilling to share. Some even believe that you may be aiding him in eluding the authorities."

"I assure you Captain; I am in no way interfering with their investigation."

"What of the other claim?"

"What proof do they have?"

He smiles. I haven't been shown any. But, let me say this; this is a very serious situation. We've never, *no one has ever,* had to contend with such a threat. You're good police. I can't afford to lose you, whether it be termination of life, or termination of employment. The mayor's even under pressure. Be careful Jessica."

"I will sir."

As Walker leaves the office, the Captain again smiles. *This is our city, go get him Jessica*!

Walker returns to her desk and sends the text she meant to send earlier. She informs Sir Good Knight of her partner's absence. Walker figures that Owens, with his team, are likely preparing to travel to Asia.

For the next four days, London has meetings with the Peace Corps, Walker keeps her eyes and ears open, Owens sets off for The Himalayas, and Pat readies his master's plan.

A lethally cold wind blows for a few minutes and then stops. Snow falls heavy and silent, undisturbed and pure. The natural white brightness hides a secret weapon; it is so cold that each flake would sting like a scorpion if it lands on skin. Visibility is no more than five feet in every direction. Everyone onboard is silent. There is no need for talk. The orders had been given, and the expectations are known. Each man is prepared. A red light comes on. Owens unbuckles his restraints and jumps to his feet. Two of his men open the doors. Wind and snow pour into the helicopter. The E.S.A.D. Agents jump out into the mountain atmosphere at an uncanny rhythmic pace. They have no concern for the turbulent weather. Each man is covered in a new age temperature resistant uniform that also allows for inner body temperature control and flexibility. Their eyes are covered with night vision goggles that also pick up heat signatures. Three helicopters in all drop a payload of E.S.A.D. Agents, ten each. As they parachute, they ready their weapons. The troop drops on a strategic location on the surface of Mt. Everest. Owens lands and immediately gives hand signals over the roar of the wind. Half the troop is sent to scout the mountain. The other half sets up base camp. This is all done without a single word. Their efficiency is remarkable. The peak is scouted and under surveillance along with camp being set all in a matter of forty-five minutes. The time is 12:01 am, two days before London makes travel to Iraq.

Early Tuesday morning, London is awakened by the phone ringing. He lifts it up and lets it fall back on the hook. London rolls out of bed and goes to the bathroom. He turns the shower on and waits for the water to heat up while sitting on the edge of the tub. Staring at the floor, London goes over his mental checklist. Twenty minutes later, he texts Walker telling her he was leaving. He knows she's up. She replies: *I still don't know how you're getting there, but if you need back-up, you know how to find me.* London laughs as he sends his reply: *Maybe next time*! Before they ended, Walker sent one last text, *Be careful*.

London and company hop in three mini-vans and head for the airport. Everything is going according to plan. London is trying to prepare himself for what he could possibly be facing once he makes it to Turkey. Dr. Bolden hands London his boarding pass. They walk toward security; London stops dead in his tracks. The Eden sword is in his bag!

"Come on London, laughing, as long as you don't have a bomb, or anthrax we'll be fine."

A security guard turns around upon hearing this. London hurries to catch up with Dr. Bolden. He feels light headed. What happens when they find the sword? It was too late to turn back. If he did, that he would not only squander his only way to get to Pat and the Ark, but he would most definitely be detained by security. He had to have faith. London reluctantly places his bag on the rollers. He walks through the arch. No problem. But he nervously looks back and watches as his bag travels through the conveyor belt and enters the x-ray machine. It slides out the other side without incident. London closes his eyes and exhales as he reaches for his bag.

"What's the problem?"

It's the same guard that had overheard the bomb and anthrax comments. London turns to face her. His behavior must have put up a red flag. He smiles.

London grips his bag; "I'm sorry, it's just that, I've never been outside of the country before. You would think I would first try somewhere safe and friendly, like Canada, or England. But I'm going to Iraq of all places! I'm starting to get nervous. I'm hoping I didn't make a mistake."

The explanation seems reasonable. It calms the suspicion that the guard was feeling.

She slowly nods. "Are you a God-fearing man?"

This surprises London. "I am."

"Stay prayerful and careful."

"I will, thank you."

As London rejoins the group, he realizes why the Eden sword hadn't set off the detector. He wanted to slap himself. Fire!

The sword was made of fire. It contains no metal at all! The Philadelphia chapter of the Peace Corps boards the plane; Final Destination: Iraq.

The trip that would never end was finally over! It was Wednesday morning. Twenty-One and a half-hours later, including a three hour layover in Germany, and the never ending trip was finally over. London looks out of his window. They've touched down at Baghdad International Airport. The military presence is great. You can't throw a rock without hitting either an armed soldier, a tank, a jeep, or a helicopter! The group exits the plane and is immediately met by American soldiers in Hum V's. The group retrieves the rest of their bags from the cargo section of the plane and is taken to the military camp that is going to be their home in Iraq. Each group member is given an emergency pack that includes: an Arabic to English translator, a fully charged cell phone (important numbers already loaded), water, a compass, and a map. The map is of most importance to London, he studies it and sees that the camp isn't too far from the border with Turkey. At least not for him. London formulates his plan.

The group eats dinner together in a large tent in the middle of camp. Afterwards, there's a brief meeting detailing tomorrow's event. Just before being dismissed the group is reassured of their safety by being introduced to the commanding officer of the U.S. Army platoon in charge of their security.

Dr. Bolden leans over toward London. "I bet you feel better now, huh?"

The Professor had obviously overheard London's conversation with the airport security guard. "Oh yeah, definitely."

London knows this would make his escape that much more difficult.

As the night came to an end, London and the rest of the Peace Corp retire to their barracks. The long travel and jetting is more effective than a tranquilizer. All are in deep REM sleep. All except for the young man with the hidden agenda. Although his roommates were out like lights, London pretends to be asleep for thirty minutes in order to familiarize himself with the security patrols. He takes one of his bags to the bathroom stall and changes into his battle gear. London knew that the weather in the desert drastically changed at night, so he was prepared. He suited up in an all-black hooded sweat suit and laced up a pair of durable black work boots. He then pulled out a tube of black face paint and camouflaged his face with a series of random lines. Next, he slipped on a pair of black leather gloves. Last was the Eden sword.

An armed foot patrol walks by the barracks. A dark figure watches closely from the rooftop. Once they pass, the figure runs across the rooftop and dives flying off into a black abyss. Thirty seconds later, Sir Good Knight's eyes come alive, he had covered a distance over 250 yards! He landed and continued his rooftop dive and glide dance over the desert floor.

Minutes later, the SoulKnight kneels down staring directly at the border, and the military obstacle guarding it. He debates with himself on how to cross it. Going over the top would seem best, but he's sure they have radar and other such technology. Digging is out of the question, and …

"Allow me to be of some assistance."

Sir Good Knight draws the Eden sword and spins around! It was the 4th Corner.

"Had those soldiers been looking in this direction, they wouldn't have had any difficulty spotting your burning red sword in the middle of nothingness."

The SoulKnight quickly conceals his sword "I'm glad to see you."

"I have come to keep a promise made."

"Promise, what promise?"

"I expressed anger toward you, And I gave my word, I am here to make amends. He points, mark that path in your memory."

He was pointing at an area between a group of tanks. There were also electric barbed wire fences.

"Have you marked it?"

"Yes, you're going to freeze them, right?"

"Stand back."

The 4th Corner's large and powerful wings appear. He bends slightly forward and beats them toward the desert floor. Clouds of sand explode up, out, and forward.

A host of soldiers guard the border. "What the... *a sandstorm*! Take cover!" The soldiers scatter.

The 4th Corner's sandstorm quickly engulfs the border. Sir Good Knight gazes in amazement. The size of the storm is remarkable.

"That is unbelievable. How did you come up with...? (he looks around)."

The 4th Corner was no longer there. The Knight instantly realizes what he is supposed to do. He holds his breath and runs as fast as he can to catch up with the rapidly moving cloud of sand. He runs toward the path that he'd marked in his memory. He holds his breath just before diving into a storm of blindness. He prays that his memory hasn't failed him. Even though the sand is blinding enough, Sir Good Knight squeezes his eyes shut. He leaves all to memory. He hops over fences, dodges parked tanks, and glides. Over a minute had passed, his lungs are at their limit. He needs to breathe. His eyes are still closed, so he doesn't know whether he's cleared the sandstorm or not. But there is no choice, he exhales and crashes to the desert floor. He takes a deep breath.

The air is clear. He opens his eyes. The sky above is also clear. The Knight looks back. A wall of sand threatens to overtake him. He jumps up into his diving dance to once again outrun the storm. It takes another two minutes before it finally calms.

Sir Good Knight is now well past the border, and very much in the country of Turkey. He pulls out the map and compass to search for his current location. He figures he's no more than thirty minutes from the foot of the mountains of Ararat. A half hour later, he is looking up at the very mountains that brought him to Turkey. This was it. The Knight looks up at his destination. He can feel the mountain top's promise to be a confrontation of epic proportions. He takes a moment to empty the sand out of his clothes and boots. He then says a quick prayer before effortlessly gliding up the side of Ararat. He stops twenty feet from the summit to listen. The only sound is wind. Still, the Knight decides not to take the chance of exposing himself on the summit unprepared. He jumps up with the Eden sword in hand, purposely landing low with the sword up. He is greeted by a cold wind and silence. The Knight scans the surface looking for movement. He listens some more, nothing. He glides along the area focused. The air is thin and frigid. Then, a faint but familiar sound catches his ear. Sir Good Knight dives in the direction of the noise. It's a voice. Pat's voice.

Meanwhile on Mt. Everest:

This was what Agent Owens desperately wanted. An opportunity to make a significant difference. Not that he wanted to be the big man, he just knew he had more to offer. And here it was, he is Field commander on E.S.A.D.'s most important and covert mission to date. The entire country, and the world for that matter, have anxiously awaited word of any progress the newly formed agency makes ever since The President announced their formation. David Owens was ready.

The weather is unusually calm on Mt. Everest. It allows E.S.A.D. to more freely investigate. Owens steps outside of the shelter erected for base camp. He is able to look around as easily as if he'd been standing on someone's porch. It is cold but clear, no snow, no wind. Agents are spread across the mountain armed with every piece of high-tech search equipment that exists. They report their findings back to base camp every fifteen minutes.

A couple of days pass without a single incident. Owens is once again outside of his shelter. He raises his portable radio to check with the units currently deployed, when he hears voices. He looks around. The voices were coming from behind a half ice, half boulder protrusion thirty feet to the left of camp. He draws his sidearm and silently approaches. One of his search units returning to camp notices him. He motions for them to join him. They too draw weapons. They slowly advance around the ice rock, then Owens motions to stop. They listen.

"... *a big waste of time*! We're the only one's dumb enough to be all the way up here looking for alien fugitives that are obviously still in Philly! I mean come on man; we've searched this whole mountain!"

"We should've known that any intelligence gathered by Owens would be unreliable. What a joke. He needs to stick to babysitting!" Says a second voice.

Owens holsters his weapon. The Agents with him do the same. They round the ice rock and confront another search unit.

They stand at attention upon seeing their commanding officer staring them down. The same person they were just dogging!

"It appears the work that you two have been given has not been adequate. You can now relieve this unit!"

"Commander Owens, we didn't mean… "

"That's an order!"

As the two units walked off, Owens clenched his teeth. He closes his eyes and exhales. He knew some of his men were getting anxious, but he didn't realize he was in their crosshairs.

Mt. Ararat:

Sir Good Knight kneels low staring down from a cliff of the Ararat Mountain. No more than twenty-five feet below was the target of his international manhunt. Pat stood triumphantly with his arms folded on his chest. He was not alone. There are dozens of shadow walkers. Some are digging, and others are pulling ropes and chains. The Knight's heart skips a beat when he sees what the ropes and chains are tied to. It looked like a giant wooden chest. It was dark in color, but not quite black. At the top there is an opening that seems to serve as a window. He was staring dead at a miracle; Noah's Ark! Even though he knew Pat was there to find it, he didn't actually expect him too. So, neither could be expect that actually seeing it would affect him so. The moment is surreal. The SoulKnight takes a deep breath before springing into the air. He converts his leap into a swan dive unsheathing the Eden sword. His anger grows as he descends.

How dare he disturb the resting place of the Ark! He isn't even worthy to touch it, and here he is attempting to steal it!

The Knight is unseen until he burns his sword through several of the ropes and chains before touching the ground. By the time Pat knew what was happening, The Knight had acrobatically burned through the rest. The shadow walkers charged swinging the chains, that they were just seconds ago pulling. Sir Good Knight glides over their attack. His new target is Pat. Pat's true form reveals itself. He stands his ground. The Knight's emotions are raging! He can barely keep from hollering out. He grits his teeth and tightens his grip around the halt of the sword. He is much too anxious, and he's been taught better. *Crash!* The Knight's plans to pounce on Pat come to a screeching halt. He is violently tackled out of the air; By none other than Dozorn. They hit the side of a rock face with the force of a wrecking ball. Debris is sent flying. Dozorn rolls down the rock face while Sir Good Knight is encased in a small crater. The Eden sword is far from his hand protruding handle up from a nearby boulder. He sees Shadow walkers advancing toward him. The Knight had not yet caught his breath but was able to reach into his pocket. Just before the creatures can attack, he pulls something out of his pocket. He snaps it. It was a flare. The closest shadow walkers scream in pain as the light from the flare disintegrates body parts. The remaining shadow walkers stop in their tracks. Sir Good Knight, now fully recovered, emerges from the hole holding the flare out in front of him. The demons run and dive into shadows like rat holes. He throws the flare in their direction and jumps down. He pulls out another one and snaps it. There's no sign of Pat or Dozorn. But even more troubling, there is no sign of the Ark. He throws the second flare toward the darkest area of the mountain top then pulls out a third one snaps it and does the same. The flares create a rather wide perimeter of light. This kept any and all shadow walkers at bay. Sir Good Knight catches sight of the Eden sword slowly burning through a boulder. He decides to wait to retrieve it, especially since it is outside of the perimeter of the flares. The Knight can feel the presence of evil around him. He listens to the air; his sensitive ears give proof to what he is feeling. There's a low grinding noise. The Knight knew exactly what the sound was. He digs his hands in the ground and grabs two handfuls of rocks. The Knight then crosses his arms, and then quickly extends them throwing the rocks so that they spread wide. Some of the rocks smack against boulders on the right. Some smack against boulders straight ahead and ricochet. But the sound of rocks making contact on the left, came much later. Sir Good Knight digs another handful of rocks out of the ground and drills them at the mountain face on the left. The rocks pass through and disappear. Then, several feet beyond what appeared to be solid, the rocks finally made contact with a rock surface. The Knight charges at the image, but before he can reach it, the illusion shakes. Dozorn explodes out of the illusion. Sir Good Knight is just able to dodge him. The beast slams all six limbs into the ground to stop his momentum. He slides fifteen feet kicking up snow and a thick cloud of dust. The Knight regains his balance and shoots through the image of stone. The Ark is now almost completely exposed. But the sight that gives him pause, is the dozens of *men,* now pulling the Ark clear.

None of the men are Pat. Dozorn charged again. Sir Good Knight turns to face him, gearing up to once again elude the blue beast with his agility. Dozorn stops his approach. The beast paces back and forth. It was then that Sir Good Knight thought of the first time he'd encountered the six-legged demon. The woodland area as a child, Dozorn displayed the same behavior when the 4th Corner had appeared. It was respect. He now regarded the Knight as a combatant he could no longer underestimate. Dozorn was contemplating his options. Sir Good Knight didn't have time for a chess match; And frankly, he wasn't interested in seeing what kind of attack the beast would come up with! He strikes the ground with both fists and simultaneously jumps up into an Arabian double front somersault. The ground explodes and swallows the beast whole. Rock fragments rain down and bury the demon. When the Knight lands, several of the men pulling the Ark run straight for him. He leaps into a perfect spinning back kick. To his surprise, his foot passes completely through the first attacker's head. The force of the misplaced kick sends him tumbling to the ground; Another illusion, which means Pat is still on the mountain. The men jump on Sir Good Knight. They scratch, claw, and even bite him. Shadow walkers! The Knight struggles to fight them off.

He is greatly outnumbered; Then there is a loud crash. Dozorn had smashed his way out of his temporary grave. The demons in disguise all look toward the noise. Sir Good Knight seizes the moment. Spinning in a circle, he sweeps his attackers off of their feet. He then dives and glides over them, toward the Ark. He lands and wishes he had gone back for the Eden sword. The rest of the disguised demons pulling the Ark rush the SoulKnight, Dozorn and the others charge from the rear. All the while a distant noise grew louder.

"Wait... wait... not yet... Now!"

Sir Good Knight reaches in his pocket, hops up, spreads his arms out wide, and spins rapidly. The sound of his last flare snapping is lost in the noise from some unknown source. The men/demons disintegrate two and three at a time. By the time Sir Good Knight lands, He and Dozorn stand alone, facing one another. The Knight throws the flare toward the Ark. There is still no sign of Pat. The two combatants circle and size each other up. The once distant noise is now all around. The wind is stronger than before. Shots ring out! Sir Good Knight hits the ground and rolls away for cover. The shooting stops. He looks up from behind a rock. A helicopter-like aircraft hovers over the Ark. Soldiers on ropes descend on the Ark. Chains are being lowered from the helicopter, and the soldiers attach them to the ancient vessel. *What was going on*? The Knight creeps to his feet, Dozorn is nowhere in sight. Again, Shots are fired. But this time, they come from ground level. Several soldiers are apparently assigned to gun him down. The Knight ducks back behind a rock face. He can hear the steps of the real men running toward him. It would be impossible to consistently dodge this many automatic weapons. Sir Good Knight runs and glides. He needs the sword! Remembering the exact place he'd seen the sword. The Knight jumps on top of the boulder that held the sword. The entire blade of fire rests inside of the rock. All that shows is the halt. Sir Good Knight triumphantly pulls the Eden sword from its prison in a scene that is reminiscent of King Arthur. But there is none to see. His pursuers had broken off their attack and ran back to the helicopter. Now it's the Knight who gives chase. The soldiers have what seems to be a safe lead, but the SoulKnight gains quickly. As he closes the gap, he is shocked to see that there are now three helicopter-like aircrafts with chains attached to the Ark. They were lifting it off of the mountain! The soldiers that Sir Good Knight was chasing, are now climbing the chains in hopes to rejoin the others. The Knight is in range and poised to attack. The soldiers on the helicopters fire at Sir Good Knight to assist their comrades. They find him to be a very hard target! The Ark is now completely in the air and moving away from the mountain. Sir Good Knight dives off the edge of the mountain. He can see inside of one of the helicopters. Pat stood staring back at him. He had changed his clothes, but why? He was wearing a military uniform like that of the soldiers. Then, out of nowhere, Dozorn also dives off of the mountain cliff, but from a different angle. The Knight hears him rushing through the air, and twists to meet the beast, while swinging the Eden sword. It burns through the beast's right arm. However, this does nothing to stop the demon's momentum. He collides into the Knight knocking the wind out of him. Sir Good Knight falls rapidly, unable to hold his breath. A sharp protrusion in the side of the mountain rapidly approaches. The Knight is spinning out of control and still can't breathe.

"Don't panic. Focus, focus."

He has an idea, at the top of every spin, he can see the sky, so on his next spin, he throws the Eden sword straight up in the air.

He then extends both arms and legs outward, effectively slowing his tumble and gaining control. Seconds before impact, Sir Good Knight is able to steer himself fists first into the protrusion. There's a great explosion! The Knight comes to a rolling stop inside of a cave that seconds ago didn't exist. He gasps as his lungs finally unlock. After a few deep breaths, The Knight runs and glides out of the newly formed cave. As soon as Sir Good Knight is in the open, he listens for the sound of the Eden sword cutting through the air. It only takes a moment. The Knight rapidly exhales to catch up to the now plummeting sword. A few seconds later, he is grabbing the sword by the halt as the blade of fire points toward the ground. He then flips once, just twelve feet from the ground, and holds his breath bringing his enormous momentum to a complete stop! The wind that his mountain top dive had created took about two seconds to reach the now stationary Knight. It blows around and through his clothes with a strong gust. Sir Good Knight then exhales and effortlessly touches his feet to the ground. He immediately turns to stare up in the direction of the now very out of range Ark. His heart drops to the bottom of his chest, and Sir Good Knight drops to his knees. The Knight looks up into the clouds.

"I have failed you my Lord!"

"*I have… failed.*" He bows his head in shame.

Chapter Eighteen:

The Dark Author's Revelation

The burn of Sir Good Knight's water-like eyes fade. London crumbles at the bottom of Ararat. The pain of failing God is overwhelming!

"WHY DOES THOU LAMENT?"

London certainly knew the voice that spoke. He raises his head.

"Lord, forgive me; For I have lost the very Ark that you gave Noah. I was responsible, it was my watch."

"RISE MY SON."

"Father I …"

"ARISE! MY SON. London stands. THE BATTLE… IS INDEED LOST. BUT IN THE MIDST THEREOF, ARE VICTORIES STILL TO BE WON."

"But Lord, I still don't know why the Dark Author wants the Ark. And how do I get it back?" He waits for a response.

"Are you still there Lord?"

London begins to pace.

"There are victories still to be won? He must mean learning from defeat, the reason why I failed."

He continues to pace.

"Dozorn, Shadow walkers, Pat, soldiers… I need an army!"

London stops cold in his tracks.

"An army. A war can't be fought alone. I need a team. Walker! It's time to make our partnership official. And maybe even the 4th Corner. *Maybe*."

London re-sheaths the Eden sword, then considers more of what the Lord had said.

"*Victories*, that's plural. There's more, I'm missing something. *In the midst thereof, are victories still to be won*. What am I missing Lord? *The battle, is indeed lost, but in the midst thereof...* (He understood). In the midst of the battle! He wants me to go back atop the mountain. My answers are there."

London's eyes set ablaze and shimmered blue. Sir Good Knight quickly scaled the mountain. As he reached the top, he wondered what he would find. He cautiously looks around but has no idea what he's looking for. A moment later he hears a soft noise. It stops as abruptly as it began. The SoulKnight slowly scans the snow-covered mountain top. He hears it again. It's a voice. The Knight reaches for the Eden sword as he heads in the direction of the voice. The voice gets louder. He looks down. There, almost completely buried in the snow is a two-way radio. Sir Good Knight's mind allows him to picture a soldier knocking it off of his equipment while throwing his weapon over his shoulder to climb. He picks it up.

"Victories."

Meanwhile on Mt. Everest:

"Commander Owens, Col. Foster is on the comm. For you."

Owens knew what the Col. Wanted; results. He wanted answers, and he wanted them now.

"Owens here."

"Commander, what news do you have?"

"All is well Col. Base camp is up and running, units are on patrol and the weather is calm and clear. It won't be long before we find something."

"Find something? Commander am I to gather that in almost 72 hours you have nothing?"

"Sir, as I stated before, I have no specific intelligence as to when the rendezvous will take place. My information is limited to this location and a seven-day window. The week is young Col. I am confident that … "

"Very well Commander. But keep in mind that we are spread incredibly thin. Your mission needs to bear fruit. Am I making myself clear Commander Owens?"

"Yes sir, very clear sir."

"You have until Saturday evening, Foster out."

Owens takes a deep breath. If this mission fails, he'll be held directly responsible. Not only was he in command, but the mission was green lighted based on his recommendation. It was also costing tons of tax dollars. The pressure was beginning to mount as high as Everest itself.

Mt. Ararat:

Sir Good Knight headed back to the Turkey and Iraq border. He performs his dive and glide dance at top speed. All the while he listens to the chatter on the two-way radio. It proves to be a wealth of knowledge. He is finally given the answer to his most burning question.

"Victory is at hand! The Ark is ours."

The Knight knew the voice. It was Pat. Then a second voice, Dozorn. But how? The beast was defeated and fell to his death!

"Too long have we been kept in the dark. Says the beast. What are we to do with Noah's ancient Ark?"

"Alas mighty Dozorn; hear the Dark Author's revelation. We have all heard and read that God cannot and will not tell a lie. It is written in the scriptures. It has also been said that before he will allow himself to tell a lie, he would sooner destroy himself! Considering God's arrogance, the Dark Author believes this to be true. So, we will make him a liar for all to witness. Mighty Dozorn, you ask why Noah's ancient Ark. The answer; it is the only thing in creation, that could withstand the great flood. That remains true to this day; and in being so, we will all board it as we once again flood the Earth!"

There is great commotion. A third voice speaks.

"How can we flood the Earth?"

"The Dark one has discovered how to once again open the windows of Heaven to pour an endless rain. And not only that, but we have also found the secret to once again break up the fountains of the great deep as spoken of in the Genesis (Gen. 7:11). As you all know, one of God's most memorable promises, is to never again destroy the Earth with water. We will destroy this very promise! The rainbow will disappear from the sky, and God will effectively become a liar. He will be forced to eradicate himself, and the Dark Author will reign supreme!"

There is pandemonium. Sir Good Knight has to turn down the volume on the radio. It is apparent that although Pat is on board one helicopter, he is communicating with the other two. *Flood the Earth*? Sir Good Knight is anxious to hear more. After the noise and commotion finally calms, The Knight turns the volume back up. Upon doing this, he sees that he's approaching the border of Iraq. He stops his dive and glide dance and hunkers down 150 yards from the heavily guarded border. Pat continued.

"Only two steps remain. We will travel to Alaska. Our purpose... the Aurora Borealis."

The Northern lights? Sir Good Knight is perplexed.

"In two days, the Aurora will burn at the height of its brilliance. The rain will fall! Until then, we will remain hidden and await time."

Sir Good Knight waits for another three minutes to be sure that there is no more information to learn. Once he is convinced, he tucks the radio away and focuses on the border. The sun had

435

not yet come up. Although his energy is restored, he does not want to engage the troops. He is confident that he would be victorious, but the fall out would be considerable. He has accepted that the 4th Corner is not going to assist him this time. He has to come up with his own creative solution. His biggest obstacle is time. The sun will be rising soon. Sir Good Knight decides to take his chances slipping through their defenses. He carefully makes his way within striking distance of the border. When he's convinced that no attention is aimed in his direction, the Knight holds his breath and explodes over the sand! He flips over the first fence and exhales just enough until he lays horizontally, face two inches from the ground, in midair. A tank is parked only fifteen feet away. Sir Good Knight reaches forward placing his hands on the ground, body still elevated, and pulls himself as if he were lying on a skateboard. He stops next to the tank and exhales. The Knight crouches low. Footsteps approach. An armed guard walks right past him. Not far off stood a second fence. This one with electric barbed wire. This was the direction he needed to go. But between him and the fence were several more armed guards. More voices approach. Guards are about to round the tank. The Knight knows he won't again go unseen; especially by several guards at once.

Still low, he walks around the opposite side of the tank, all the while watching his every angle. Once he makes it around, he now finds himself six feet behind three soldiers walking in the same direction. No one sees him. He now has a somewhat clear path to the fence. He takes off. His plan is to simply hop over it and the soldiers on the other side with their backs facing him. Then his eye catches sight of another tank on the left. The sight of it while running makes him think of the nights he used to sneak out of his dorm, run down the street and jump off of the mailbox. The Knight changes course and springs off of the tank! This time he makes sure to hold his breath right before his foot lands, so as not to make a sound. The moment his foot landed, he catapulted silently away. On the other side of the tank stood four armed soldiers who would've seen the Knight had he hopped over the fence from the angle that he had first planned.

It wasn't long before Sir Good Knight made it back to barracks. Sneaking into camp was much easier than sneaking across a guarded border. London packed away his battle gear and quietly got back into bed. But his sleep was hindered by one thought. *How in the world was he going to get to Alaska from Iraq? And in two days no less.*

Thursday morning, Owens stands on a cliff atop Mt. Everest. He stares through a pair of heat sensitive binoculars scanning the mountain side. There's a subtle hum in the distance. He turns his attention to the sky and readjusts the binoculars. Some type of aircraft is approaching. Owens sprints at full speed! He yells on his communicator, *Omega Dawn all hands to base camp, Omega Dawn!* Owens pulls his laser sight rifle off of his shoulder and joins his men, who were on hover-forms outside of the shelter of base camp. The Agents patrolling the mountain knew what was expected of them. In the event of Omega Dawn, they were to hide around the perimeter of the target and wait to ambush. As the aircraft grows closer, Owens realizes that the ship is much larger than he had anticipated.

"This is it men. No retreat, no surrender!"

"That has to be the mother ship! Commander we're going to need reinforcements."

An enormous saucer shaped aircraft comes to a hovering stop no more than one hundred feet from base camp. Owens walks toward the ship. His men cock and aim their weapons to cover him.

"Commander Owens, what are you doing?"

Owens doesn't respond. A door in the middle of the ship's floor slides open and stairs extend to ground level. Col. Foster walks down the stairs. Owens is not surprised. Nor is he amused. Unlike his men, he knew of the prototype Saucer craft. Upon seeing Col. Foster, Owens' men stand down. They're confused.

"Commander."

"Col. Owens salutes. Sir have you brought reinforcements?"

"No. We're here to take you all back."

"But sir, you gave us until Saturday."

"Yes, I did. But unfortunately, Gen. Morris saw things differently."

Owens is furious.

"Sir with all due respect, how can we be expected to apprehend these beings, if we aren't given the proper opportunity?!"

"Commander Owens ... "

"Who's going to take the blame when we miss this rendezvous? We owe the general public, all of whom depend on our protection, and trust us with their tax dollars. What will the General ... "

"*COMMANDER OWENS!* That is enough. Have your men strip the mountain and load the Saucer craft. That's an order!"

Owens takes a deep breath. He had just yelled and second guessed his superior officer. And he had done all of this in the sight of a host of E.S.A.D. Agents. Owens turns around and calmly walks toward his men. They'd pretty much seen and heard everything. With swallowed pride, Owens gives the order.

Earlier the same morning, London and company were woken up at 6:30am, much to London's chagrin.

"Mr. Bishop after you've gotten dressed, I need to see you in the mess hall."

London didn't know quite what to think. They couldn't know of his overnight exploits; could they? But why is he the only one being singled out? Maybe it's because he's the new guy. He pondered all of this as he showered and got dressed. Twenty minutes later, London walked into the mess hall.

"London come in, please have a seat. London, what I'm about to say, is going to seem unfair. It seems that we've made a mistake. On last night, London's heart stops, we made the discovery. The mistake directly involves you."

"What kind of mistake?"

"We miscalculated our budget. We were under the impression that we had enough remaining to cover the cost of fifteen relief workers. But as it turns out, we only have enough for fourteen. We tried to rearrange as much of our spending and research as possible to compensate, but it wasn't enough. London, what I'm trying to say is, we're going to have to send you back. I don't know how this happened, but I take full responsibility. If it were up to… "

London had to fight hard to restrain his smile. He wanted to jump out of his chair and shout, but he was able to manage a solemn look.

"… me, Listen London, I promise I'll make it up to you. I'll … "

"It's not your fault Dr. Bolden. I still appreciate the opportunity that you've given me. How many civilians can say that they've been to visit our troops abroad, let alone in Iraq. I feel fortunate … "

For the next thirty minutes, Dr. Bolden found different ways to apologize, and London kept assuring him that it was okay. When London returned to the barracks and informed his colleagues of the new developments, it was déjà vu. London ate breakfast with everyone and within 2 ½ hours, he was in the air. Although he was forced to fly in a cargo plane, London was finally able to smile. He unpacked the two-way radio he'd found and turned it on for the entire flight. He was seated in the rear of the plane. It was impossible for the pilots to hear. London propped his jacket like a pillow and laid back. Before long he was asleep. He had a long trip home.

Chapter Nineteen:

Confrontation

Friday morning. It had been seven days since Detective

Jessica Walker had seen Sir Good Knight. She'd talked to him the

morning he'd left for Turkey, via Iraq, but it was very brief. She

knew that he was more than capable of taking care of himself, but

she couldn't help but worry a little. However, she did find time to

consider a few other things. One being her supposed to be partner,

who turned out to be an undercover E.S.A.D. Agent. Walker had

no idea that Owens had been manipulating her. She felt like a

victim. Was he that good, or was she just off of her game? After

all, she was dealing with unprecedented circumstances. The other

thought that she just couldn't shake, was what Sir Good Knight had

said to her. Not only the part about him being human, and being

sent by God, but more so the question that he had posed to her.

Why was it so much easier to accept Sir Good Knight and his foes

as aliens? Before recent events, most people would probably

consider an extra-terrestrial invasion farfetched and improbable, including Walker. At the same time the vast majority of the world's population believes in the existence of God, and his power. Walker was never a religious person. She was practical. She always believed that everything has an explanation, and she controlled her own fate. Destiny was a myth. Walker believed that numbers didn't lie. She's a detective for crying out loud! Therein lied her dilemma. Could so many people be wrong? She covers her eyes and sighs, before refocusing on her caseload.

A couple hours pass. Walker's phone vibrates. She pulls it out and reads the message. *Be home in about two hours. Need a favor. I have to get to Alaska ASAP! I'll explain later, thanks*!

"Alaska?!"

Thursday evening, Owens and company were back in half the time that it should've taken them; well before London, thanks to state-of-the-art technology. Upon landing, Col. Foster assembles everyone.

"Listen up. Each of you need to get as much rest tonight as possible. Unfortunately, we're on our own for tomorrow."

"What do you mean Sir," an Agent asks.

"I would love to give you all a day off, and you deserve it, but the fact is we're not at full strength."

Not at full strength? Owens is confused. The rest of the men moan and groan as they exit the aircraft. Owens' team was the only one out on a mission. Now that they've returned, why wouldn't E.S.A.D. be at full strength? He needed to know more. The Saucer craft sat in a wide-open field behind E.S.A.D. headquarters. Owens stays out of sight as his men rush off to get some rest. When he is sure all his men are off the Saucer craft, he makes his way to the cockpit /control room. The door is open. He can hear Col. Foster.

"With all due respect General, the best intelligence we have, pointed to Mt. Everest. I don't feel we gave our men enough time to… Sir, forgive me for asking, but how do you know that they had bad Intel?"

This upset Owens. He was the one on the inside, how could they second guess him?!

"I understand sir. One last question sir, how long will we be without the rest of the men? Fairbanks? But Sir what's happening in Alaska?"

Owens stretches to hear more, while at the same time trying to keep from being seen. As he does this, he stretches a little too far and stumbles. Although he only makes a subtle noise and is still able to keep from being seen, he is sure that Col. Foster has heard him. As if to confirm his suspicion, Foster quickly changes his tone and subject.

"That's as much of an update as I have now, General. I'll be sure to ..."

Owens has to react. He can't let himself be caught spying. He knocks on the door.

Col. Foster looks to the door. "... Contact you immediately with any updates. Thank you, sir, Foster out. Come in Commander."

Owens enters at attention and salutes. "At ease Commander. I was expecting you."

"Sir, I came to apologize for my behavior on the mountain. I was incredibly insubordinate. I assure you that it was totally out of character, and nothing like that will ever happen again. I accept whatever consequence you deem necessary."

"Have a seat Owens. I understand your anger. I probably would've reacted in much the same way. You feel betrayed. He sighs. Between you and I, I too question the General's decision. But soldiers follow orders. We don't have to agree with the orders."

"Yes sir. Col, may I ask a question?"

"What is it?"

"What could possibly be so important, that it would justify taking my squad and I off the mountain prematurely, and at the same time sending a team large enough to leave us vulnerable, on some ghost mission?"

"I have yet to be fully briefed."

"Col. May I ask a favor of …?"

"No Commander. Foster stands. I will not report to you once I've learned more! You will be told what you will be told and that is all."

"Sir, I would never ask such a thing. I beg your apologies for giving you that impression. I was going to ask if you could speak to the General on my behalf?"

"Let's get one thing clear, even though I do understand your anger, the only thing you need to be concerned about is making damn sure that you never again even dream of such audacity; to speak to a commanding officer in the manner in which you dared! Especially, not me. Do you get me?"

"Yes sir."

"Dismissed."

Owens felt no animosity toward the Col. as he exited the Saucer craft. Foster was a military man through and through. He believed in the system. The same system that Owens was now losing faith in. He decides to get some sleep. It has been a long day, and tomorrow will likely be worse.

It was now early Friday afternoon. Owens had overslept. He sits up and walks to the bathroom. He turns the shower on then turns to face the mirror. An envelope is taped to it, his name is written on it. *Agent Owens;* It was clear. He is no longer a Commander. He takes it down and opens it. Inside are orders to resume his surveillance of Detective Jessica Walker. Ironically, she's the first person he intended on seeing.

An hour later Owens walks into the police station silently searching for his partner. He hopes to see her before she see him. She has to be at least a little suspicious of him. After all, he did abruptly disappear without as much as a hint to his partner. He doesn't see her anywhere. Good. He quickly walks to the Captain's door and lightly knocks. He sticks his head in.

"Detective Owens come in. Are you just visiting us today or do you plan on doing some police work?"

"I'm back on duty sir, he laughs; back on the job. I was looking for Walker. Is she in today?"

"Yeah she's around here somewhere. She's been steady at work picking up the slack while you were out. I'm sure she'll be glad to see you."

Walker was trying to find a way to Alaska, and track down leads on a case, all without arousing any suspicion. It was hard work. In fact, she'd been steady multitasking while her bookend partners were playing plant the flag on separate mountains. She needed to release some tension. The best way she knew to do that, was to let off a few shots. Walker put everything on hold and got on the elevator. She got off on the lowest level, the shooting gallery. After signing in, she puts her goggles and headphones on. Walker wastes no time, she squeezes off round after round into the torso of her target. Her aim is impeccable. Three clips later Walker feels renewed. She gets back on the elevator and heads back upstairs. Walker sits down at her desk and takes a deep breath before diving back into the depths of multitasking. Then …

"How've you been?"

Walker slowly turns in her chair to face none other than Detective David Owens, undercover E.S.A.D. Agent.

"I've been just fine, how about you?"

"I know I should've come to you about having to leave, I apologize for that. You should've heard it from your partner not your Captain."

Walker turns her chair back around, "Yeah."

Owens walks around to the front of Walker's desk. He whispers.

"Jessica, I need to talk to you. It's urgent."

Walker looks up. This was the first time Owens had ever used her first name.

"Well, what's this all about *David*?"

"It's a highly sensitive matter. I would rather go someplace else to discuss it. I told the Captain that I would like to check out an old lead and could use your help. Will you please come?"

Walker just stares. She can't believe his audacity! What are his orders?

"Please Jessica."

"Come with you where?"

"Away from ears."

Walker considers it. She decides to go. She'd imagined confronting Owens since the day she found out that he'd been playing her. This was an opportunity to work off some tension right at the source!

"Alright, I'll go. But I'm driving. I know just the place. Follow me."

Walker drives for twenty minutes on the highway before getting off at an old weigh station. She stops the car and jumps out. Owens pulls up. She motions for him to let his window down. He presses the button and turns the car off. Walker draws her Glock!

"Walker, what the ...!"

"Don't move!"

"What are you doing?"

"I'll ask the questions; you just concentrate on the answers! Now give me your pistol, and don't be slick *David*, handle first. He complies. Good, now hand over your radio, and keys. Okay now open your door. Cuff yourself to the window frame."

"Have you lost your mind?"

Walker extends her Glock towards Owens "I'm not going to tell you again."

Owens does as she orders.

"Now, you wanted to talk... talk. But only my friends call me by my first name, and the last time I checked, I didn't have any friends who were E.S.A.D. Agents."

Owens straightens up.

"That's right. I know who you are. So, why don't you tell me the real reason you wanted to get me alone?"

"How long have you known?"

"It doesn't matter?"

"How did you find out?"

"It *doesn't* matter!"

Owens sighs. "My orders were to shadow you. We wanted to monitor any communications you have with the humanoid alien."

"I told your people that I didn't have communications with the humanoid!"

"You stayed a step ahead of us for a while."

"A while, then what?"

"I eventually learned that the two of you were planning a trip to Asia."

Walker begins to pace, "Go on."

"That's where I've been. I lead a team of E.S.A.D. Agents to the same mountains in hopes of ambushing the alien and detaining him. But things didn't go according to plan. In fact, that's what I wanted to talk to you about. I need your help."

"My help? You've been spying on me all this time, and now you ask for my help? Now who's lost their mind? Again, Walker paces. What did happen up there?"

Owens explains how he and his team arrived on the mountain, set up camp, and put the entire rock under surveillance. He describes how still and silent everything was, and that there was no sign of the target. He then tells her how the silence was finally broken. Walker stops pacing.

"The aircraft came into full view. It was immense! This was it; the mother ship! That's what we thought. But, as it neared, I saw that this was no alien ship."

"Then what was it?"

"It was one of our very own."

"E.S.A.D.?"

"Yes. We call it the Saucer craft. I was one of the select few with knowledge of its existence. I was under the impression that they were bringing back up, but I learned that they were there to pick us *back up!*"

"What about your mission"?

"It had just begun! Sure, we'd secured the mountain and kept watch, but we were sent to engage and apprehend the alien threat. Or so I thought. It was my Colonel who came. He'd been ordered to end our mission prematurely. I got a chance to speak with him later in private. I found that he felt much the same as I did."

"And how did you feel?"

"I felt something was off, very off. And so, did my Colonel, though he wouldn't speculate."

"So, what are you saying?"

"I believe there's a conspiracy taking place. Before I spoke with the Colonel, I overheard him speaking with the General. The General said that the Intelligence that I'd gathered was no good and he had proof. Not only that, but he, without the knowledge of even his trusted Colonel, took half of E.S.A.D. on some covert mission. He set out on this mission while Colonel Foster was on his way to retrieve my team."

"Hold on, let's rewind. You said you needed my help. Just what were you hoping that I would do?"

"I want you to help me uncover the truth; You and your friend."

"My friend?"

"Friend, acquaintance, whatever. I bet he gets to call you by your first name!"

Walker realized that denying her association with Sir Good Knight was useless; at least to Owens. Then she has another thought, *what if she isn't talking to only Owens.* He could still be playing her! Walker retrains her gun on Owens.

"What?!"

"You wearing a wire?"

"Of course not. I need your help!"

Walker searches her partner with her off hand until she's certain that he isn't wearing a conventional wire.

"Okay you're not wearing any wire that I'm familiar with. But then again, I wasn't familiar with those futuristic vehicles that you and your spy friends ride around on either!"

Owens sighs. "Walker you're a detective. Trust your gut! What does it tell you?"

He was right. Walker's gut had long since decided that he was telling the truth.

"Alright Owens. You've got me. You're right. I have been in contact with the humanoid."

Owens nods.

"But if you don't want him in custody, then what do you want with him?"

"I'm sure you remember our introduction?"

"Of course, that was the same day I made Detective."

"Uh yeah, umm… well what you didn't know, was that wasn't our first-time crossing paths. I first saw you at The Encounter Point."

"The what?"

"The Encounter Point. That's E.S.A.D.'s official name for ground zero of the first alien battle. You know, *close encounters*."

"Yeah of the fifteenth kind!"

"Indeed. Well, you were obviously there and so was the humanoid. Not to mention another alien who stood on two feet, but that was the only humanoid feature about him."

"Bloodsport," Walker whispers.

What was that?

"His name was Bloodsport."

"Was?"

"Was. But go on."

"I was also there. I was the Agent who chased the humanoid."

Walker thinks back. She remembers.

"What assurances do I have to help me trust you?"

"In my Inside jacket pocket, I have classified E.S.A.D. documents. Some are even concerning you."

Walker carefully takes the papers out of Owens' pocket.

"If you were to go to the press with those, my career would be finished! I'm putting my future in your hands."

Walker fishes through the folded papers looking for her name.

"Look on page twelve."

Walker glances at Owens then turns to page twelve.

"No. No this isn't true. I earned my promotion! I made Detective on my own merit! I'd been up for promotion for more than two years!"

Owens doesn't respond. Jessica turns to face the other direction. Her eyes well up. She struggles to regain her composure. Walker takes a deep breath and wipes her tears before turning back.

"I'm sorry. For what it's worth, you've shown that you possess the elite skills necessary to be a Detective. You deserve that gold shield."

"Finish the story! You said you were chasing Sir Good Knight!"

"*Sir Good Knight*? Is that its name?"

Walker clenches her teeth. It was too late now.

"Yes. Yes, that is *his* name."

"Well I chased *him* into a parking lot. Somehow, he got the drop on me and totally destroyed my Hover-form. He could've taken me out in a blink! He could've even let me crash with my Hover-form. But instead, he snatched me off and sat me down unharmed. I had been firing at him! That showed me that he had no hostile intentions. At least none toward humans. Now knowing this, along with his abilities, I believe we can all help one another."

Again, Walker paces. "I don't know. I'll have to talk to Sir Good Knight."

"Please do. Oh, and there's one more thing."

"What now?!"

He dangles the cuffs, "I could've taken these off at any

time."

Chapter Twenty:

Then there were three

London is awakened by the Captain's voice on the intercom.

"Twenty minutes until touchdown."

He had slept for nearly the entire flight. The two-way radio was still all static. London turns it off and hopes that he hadn't missed anything while he was asleep. He stretches and pulls out his phone to send a text to Walker: *I'm back. When and where can we meet?*

"Glad you're safe. You won't believe what I've learned! My place, one hour."

"You sure?"

"I'm sure."

"See you there."

Forty-five minutes later, Walker looks at the clock on her living room wall. She walks to her front door and opens it. It was dark. She steps out on the porch and down the stairs.

"You coming in?"

Jessica turns around. Sir Good Knight is standing in her doorway.

She shakes her head. "You just love sneaking up on people, don't you?"

The Knight grins. Jessica climbs the stairs; with each step her face grows more serious. This wipes the grin off of the Knight's face. Something is wrong, he draws his sword and looks around.

"Good Knight, do you trust me?"

Jessica looks into the glow of the Knight's shimmering water-like eyes, wondering what he will say. After five seconds, which seem like an eternity to Jessica Walker, Sir Good Knight nods. Jessica is relieved.

"You can put your sword away."

Sir Good Knight re-sheathes his weapon. Jessica keeps her eyes glued to the Knight's as she speaks her next words.

"I need you to meet David Owens."

Sir Good Knight immediately brakes from Jessica's stare and fixes his intimidating glare on the undercover E.S.A.D. Agent who now enters the room. This was the one Agent who was tasked with shadowing Detective Walker in order to find him! And he was good, very good. This is who now stood just five feet from the Knight. David Owens freezes.

The last time he was this close to the humanoid, he had his Hover-form cut in half! The tension threatens to blow the roof off.

"Just hear him out Good Knight. Believe me, you'll want to hear this."

For the next hour, Owens explained the entire situation to Sir Good Knight. The three of them stood the whole time. Walker showed the Knight the documents that Owens had given her.

"I believe him Good Knight."

He looks over the documents and considers what he'd just been told. But his attention is truly on just one thing. The Lord had assembled his team! A Detective, an E.S.A.D. Agent who was now a triple Agent, and a SoulKnight. Sir Good Knight hands the documents back to Jessica and approaches Owens. He stands a little taller than Owens. The Knight still hadn't spoken a word. Owens stands his ground, even though he feels like stepping back. The Knight stares, then sticks his hand out. Owens does the same, they shake. Sir Good Knight nods. Jessica Walker finally exhales.

The newly formed team sits at Jessica's dining table. Owens hears Sir Good Knight speak for the first time.

"There's still something that doesn't add up."

"What's that?"

"You say your team was pulled off the mountain without seeing any action."

"That's right, it was midnight quiet up there."

"I fought hard against a team of soldiers up there. But they unfortunately accomplished their goal."

"You saw battle?"

"Fierce battle."

"When did this take place?"

"Two nights ago."

"That's impossible! I was still there Wednesday night. We had all of Mt. Everest under lock and key."

Sir Good Knight and Walker make immediate eye contact.

"I'm telling the truth!"

"It seems your General was also telling the truth. Your intelligence was not accurate." Walker says.

"How do you mean?"

"The battle did not take place on Mt. Everest. We were in the nation of Turkey, on the mountains of Ararat."

Owens slowly lowers his eyes. "Turkey?" He stands and walks to the window. He's been played. He ironically felt the same way that Walker did when she discovered, *he* had played her.

"General Morris. He approved the Everest mission in order to distract the rest of E.S.A.D. from his true intentions. You fought with the other half of E.S.A.D. *You* were the ghost mission. Wait a minute. You said they accomplished their goal. Our goal was to apprehend you. So how could they have accomplished their goal?"

Again, The Knight and Walker make eye contact.

"They have captured the Ark of Noah."

"The Ark of Noah? Wait... *Noah's Ark?!*"

"I'll explain later."

The SoulKnight turns to Walker. "Any developments on Alaska?"

" No, I'm afraid not."

"Alaska, what about Alaska," Owens asks.

"That's where the next step of their plan unfolds. Something to do with the Northern lights. I just don't know where in Alaska."

"I overheard my Colonel and General speak of Fairbanks."

Sir Good Knight turns to Walker. "This time, I won't go alone."

"I don't mean to impose, but if you allow me to tag along, I may be able to help with the transportation."

Sir Good Knight smiles.

"*For there are three that bare record in Heaven...* (1st John 5:7)."

"What?"

"Three is perfection."

An hour later, Owens hands a couple twenties through a plastic-glasslike barrier. He then steps out of a cab. The triple Agent is roughly three blocks away from E.S.A.D. headquarters. He walks the rest of the way. He doesn't want to draw any attention to himself. It is a rare occasion to see a vehicle pass by the once abandoned warehouse. Owens is sure that he can approach the building undetected if on foot. Especially since he knows the location of the cameras. He walks around back to the shipping and receiving area. This is the section of the warehouse where E.S.A.D. house their vehicles. Owens knocks on the only standard door. A security camera slowly scans the rear perimeter. Owens steps into a shadow just before the camera points in his direction. Although he is still a member of E.S.A.D, and no one knows of his new allegiance, that still didn't give him authority to take a vehicle without direct orders from Col. Foster.

"Who's there?"

"David Owens."

"Commander Owens? Why don't I see you on the monitors?"

"I dropped my phone back here somewhere. I'm looking around for it."

The door opens.

"Yeah I dropped mine back there at least twice now."

Owens keeps his eye on the camera while he hides in the shadows. He isn't just thinking of the guard on vehicle watch, he was thinking ahead. Owens knows that if he's successful, that the security cameras would be reviewed when the incident was investigated. As soon as the camera pointed away from the door, Owens came out of the shadows.

"Got it!"

Owens greets the guard and enters the compound. The camera never catches a glimpse of him.

"What's going on, why are you down here?"

"I need a favor."

"What kind of favor Commander?"

"Well for starters, I doubt they'll allow me to keep that rank. Obviously, things didn't go quite the way I'd hoped on Everest. It was my responsibility. To make things worse, I go and blow up on Col. Foster; and in the open!"

"Yeah, that wasn't your best moment."

"Tell me about it."

He Sighs. "So, what do you need?"

"I need to prove myself. I have to get back in the good graces of Foster and Morris."

"And how does that involve me?"

"I need a R.A.M. shuttle." (Rockets and Missiles).

"Without authorization?!"

"Listen, Detective Walker has a pilot's license, and she's arranged for a flight tonight. Within the hour no less! I know who she's going to meet with, but I have no proof. I have to follow her. I need this Cooper."

Agent Cooper scratches his head and walks to his desk.

"I don't know Commander."

"No one will know. We've never even used them, besides there's two more."

"Alright, alright but here's the deal. If you don't have it back here by eighteen hundred hours, you're on your own; I'm not covering!"

"I owe you one Cooper."

Owens wastes no time. He jumps in the R.A.M. shuttle and waits for Agent Cooper to open the dock doors.

"I'll take care of the cameras."

Agent Cooper opens the doors and repositions the cameras. Owens fires up the engines and puts the shuttle into hover mode. This allows for a low speed and low altitude transport. It also allows for take-off from a stationary position. Noise from the high-powered engines will not be an issue. R.A.M. shuttles are equipped with several prototype technologies. One of which is a whisper quiet exhaust system. Another feature are its name sakes, Rockets: powered by high efficiency jet rocket engines, and Missiles: four state of the art mini-missiles. Along with a couple other features. In short, it is a compact four-person speedy attack jet! Owens maneuvers the R.A.M. Shuttle out of the dock doors and into the open. He then looks back at Agent Cooper and salutes. Two seconds later, he is off!

Owens reaches the rendezvous in no time at all. He hovers the shuttle to a remarkably silent landing. Sir Good Knight and Detective Jessica Walker emerge from their hiding place and board the shuttle. Just as quickly as the prototype jet had landed, it was off again. Walker places a sack in the open seat.

"What's in the bag?"

Walker reaches in the sack and pulls out flashlights and duct tape.

"I thought we were expecting a fierce battle? Where are your weapons?"

"You've never encountered Shadow walkers."

"Shadow walkers?"

"Yeah, they're small gargoyle-like creatures who are... let's say deathly allergic to light."

"Light? What about crosses and Holy water?"

The new allies all laughed. It was the first time since teaming up that the mood had allowed for a light moment. They needed it.

"Your bag of treats looks more like a science project than an arsenal."

Walker opens her jacket revealing her double shoulder holster complete with twin 9 millimeters. She also revealed a third Glock in a waist holster.

"And not to be left out, is my *Bodyguard*."

That was the name Walker had given to the assault rifle she pulls out of her sack.

"And where's your arsenal?"

"Everything I need is in the weapons carousel in the back. I guess you don't need anything other than that sword of yours?"

"Actually, you and I would both be wise to utilize a couple of Jessica's flashlights."

"I knew he called you by your first name!"

The rest of the flight is rather quiet. Walker duct tapes a flashlight to each of her weapons. Owens takes the Knight's advice and asks if she would prepare his weapons the same. He presses a button and the floor behind the last seat opens up and elevates his carousel of weapons. Sir Good Knight had Walker tape a flashlight to the top of each of his shoulders.

"So, Sir Good Knight, *can I call you Good Knight for short?*"

"You may."

"Good Knight, seeing as how we have a little time before we reach Alaska, is it too much to ask about your people and your planet?"

Walker looks directly at Sir Good Knight. She's still having issues with what he'd told her. He knew what her look meant. She didn't think Owens was quite ready to hear everything that she had. The Knight nods to assure her that he understands.

"I am in this world, but not of this world. My people are sons of Light, royalty; kings and queens who will one day receive our crowns."

The Knight grins at Jessica.

"That is so cool!" A wide-eyed Owens says.

An open field appears in the distance.

"That is where our destiny lies."

Three military helicopters, sharing one cargo load, began their descent. The Ark of Noah is lowered to Gen. Morris' specifications. E.S.A.D.'s ghost Agents climb down the chains and disconnect them. Morris speaks over the radio.

"Land the choppers in a wide perimeter around the Ark."

Pat, Dozorn, and the ghost Agents of E.S.A.D. step out of the choppers and walk toward the Ark. Pat, using his powers of illusion, is dressed in uniform as Morris was. He gives the ghost Agents their orders. The Agents are oblivious.

"Secure the area. Leave none alive. We have one hour until the Aurora is in full glory."

As the men run to follow orders, Pat turns to Dozorn, whose severed limbs had grown back.

"The Dark Author will reward the three of us greatly!"

Dozorn growls with a wicked grin.

Gen. Morris now de-boards one of the helicopters. He looks to the sky.

"Today is the day the God of man meets retribution. The price for banishing Lord Lucifer from Zion shall be paid before another sun rises!"

Morris walks toward the two and greets them.

He pats the beast on the back, "Mighty Dozorn;" Then he turns to his twin, "Brother."

Gradually the ghost Agents return; men loyal to Morris. Morris had specifically recruited these men because of their commitment and worship of the Sin Father. The evening shade had all but swallowed the light of day. Morris steps forward. His Agents are seeing that he has a twin for the first time. They are visibly confused.

"Do not concern yourself with what you now see. A two headed cobra will catch more prey than any single serpent. This revelation of The Dark Author was planned long ago, and now it is coming to fruition."

The Ark sits directly beneath the place where the Aurora will burn its brightest.

"Now, we must encircle the Ark of Noah. But, if there be any among you, who does not revel in wickedness, if your every imagination and thought of your heart is not evil continually; (Gen. 6:5) you may not join our circle. For you are not true evil. These are the things that the God of man perceived when he first flooded the Earth, and this is what must surround the Ark when the Aurora burns in full glory. If your wickedness is not whole, your evil not pure, *STEP- BACK- NOW!*"

No one blinks. Pat turns to Morris with a grin of fangs.

"You have done well in your recruiting brother."

"Now, surround the Ark!"

As they circled around the vessel on the ground, another circle begins to form. Ten feet above the first circle, a swarm of vampire bats spun. Everyone on the ground looks up.

"All hail the Dark one of the under!" The beast yells.

Morris' men are in awe to be in the presence of the Dark Author.

It's real! Walker says.

Sir Good Knight and his newly formed alliance are now in Alaska, just minutes from Fairbanks.

"According to the navigational system, we'll be entering Fairbanks in two... "

"Look!"

The Northern lights began to surge. Then an unending Aurora wave explodes in every direction. It covers the entire sky. And in seconds, the wave reaches every corner of the Earth's skies. Then it disappears. However, in its place a thick cloud cover now looms.

"What was that?!"

"Go to where the Aurora began!"

They near the location of the original phenomenon.

Then all at once, the rain fell. Though not as heavy as the rain that fell on the Knight in his second battle with Bloodsport, it is hard. It is steady, and it is the same across the globe.

"There... Noah's Ark."

"What in the world?! You two still have to explain this to me!"

From the sky, Sir Good Knight and company can see men in uniform celebrating like happy children. They were jumping around and running in glee.

"Are we too late?"

The Knight knew the answer in his spirit "No. We take the Ark!"

One of E.S.A.D.'s ghost Agents looks to the sky and sees the shuttle.

"General, isn't that one of ours?"

Morris looks up. "It is. But who's piloting it?!"

"It makes no matter, destroy them!" Commands the bats.

The Ghost Agents open fire on the shuttle, and The Dark Author, in the form of bats, attack the windshield. The bats completely cover the glass and hang onto the ship.

"What are these things?! I can't see!"

"They look like bats!"

"The Dark Author." Sir Good Knight says.

"They're firing on us. I can't see to dodge! We're taking too much damage. Put on your parachutes and grab your weapons, we have to eject!"

Walker and Owens quickly strap their parachutes on. Owens looks at Sir Good Knight as if to say, *what are you waiting for?!*

"I need no parachute."

Owens pulls a ski mask over his face. Walker responds likewise.

"On three; One, two… "

"I'll see you all on the ground. Fight valiantly, and may the Lord bless our battle."

"… Three!"

The top of the shuttle blows off and all four seats shoot out. A fifth object also shoots out, a kind of chest. Sir Good

Knight is the only one of the three not wearing a seatbelt securing him to the seat. When his seat ejects, he holds his breath and uses the force to propel himself high up into the sky. And as his seat succumbs to gravity, the SoulKnight continues upward. Once he is high enough to see the entire perimeter, the Knight allows himself to pause in midair. The shuttle crashes further in the field. There's an explosion. The Knight, now clear on his plan of attack, positions himself upside down, and exhales. He rips through the rain at an ever-increasing speed. He does a series of breathing exercises until he is able to manipulate his assault dive into a diagonal line to the Ark.

His partners were strapped to their seats as they were shot out of the R.A.M. shuttle. They only ascended a third as high as Sir Good Knight, at peak height. Then their parachutes deployed. Both Walker and Owens began a slow descent through the rain. They watch as Sir Good Knight rockets toward the enemy.

Gen. Morris spots the SoulKnight. "It's him! Men get to the choppers, get the Ark in the air!"

"Shadow Walkers!" Pat yells.

At his call, the creatures pour from countless shadows. Dozorn climbs to the top of the Ark awaiting the Knight. Sir Good Knight is focused. His true target is the men running for the choppers. He anticipated Dozorn's interference. Once again, the Knight manipulates his dive, it seems that he will now clear the Ark. Dozorn sees this and runs the length of the Ark to build momentum. He then leaps to clash with his now deemed worthy adversary. But just before they collide, Sir Good Knight inhales, in effect slamming on the breaks. He then exhales avoiding the Blue demon. An angry Dozorn roars as he continues to race through the air. The Knight unsheathes the Eden sword, and lands weightlessly atop the Ark. This all happened so quickly, that Walker and Owens still hadn't touched the ground.

The rain begins to saturate the soil. The land would soon flood. Especially since the Tanana River is so close. Although the Ark is solid, there are many sections that tell her age. But, right before the Knight's water-like shimmering blue eyes, the rain miraculously restores every weak spot. The Ark is now as sturdy as it was the day Noah finished building it.

Pat jumps on top of the Ark in his true form.

"I believe the expression is … a day late and a dollar short (he chuckles). How fitting that you, the one that caused me such stress, would now amuse me. My laugh shall be the last one Knight!"

Shadow walkers crawl up each side of the Ark, surrounding Sir Good Knight.

Morris and his ghost Agents reach the choppers and lift off the ground. Dozorn lands with all six limbs splashing water. Again, the Knight has made him miss! In his anger, he throws his head back and roars! There in the midst of the rainfall, is his consolation prize. Two humans with parachutes are descending before his eyes. They are no more than twenty feet in front of him, and thirty feet up. The beast runs full speed and leaps in the direction of David Owens. Walker has her sack of weapons slung over her shoulder and head. She pulls out her assault rifle, aims for the beast and fires three shots. The force is enough to throw the demon off course, and at the same time, sends Walker flying backward. Her parachute tangles from the sudden jerk, and she falls to the ground. Luckily, she wasn't at lethal falling height, plus the ground has begun to flood. Dozorn hits the ground and rolls. Owens finally touches down. He quickly pulls his 'chute off and runs to the aide of Walker. She is trying to free herself from the ropes of her parachute.

Dozorn stands and turns to face his enemies. "Foolish mortal. Your weapons do nothing but annoy me!"

Using a knife, Owens frees Walker. She stands and raises her rifle.

"Well I've got plenty more to annoy you with!"

Owens also takes aim at the demon. However, he only holds a handgun. His assault weapons are in the chest that was shot out of the shuttle when the team ejected. He looks around for the blinking light that signals the location of the chest.

"Walker. He whispers, do you see that light blinking behind us?"

She glances, while keeping an eye on the blue beast. "Yeah, I see it. What is it?"

"It's my weapon's carousel. We need it. I have some specialized weapons in it."

They began to inch backward in the direction of the chest. They still hold their weapons on the beast. Dozorn roars. This causes Walker and Owens to speed up. Dozorn pursues.

"Cover me!"

Owens runs for the chest. Walker stands her ground and fires. She is dead on! The shots make Dozorn stop and shield his face. He again roars and this time charges at Walker with a new fury. She keeps shooting, but although her bullets are still hitting their target, Dozorn will not allow them to dissuade him. The beast splashes toward the courageous Detective, and swings smacking her rifle out of her hand. His next swing would pulverize her gossamer-like frame (in comparison to his)! However, a fraction of a second after the demon smacked Walker's weapon away, Owens fired one of his prototype weapons at the beast. It was an electric spray. It traps him to the rain-soaked ground in an electric net. The beast struggles to free himself, but every time he makes a move, the net shocks him. Walker had seen her life flash before her eyes. She breathes heavily. Owens, standing in front of the open chest, grabs two supply belts and straps them on. One around his waist, the other diagonally around his torso. He also grabs the assault weapons. Walker takes another look at the trapped demon before joining her partner.

"Are you okay?"

"I'm fine. How long will that hold him?"

Owens looks back at the struggling beast. "I don't know."

"We have to find Sir Good Knight."

The drenched duo run for the Ark.

The Knight waits for the Shadow walkers to close in. The helicopters are now overhead. They lower chains to once again carry the Ark. The Knight's eyes are fixed on Pat, peripheral vision on the Shadow walkers, and ears on the helicopters.

"There he is, he's outnumbered!"

"I have an idea, you keep on, and I'll catch up."

Owens kneels down in the now shin deep water and pulls a weapon from around his back.

Dozorn was determined. He would not be a prisoner. But it was clear that fighting would not free him. The beast stops

489

struggling and contemplates his predicament. He breathes deeply. Suddenly he has his answer. He shoves his hands into the mud and begins to dig. The combination of saturated soil, and six powerful limbs, makes the task a simple one.

Owens extends the barrel of his weapon and lets it rest on his shoulder. He looks through a scope, and fires. The blast knocks Pat down off the far side of the Ark. Owens stands and then turns as he hears splashing from behind. A second later Dozorn bulldozes him. The only thing that kept David Owens' head attached, was the fact that he was lucky enough to have seen movement out of the corner of his eye when he began to turn, thus giving him a microsecond to react. He was able to slightly duck. But he is hurt. The beast circles back for more. Owens, lying half submerged, reaches in his pocket and pulls out an object that resembles an ink pen. He clicks the back end of it, and then sticks it in the ground next to him. Once again, the beast is bearing down on him. An energy dome forms around the triple Agent's entire body. The blue demon crashes down on top of it. Owens is unaffected. Dozorn can't reach him. The beast punches and claws at the energy dome to no avail.

"Coward!"

Dozorn roars and decides to abandon Owens and runs after
Walker.

Sir Good Knight had already begun to engage the slowly
converging Shadow walkers, when Owens shot Pat off the Ark.
Upon seeing this, The Knight turns the flashlights mounted on his
shoulders on and spins in multiple circles disintegrating dozens of
Shadow walkers. He then jumps in the air swinging the Eden
sword burning through the chains of the closest helicopter. All
three of the prototype copters fire on him. Still in the air, he
swings the sword deflecting both bullets and lasers, before landing
back on top of the Ark.

"Hold your fire! Do not shoot while he stands atop the
Ark!"

Gen. Morris, sitting in the cockpit of the lead helicopter,
looks down at the Knight. Sir Good Knight stares back in
disbelief. It was Pat, or so he thought it was. But how could he
board the airborne copter, and change back to human form all
while being shot to the ground? Walker, now standing at the base

of the Ark, fixes the high-powered flashlight attached to her assault rifle on the windshield of the lead copter preparing to shoot.

"It's Gen. Morris! Owens was right."

Gen. Morris?? The Knight says to himself.

She fires on the windshield of the copter with no effect. Pat climbs back atop the Ark. Sir Good Knight makes eye contact. Pat looks up at the lead copter. He laughs.

"I see you've met my twin."

Sir Good Knight grips the Eden sword with both hands and engages the enemy. Shadow walkers emerge from behind the detective and knock the rifle from her hands. Another one jumps on her back. Walker digs in her pocket and pulls out a smaller flashlight. She directs it over her shoulder. The creature screeches in pain. It lets go and drops into the newly formed lake. She aims the flashlight at every Shadow walker in sight. Some are disintegrated, while others run and jump into shadows. Walker draws her hip gun and splashes through the water watching her back. She never sees Dozorn approaching her. He looks up and sees the fight taking place on the Ark. He then sees three Shadow walkers waiting to pounce on the detective. The helicopters hover above the Ark awaiting an opportunity to attach the chains. Dozorn realizes this and reacts. He runs to the Ark and jumps up tackling both Sir Good Knight and Pat! The three of them fall to the ground.

General Morris orders his Agents. "Lower the chains!"

The choppers all lower chains, and E.S.A.D. ghost Agents onto the Ark. They quickly make the necessary connections and the copters begin lift off. Pat and Dozorn keep Sir Good Knight from interfering.

The sky grew darker and the rain refused to let up. Walker hears a big splash. She knew someone, or something had to have fallen off of the Ark. Hoping it wasn't The Knight, she runs toward the noise and hangs off the side of the Ark and let's go landing in the now much deeper waters below. Shadow Walkers pounce pulling both her arms away from her flashlights. The cunning Shadow walkers attacked. Both of her arms are pulled away from her weapons. She is then knocked to her knees and snatched by the hair. A Shadow walker forces her head under the water. They were drowning her. She struggles, but the Shadow walkers are too strong.

Sir Good Knight, Pat, and Dozorn all stand unaffected by the fall. The demons stand on either side of the Knight. Six feet away from the stand-off, steam rises from the now nearly knee-deep water. Sir Good Knight knew from experience that this is the Eden sword. Oblivious to the steam, and more importantly what it meant, the demons circle the Knight.

Walker is ready to give in. She'd accepted the fact that this was it for her. Her mother never wanted her to become a cop. She always said that it would be the death of her. Jessica never thought of her mother as clairvoyant; until now. Then suddenly, the grip on her right arm releases. Then her head and left arm are free. Walker rises to her knees and takes the deepest breath of her life before coughing uncontrollably.

"Are you okay?"

In between the coughing and gagging, Walker looks up and sees David Owens. He helps her to her feet.

Sir Good Knight slowly turns as his enemies ponder their attack. As Pat circles left, he opens a clear path to the Eden sword. The Knight wastes no time, with unearthly speed, he dives into the rising water and races to his weapon.

Gen. Morris isn't interested in the action below. He has to complete the final steps, in order for the Dark Author's revelation to be fulfilled. The choppers fly off with the Ark; but something shoots out of one of them.

Sir Good Knight stands from beneath the water weapon in hand. Water runs down his head, shoulders, and body, but does nothing to cool the burn of his eyes and sword. Pat charges and swings a hand of claws. The Knight ducks and drop kicks the demon knocking him several feet back and into the water. But Dozorn snatches the Knight, before his feet can touch the ground. He wraps his enormous arms around the Knight and squeezes!

"You struggle in vain Knight! It's a shame that you will meet your end before the Dark One's revelation is full!"

Sir Good Knight can't move. Dozorn's grip is even tighter than Bloodsport's! Breathing is out of the question. He still holds

the sword but can do nothing with it. All he can think to do is head
butt the beast. Though it has some effect, it hurts Sir Good Knight
even more. Still, it is his only recourse. He does it again. Dozorn
drops him and reaches for his face. The Knight is nearly
unconscious as he hits the water. The demon enforcer shakes his
head in effort to clear it. Enraged, he pulls the Knight out of the
water, but his retribution is cut short by an energy blast from
Owens' laser cannon. The blast separates Dozorn from Sir Good
Knight. Walker locates her rifle and rushes to his aide. Owens
raises from his knee, and as he does, he comes under fire. The
source is the object that had come from one of the choppers
carrying the Ark. It was a Hover-form. Walker raises her rifle to
return fire, when Pat suddenly emerges from the water and knocks
her down. He then leaps into the air to rendezvous with the ghost
Agent piloting the Hover-form. Sir Good Knight holds his breath
and takes off like a rocket out of the water in pursuit of the master
illusionist. The Knight quickly closes the distance between himself
and the Hover-form. Pat had anticipated this. As he glances down,
he waits until the SoulKnight is a mere six feet away, and then
throws the Agent off of the Hover-form into him. Pat conveniently
takes over the piloting duties of the Hover-form and speeds off in

the direction of the Ark. Sir Good Knight manipulates his fall and uses the momentum to fling the Eden sword. He hollers in fear. In his anger, the SoulKnight wants to let the Ghost Agent fall to his much-deserved death, but his mercy wins out. He exhales, allowing himself to cut through the air much faster and to catch up with his fellow sky diver. As a collision becomes imminent the Knight grabs the ghost Agent and immediately holds his breath. There's a gentle jerk.

Meanwhile, Dozorn readies to engage Walker and Owens.

"You mortals should've run when you had the chance."

The two take aim at the beast.

He laughs. "A fool's courage begets a fool's death!"

The beast coils to pounce; Walker and Owens squeeze their triggers. Dozorn never gets a chance to jump. Though they indeed hit their target, Walker and Owens lacked the force needed to inflict fatal damage. The fatal blow is inflicted by the burning blade of the Eden sword. It swiftly burned through the darkening sky, blade down and stabbed the beast through the back of the neck, exiting through his throat. The sword sticks in the ground pinning Dozorn's head and half his body under water. Both Walker and Owens are speechless.

Sir Good Knight silently lands with his prisoner.

"Secure him."

Jessica Walker cuffs the ghost Agent. Sir Good Knight walks through the water toward the body of Dozorn. He'd thought the beast was dead once before. This time, he was taking no chances. He grabs the sword by the halt and pulls. The head of the demon emerges from the water. Sir Good Knight yanks the sword free and swings it, decapitating the beast before its head hit the water! Walker and Owens flinch at the brutality. The water around the body of the demon begins to part. The Knight steps back. The ground opens and swallows Dozorn's head and body. It then closes. Sir Good Knight turns his burning gaze on the ghost Agent.

"Wait, wait, hold on, wait a minute!"

The Knight approaches the prisoner through the knee-deep water. The Eden sword steams and sizzles in the rain.

"I'll tell you whatever you want to know!"

"Where are they taking the Ark?"

"To England, Stonehenge!"

"Stonehenge?!" Walker and Owens yell.

"Yes, it's the last piece of the puzzle. Now please… may I go?"

"What role does Stonehenge play?" The SoulKnight asks.

"It's key to opening the fountains of the deep. In order to completely flood the Earth, the fountains must be opened. Now please, that's all I know!"

"Go." The Agent runs off.

"Flood the Earth? How can the entire Earth be flooded? You can't seriously believe that is *The* Noah's Ark!" "Owens yells!"

The Knight looks up. "It is raining in all the world."

Owens looks to Walker. She says nothing.

"Those copters can achieve remarkable speeds. We need your alien technology. He points to the sky. "Like the kind that can make rain fall... everywhere." And if it's truly raining everywhere, hundreds of thousands and possibly more will drown before we can even get out of Alaska, not to mention England!"

Walker wades through the water. "We don't even have a vehicle! She turns to Sir Good Knight. How do we stop them?"

The SoulKnight stands emotionless as he listens to his partner's concerns. Then he responds.

"Have Faith."

Owens looks at Walker, "*What did he say?*"

"He said, have Faith," says an unknown voice.

Just then, a being with the likeness of a man descends out of midair. It is not the 4th Corner.

Chapter Twenty-One:

Line in the Sand

Although he does indeed resemble the 4th Corner, glowing eyes, ability to fly, uncanny calm in the midst of chaos; he is clearly not him.

"*What the…* where did you just come from?"

"Greetings Sir Good Knight, it is an honor to meet thee. Much you will do in the name of the Lord. Peace be unto you Jessica, daughter of Jerome. And peace be unto you David, son of Kenneth. I am Guardian of the 3rd Corner of the Earth."

"What?! You're who? How do you know my name, how do you know my father's name?! How… "

Sir Good Knight holds a hand up to Owens, then approaches the visitor. The Knight had never thought he'd encounter another Corner's Guardian.

"Where is the 4th Corner?"

"Earth's rotation has brought you to the 3rd Corner. I am Guardian. Though thou art not my task, the Lamb hath sent me. He knows what thou hath need of."

He looks past the SoulKnight and makes eye contact with Walker, and then Owens.

"What?"

Walker understood. She grabs Owens by the shoulder and pulls him in arms' length of the 3rd Corner. The Guardian's immense wings appear. He stretches them out to touch the Knight and his team. The four of them disappear.

The world's media is in a frenzy! *A second great flood?* Is the headline. The lower elevations are already under three feet of water. Rivers are overflowing, and so are lakes. Scientists are baffled, they have no answers. The consensus is that this shouldn't be possible. How could it rain in every city, in every country simultaneously? It hadn't been raining long, but the fact that it was raining everywhere, no boundaries, it accumulated quickly. The ground and sewer systems are like a thin sponge. In only an hour, they could take no more. There were mudslides, landslides, and avalanches. Many deaths are reported. People unanimously believe it is the end of the world.

But through it all, there are those who knew better. Though they didn't know what *was* going on, they knew what wasn't. They knew the written word. They knew of the promise. The promise to never again destroy the world by water.

The 3rd Corner, Sir Good Knight, and his team appear in the center of the rock formation known as Stonehenge.

"Oh my God, that was some Cpt. Kirk beam me up type stuff!"

The Knight looks to the sky. "How do we stop the rain?"

"Gather the true believers. Completely surround the Ark with them."

"True believers of what?"

Sir Good Knight glances at Owens. He then turns back to the 3rd Corner.

"How will I know …"

He is gone.

"What's that noise?" Walker asks.

They turn and look behind them. There are two objects approaching the formation from ground level. They are moving fast. Owens pulls a small device from his belt and looks through it.

"It's a couple of teens on jet skis."

"Jet skis? She has an idea. Owens do you have your badge?"

"Yeah, why?"

"Follow my lead. Walker takes her ski mask off. "Good Knight, you hide."

A minute later, the two jet skis speed through separate openings in the rock formation. Walker fires a shot in the air. The teens are so startled, that when they hit their breaks, they each flip over. Walker flashes her badge and speaks with her best English accent. Owens follows in tow.

"This is a police emergency! We need one of your jet skis!"

"The two of you ride together on the other one. Get to high ground, it's dangerous out here!"

Sir Good Knight yells out from behind one of the vertical stones. How do we get to the nearest Church?

Walker repeats the question. Though confused, the teens give the Detective the directions.

Owens opens one of the compartments on his waist's supply belt and pulls out a GPS device. He plots the information then sends the boys away. Sir Good Knight watches while all of this unfolds. He couldn't have come this far alone. He looks to the sky thankfully. The Knight joins his team.

"Why did you want a church address?"

"To gather the true believers."

Owens just stares.

"The tank is nearly full."

"You two will remain here. Just in case the Ark arrives before I return."

Owens hands him the GPS and shows him how to use it. Sir Good Knight walks to the edge of the rock formation, before riding off he turns to look back at his team.

"I'm honored to have you as partners. Be careful."

He takes off. Time is short. Worldwide the water is from three to almost four feet in depth; some places it is even deeper. With the water rapidly rising, Walker and Owens climb to the top of the massive stone blocks. Atop the stones, they reload their weapons. The element of surprise belongs to them, and they are well aware that ambush is their best strategy.

Owens reloads his last weapon and asks, "True believers of what?"

Jessica Walker had finished reloading and was fully expecting this question.

"What do you think is going on Owens?"

"X-files in the flesh!"

"Yeah… it just might be that."

"Okay, but what is this *Have faith* nonsense, and asking for directions to the nearest Church? How does all of this fit in? And what are these so-called true believers supposed to believe in?"

Jessica sighs "Good Knight claims that he is not an alien."

"What does he claim to be?"

"A man."

"A man? Come on, no man can do the things that he does! No man. He is not a man."

"He says, God gave him his powers, for times such as these."

"What? That's ridiculous! You don't believe him, do you?"

Looking up at the unending rain pouring sky, "I don't know."

Twenty minutes later, Sir Good Knight glides to the rear of a Church. He'd seen a few people in route, but no one noticed him, being that they were dealing with a catastrophe. He can feel that there are people inside. Then he notices a speedboat tied to a fence. That confirmed it. He runs to the front of the Church. A woman inside, on the upper level, happens to look out of a window, and sees the Knight run by. She calls to someone.

"How high did they say the water level was?"

"I'm not sure, it's rising rapidly. But help is on the way! Pastor has a friend with another speedboat."

"Yeah, I know that, it's just … you're not going to believe what I just saw!"

This gets the attention of the rest of the people who had come to the Church when it was reported that the entire planet was flooding. Sir Good Knight heard everything.

"What did you see?"

"There was a man … walking, well actually running on top of the water."

"I think we're all just frightened and looking for answers."

"I know how it sounds, but I know what I saw."

"Did Peter not walk on water when Jesus told him to come?"

The people turn to face the voice. Upon seeing Sir Good Knight: water-like eyes, sword on his back, dressed in all black, hood on his head; the congregation gasps. *A DEMON!* Most step back in fear.

"Be not frightened Saints. I am sent of the Father; Rest assured the end has not yet come. Your deliverance is at hand."

All are silent.

"Which of you is the Angel of this Church?"

A man in his early sixty's steps forward. "I am the Pastor. Just who are you?"

"Like you, I am a servant of the Most-high. As you know Pastor, The Father has promised to never again destroy the world by water."

The Pastor responds but is suspicious. "Indeed. I've been reminding the people. But what is it that's happening?"

"This is the work of the enemy. The Sin father has caused this calamity."

The Pastor looks at the congregation, then turns back to Sir Good Knight.

"How will we be delivered?"

"Seven pure in heart believers must come to the formation known as Stonehenge. The rest is my task; mine and those with me."

"Stonehenge? What must we do?"

"Have faith, nothing more. All that is needed is your presence; the presence of true believers."

The Pastor swallows hard, then turns back to his congregation.

"The Lord is calling. He is calling… for his people. We must answer his call!"

There is great commotion among the congregation. The Pastor turns to the SoulKnight.

"When do you need us there?"

"Time is short, come soon as possible." Before departing, the Knight stops in his tracks. "When you arrive, you will see many wonders. Let nothing dissuade you."

Sir Good Knight then explodes into a dazzling array of acrobatics leaping off of the balcony and lands silently atop the surface of the water that covers the first floor's pews. There was no splash, no disturbance of the water. The congregation oohs and ahhs. Sir Good Knight exits through the front entrance and glides off. He suddenly realizes that his request for *seven* true believers was made without thought. Why did he say seven? He had no answer until he was halfway back to Stonehenge. He remembers that the number seven, is the number of completion. The 3rd Corner gave instructions to *completely* surround the Ark. The Knight smiles. It was the Spirit that led him to say seven.

Minutes later, Walker and Owens spot the SoulKnight speeding toward them. He enters the circle of rock.

Walker looks down from a stone block. "What happened?"

"Seven true believers will soon come."

"But the ship is huge! How can we surround it with only seven people?"

"Seven is completion."

"What? Listen, you said three is perfection, and now seven is completion, but if you add the two together, we're still outnumbered! So, what does that mean?"

"Salvation."

Both men turn to Jessica Walker. Owens sees sarcasm. Sir Good Knight sees epiphany.

"Walker and I feel that our best strategy is to use these stones to ambush. They're large enough to hide us."

"I agree."

Owens had much tactical experience. It was second nature for him to come up with a plan of attack. Sir Good Knight and Walker keep quiet as Owens sets the chess board.

"Disabling the copters is the first-priority. We can't allow them to fly off with... the Ark again. Walker you'll take the Jet Ski and hide behind one of the stones. You'll primarily be covering me. I'll be hanging on the side of one of the lateral stones waiting for the signal. Good Knight, you are that signal. You submerge yourself in the middle of the formation. When you see the best opening, strike. Go for the propellers. Disable as many copters as possible. I'll then pull myself up and run around the top of the formation firing on the gunmen. Walker when you hear gunfire, speed in and take out any remaining threat.
We have to ..."

The Knight holds up his right hand. His ears operate as they were trained to.

"They've arrived."

"Take your positions." Owens says.

The team hides. Walker and Owens put their masks back on. The rain is unrelenting. From just beneath the surface of the now dark water, Sir Good Knight sets his stare upon the trio of prototype helicopters carrying Noah's Ark. One copter is in the front, two in the rear. Pat and company pass over Stonehenge. Sir Good Knight waits until the Ark clears the formation, then like a bullet, he shoots out of the water aiming for the lead copter. He strikes so fast and sudden that the rear propeller is burned off of the copter before Owens and Walker know to engage! The lead copter loses control and its chains that are connected to the Ark snap. This forces the other copters to release their chains to keep the Ark from yanking them to the rain flooded ground. The Ark crashes through the water to the ground front first, followed by the back end with a great splash. The flood waters and the saturated soil cushion the fall. One of the rear copters opens fire on the Knight, who is running on the surface of the water. He deflects many of the shots with the Eden sword. Owens, now aware, pulls himself from his hiding place and kneels atop one of the stone blocks. He takes the weapon off his back and mounts it on his shoulder. He takes careful aim and fires, direct hit! The copter that was shooting at Sir Good Knight, pours smoke from its side. The lead copter, which Sir Good Knight had disabled, crash lands. Several of the Agents on board jump out before it hits the ground. The second copter, which Owens had fired on, breaks off its pursuit of the Knight as it now struggles to remain airborne. The third copter takes evasive maneuvers as Owens now sets his sights on it. He's unable to get a fix. Those who bailed out of the lead copter are unharmed. They group together in the now five feet of water. Too deep for Shadow walkers. This group includes both Pat and Gen. Morris. Morris gets on his radio and orders the pilot of the last properly functioning copter, not to fire toward the stone formation. Owens fires on the second copter again, and again a direct hit. Only a few ghost Agents make it out before the copter takes a nosedive and crashes a half mile away. There's an explosion. Sir Good Knight doubles back and joins Owens atop Stonehenge.

"I told Walker to remain hidden since the third copter didn't attack."

"Good call. Sir Good Knight thinks for a second. "Why hasn't the last copter fired on you?"

"Maybe they don't wish to suffer the same fate as the other two."

"No, I believe there's more to it. (He looks down) *The key! They won't risk damaging the key!*"

Still hidden, "What's going on out there?!"

"The Agent we questioned said that Stonehenge was key to opening the fountains of the deep. If they fire on us, they'll hit the stones. We're standing on the key! Owens do what you can to keep the last copter from deploying more Agents. I'll take care of those already on the ground. Walker...

"It's about time!"

"You clean up what we miss."

All while the Knight instructed Walker and Owens, his eyes stayed fixed on Pat. Pat, along with Gen. Morris, and several E.S.A.D. ghost Agents stand in five feet and rising flood waters. Pat's empty black eyes are likewise fixed on Sir Good Knight. He also instructs his forces. The ghost Agents ready their weapons. They make their move and approach the formation.

"We cannot allow them to manipulate the stones in any way. (He then whispers to himself) Endgame."

Pat's forces form a V around him, with the point in the direction of Stonehenge. All but Pat are armed. Sir Good Knight hops from one stone to the next to build momentum. He then jumps down to the water's surface holding his breath. He slides across it. He achieved this by placing one foot in front of the other; heel to toe like water skiing. The Knight unsheathes the Eden sword. The ghost Agents open fire. So, does the last copter. Atop Stonehenge, Owens returns fire. Sir Good Knight ducks, dodges, bobs, and weaves around as many shots as he can. The sword takes care of the rest. He approaches their V attack. The Knight swings the sword at the point man. He finds no resistance. The sheer force of the Knight's swing spins him in circles. He immediately understands the situation. It was one of Pat's mirages! He had forgotten to account for that. As he spins, he hears shots fire in his direction. They came from the third copter. Sir Good Knight exhales allowing himself to fall underwater, making it appear that the copter had hit its mark. Underwater, The Knight can see the submerged halves of some of Pat and Morris' true forces. Believing they are still hidden by Pat's illusion the ghost Agents await further instruction; Until an unseen blade burns through them and expedites their meeting with the Dark Author.

Undetected and with amazing speed, Pat had swum into the center of Stonehenge. He stands and emerges to face the very stone that Owens stood atop firing on the last copter. Walker, anxious to join the battle, peaks from behind her stone, and sees Sir Good Knight in the clearing. He had come up for air. Rain still falling, he is obviously searching for someone. Then her attention is stolen by a loud splash.

Without warning, Owens is thrown off of his feet and into the water! Pat had twisted the stone Owens was standing on, causing him to lose his balance and fall. Walker looks to see what caused the splash and sees Pat. The huge stone block then drops into a previously hidden hole beneath it, leaving only a portion above ground, though not enough to be seen over the flood waters. The Earth shakes as the stone lowers. Sir Good Knight turns to the stones. Walker fires shots at the demon and powers the Jet Ski from around the stone she'd been hiding behind. Owens emerges from the water blocking Walker's view of Pat. The demon hurls himself at the next stone. Walker adjusts her aim, and hits Pat in the shoulder. However, Pat is still able to twist a second stone, causing it too to lower.

Sir Good Knight is now contending with the remaining copter as it finds itself free of Owens' artillery. His highly tuned ears pick up on a noise in the distance. The copter is attempting to keep the Knight away from the key that is Stonehenge. Two well-armed ghost Agents are lowered to the water's surface as the copter continues to fire on the Knight. But they are merely a distraction. The Agents advance on their target as the copter pulls up from just above the water's surface. The Knight zips through the water as easily as he does the air, untouched by his enemy's weapons. Sir Good Knight disarms the two Agents, *literally*, then shoots up in the direction of the last copter. Then the reason for their distraction is revealed. An energy blast hits the Knight squarely in the back, knocking him out of the sky. Gen. Morris had been waiting for the right opportunity to make his presence known. He'd been hiding, but not in one of his brother's mirages, he was using his one demon ability. When Morris remains perfectly still, he can blend in with any background, thus making him completely invisible. Gen. Morris signals for the copter to come down for him.

Still firing, Walker speeds toward Pat. Slugs penetrate his demon form before he can reach a third stone. He slumps underwater. Walker stops the Jet Ski in the area where the demon fell. There is no sign of him. Owens fishes his shoulder cannon out of the water ever deepening Neo Lake. Just then, Pat emerges from under the Jet Ski flipping both it and Walker. Jessica hits her head on the Jet Ski and is knocked unconscious. Owens shoots at the demon but misses as Pat ducks. He fires again as Pat charges, and again he misses.

Gen. Morris jumps on the copter.

"Take us up, quickly!"

When Morris feels they're a safe enough distance from the Knight's leaping ability, he gives further instruction.

"Shine the spotlight where he fell."

They see nothing.

Now too close to use his shoulder cannon, Owens swings it like a bat. He makes contact with the side of Pat's head. Pat staggers. Owens swings again. The demon blocks it with one hand and strikes Owens with the other. Wasting no time, the demon turns to the nearest stone and bear hugs it, twisting it. It drops with a tremor. As he turns to a fourth stone, the Eden sword

pierces the surface of the water from beneath, between the demon

and the stone block. Sir Good Knight immediately follows it and

swings his weapon burning clean through the demon's body from

the left side of his neck, through his right hip. The water parts, as

Pat's body falls in two. The Knight jumps to the top of the stone

block that Pat was reaching for.

Morris witnesses his twin cut in half.

"Retreat."

The last copter shoots off into the rain falling sky. Sir

Good Knight, however, isn't concerned with Morris' escape. He's

looking for the speedboats his highly tuned ears had picked up ten

minutes ago. He lifts the Eden sword high in the air. It burns an

even brighter red.

"I think that's our sign. Let's go!"

Owens isn't badly hurt. He picks Walker up out of the

water and snatches her mask off. He then snatches his off and

performs CPR. After a couple seconds she coughs up water.

Owens helps her onto the Jet Ski and climbs on with her. The water is approaching six feet in depth. They ride across the inner circumference of the formation to the stone supporting the SoulKnight.

Two speedboats stop just outside of the Stonehenge.

"My God! Is that... it can't be ...Noah's Ark!"

Sir Good Knight lowers the Eden sword and it immediately cools its bright red burn. As the Knight looks on the two speedboats, he notices two things. One, there is a halo-like glow above the heads of the Pastor and his people. And two, all which were on the boats, numbered only five.

"Quickly, follow me."

Sir Good Knight jumps to the water's surface and runs to the Ark. The speedboats trail him, followed by Owens and Walker on the Jet Ski. As he reaches the Ark, he says a silent prayer.

"Guide me Lord." "We only have five, make a way Father." Please Lord supply our needs, hear your servant's cry O' Father."

Standing atop of the Ark, Sir Good Knight turns to face the others. He now sees the glow of six! He yells down to the speedboats.

"You must all jump out of the boats and surround the Ark."

"But we have only three life preservers."

"Give one each to your two weakest swimmers."

There are three men, and two women on the boats. One preserver goes to a woman, and the second goes to a man. The Knight descends on one of the speed boats.

"There is another that requires the third preserver."

The Knight takes the last vest and turns to the Jet Ski. Jessica Walker is the sixth halo glow.

"Jessica, she looks up still coughing, The Lord hath need of thee."

Walker looks into the Knight's solid blue water-like eyes.

"I believe."

Sir Good Knight smiles and throws the preserver to Owens.

"Help her put that on and get her in the water next to the Ark. You must then take the Jet Ski and get far away. Everyone else, surround the Ark. Move quickly!"

Owens counts," But you said that seven was completion."

"I am the seventh."

The Pastor and his four members climb out of the speedboats and lower themselves into the flood waters that are now above most everyone's heads. The seven true believers surround the Ark of Noah. Sir Good Knight stands on the water in front of the Ark. He motions for Owens to depart. Owens motors up, and jets away full speed. When the SoulKnight feels that Owens is far enough away, he exhales and submerges all but his head and shoulders. He hollers instructions to the other six.

"Look to the heavens and open your heart to the Father!"

Everyone looks up to the dark rain pouring sky. Owens looks back, still speeding away. A small light begins to glimmer in the sky. Then, the same unending Aurora wave that preceded the rains, explodes again. However, even though the wave once again touches every sky on the Earth, this time it is not extending outward. It is returning. The wave is being sucked into the small light in the sky that glimmers above the Ark. The seven in the water marvel at the scene. When the Aurora wave is completely swallowed, all that remains is the small light that glimmers in a now perfectly clear English night sky. The rain has stopped. Six of the seven had just begun to cheer, and then the small glimmering light went nova! Its brilliance blinds the sky of every nation. Every open eye on Earth shuts tightly. In the midst of this wonder, the seven are lifted out of the water, and placed atop the Ark. Sir Good Knight was wise to direct Owens to get far away, for everything in a one-mile radius of the Ark is disintegrated. This includes the wreckage of the two E.S.A.D. helicopters, the bodies of the slain ghost Agents, the speedboats, and even the trees. The only exceptions are the seven, the Ark, and Stonehenge.

When the nova light finally burns out, it is daylight on all the Earth. The seven open their eyes and look up to a medium blue cloudless day sky. And then…

"WELL DONE MY GOOD AND FAITHFUL SERVANT, WELL DONE."

The Pastor, his four members, and even Walker shed tears. The Knight smiles.

The flood waters which had risen to over six feet, higher in some places, is now down to a more manageable two. The light that had shut every eye, caused an accelerated mass evaporation.

The Pastor is amazed. "Glory be to our awesome God, Glory! And blessed be this day!"

He turns to the SoulKnight.

"Just who are you?"

"I am a servant of the Most-high God, and I am your brother. I am called Sir Good Knight."

One by one, the Knight helps the Pastor and his members to the ground. When he goes back up for Jessica, the 4th Corner is standing with her.

"Greetings Son of James. Truly, thou art blessed among men. Well done."

"None of this could I have done without you; (he turns to Jessica) and my team."

"Bring now David Owens atop the Ark, and inform the Pastor that help is near for him and his people."

"I sent Owens away. He's probably... "

"Hey, is everyone alright up there?"

Owens is twenty feet to the left of the Ark, wading through the water. Sir Good Knight leaps down, and water dances across the field toward Owens. He wraps his arm around Owens' back and races back atop the Ark.

"Whoa, you again. Hold on, you're someone different. You had something to do with that light, didn't you? One second I'm jet skiing my way to safety, the next there's this blinding flash and I'm sitting stationary in two feet of water!"

The Knight looks down at the five. Help is on the way. Thank you all, peace be unto you."

The Ark and everyone on it, disappears. The Pastor and the four that are with him worships in that same spot. The three stone blocks that Pat had managed to insert into the ground, rise and twist into their previous positions.

Sir Good Knight, Walker, and Owens all look up to find themselves back in Philly. Owens is sitting in an office at E.S.A.D. headquarters. The half of E.S.A.D. that remained in Philly with Col. Foster, are out assisting local authorities with the flood. Walker is on the second floor of a shopping mall alongside a ton of other cops and detectives, dressed in riot gear, keeping order in one of the many facilities the city is using to shelter its citizens. Sir Good Knight is now London again. He is standing in the hideaway he'd recently secured for himself. The 4th Corner is with him.

"Be ever ready London son of James; For the Dark Author is resilient. He will return. Keep your identity as SoulKnight hidden. Discretion is essential. Be blessed. (He fades out of sight)."

Worldwide, the daylight lasts for 72 consecutive hours. As the final second ticked, the last of the flood waters had totally evaporated. On the fourth day, calm is restored. In the months that follow, the media, politicians, scientists, meteorologists, and scholars, all weigh in on the recent events. They give their theories, opinions, and offer research on everything from: The Philadelphia creatures, to the global rainfall, to the blinding light, to the 72 hours of global daylight. No one had a clue. The only enlightened souls outside of London and his team are an English Pastor and the inner circle of his congregation. They are exceedingly amused with the world's most generally accepted explanation, an Alien invasion.

SOUL OF A KNIGHT: The Knight's Birth

M. J. FELDER

About The Author

M.J. Felder's love for the creativity and emotions that words can produce was sparked at an early age, as his father was known to regularly play masterpieces from Stevie Wonder, Earth Wind & Fire, and many other geniuses of the day. He would later begin writing short stories and rhymes on index cards he "borrowed" from his mother's dining room buffet lol. A few years later, M.J. advanced his rhyme writing into full songs (following in the path of his mother) and began recording as a Rap artist. This was accompanied and later evolved into writing and performing spoken word. Ever focused on words and a better way to put them together, M.J. found himself becoming critical of song lyrics, and movies. He'd routinely tell friends and family "They should've said this, they should've taken the story that way, It would've been so much better if…" One summer day after graduating high school, and eager to get to the playground to play ball, M.J. was angered over the fact that his friends were all busy. Out of sheer boredom, he would pick up a *certain Novel* his mother and sister had been trying to get him to read. His mind was completely blown from the character development, plot twists, and the effectiveness of how the author drew him in with vivid descriptions and powerful dialogue. M.J.'s world was now open, and he introduced it to Stephen King, Walter Mosley, Tom Holland, Dean Koontz, Sistah Souljah, Neil Gaiman and others. The next phase of his love affair with words began to take shape. He decided to try his hand at writing a Novel! An enormous fan of Marvel and Star Wars, his first attempt was a Sci-Fi thriller that takes place on a newly discovered planet. M.J. would eventually abandon it, and continued writing poems, songs, and speeches. Then years later, he would again decide to try his hand at writing a novel. This was motivated by his creation of a new character and an original premise for a story. But it all became real when he came up with the title… SOUL OF A KNIGHT. M.J. began writing such an extensive outline that it became obvious to him that it was too much for just one book! SOUL OF A KNIGHT would have to be a trilogy. Much research would ensue, followed by countless rounds of rewrites, tailoring, and query letters. Finally, M.J. would find the right weapon to slay the beast that is *Procrastination* and put his full effort into getting his Epic published.

M.J. Felder resides in Buffalo, NY where he lives with his two sons and is a career Firefighter in the Buffalo Fire Department. He's worked with the inner-city youth of Buffalo for over twenty years in the capacities of Residential Treatment, Buffalo Public Schools, Head Start, and more. He is an avid music and sports fan and loves to travel the U.S.

Made in the USA
Middletown, DE
08 June 2020